Put a female bounty hunter with a huge chip on her shoulder in late-1800s Colorado, add the skilled writing of DiAnn Mills, and you have a winner for sure. High-paced action, tension that twangs on every page, an impossible romance, and Sage, a character who will move into your heart and stay there. DiAnn Mills keeps getting better and better.

> Lauraine Snelling, author of the Red River of the North,
> Return to Red River, and Daughters of Blessing series

DiAnn's phenomenal and has a focused heart for God. Her love of story and desire to share biblical application for daily living through her books is a tremendous blessing.

> Tracie Peterson, bestselling author of
> Dawn's Prelude and the Brides of Gallatin County series

Once again, Mills delivers. A Woman Called Sage is a well-blended story of love, trust, and faith that you will remember long after you've read the final page.

> Judith Miller, author of the Daughters of Amana series

From the first draw of the pistol to the last turn of the page, the tale of A Woman Called Sage left me breathless.

> Kathleen Y'Barbo, author of Beloved Counterfeit
> and The Confidential Life of Eugenia Cooper

DiAnn Mills has created an unforgettable heroine in A Woman Called Sage. An engaging tale that will keep any reader turning pages until the unexpected ending. Don't pass on this one.

> Lyn Cote, author of the Texas Star of Destiny series

A Woman Called Sage expertly combines the essential elements of storytelling: compelling characters, an intricate plot, and stakes as high as the Rockies themselves.

> Nancy Moser, author of Just Jane and Mozart's Sister

Sage is such a well-balanced character of woman and bounty hunter, and the intrigue keeps the pages turning. Still, God's hand is clearly at work through all the conflict. A good read on every level.

Loss and revenge, love and forgiveness. *A Woman Called Sage* brings it all to light in Colorado's rugged and majestic Rocky Mountains. Another riveting story by DiAnn Mills that has me waiting for the next Timmons family tale.

DiAnn Mills once more delivers a winner. In *A Woman Called Sage*, she has woven a historical saga destined to capture readers' hearts.

A WOMAN CALLED SAGE

A NOVEL

DiAnn Mills

ZONDERVAN®

ZONDERVAN.com/
AUTHORTRACKER
follow your favorite authors

We want to hear from you. Please send your comments about this book to us in care of zreview@zondervan.com. Thank you.

ZONDERVAN

A Woman Called Sage
Copyright © 2010 by DiAnn Mills

This title is also available as a Zondervan ebook.
Visit www.zondervan.com/ebooks.

This title is also available in a Zondervan audio edition.
Visit www.zondervan.fm.

Requests for information should be addressed to:

Zondervan, *Grand Rapids, Michigan 49530*

Library of Congress Cataloging-in-Publication Data

Mills, DiAnn.
     A woman called Sage / DiAnn Mills.
          p.   cm.
     ISBN 978-0-310-29329-3 (pbk.)
     1. Revenge — Fiction. 2. Women bounty hunters — Fiction. 3. Colorado — History —
Fiction I. Title.
PS361.I567W66 2010
813'.6 — dc22   2010001909

All Scripture quotations are taken from the King James Version of the Bible.

Any Internet addresses (websites, blogs, etc.) and telephone numbers printed in this book are offered as a resource. They are not intended in any way to be or imply an endorsement by Zondervan, nor does Zondervan vouch for the content of these sites and numbers for the life of this book.

Published in association with the Books & Such Literary Agency, 52 Mission Circle, Suite 122, PMB 170, Santa Rosa, California 95407-5370. www.booksandsuch.biz

Cover design: studiogearbox.com
Cover photography: Steve Gardner/Pixelworks
Interior design: Christine Orejuela-Winkelman

Printed in the United States of America

10 11 12 13 14 15 16 /DCI/ 21 20 19 18 17 16 15 14 13 12 11 10 9 8 7 6 5 4 3 2 1

To Allison Egert, who is more amazing, more beautiful, and more special every day.

A new heart also will I give you, and a new spirit will I put within you: and I will take away the stony heart out of your flesh, and I will give you an heart of flesh.

Ezekiel 36:26

ONE

L ife didn't get any better than having the love of a good man and his baby kicking against her ribs. Add a summer breeze to cool the heat of a southern Colorado sun and a bed of soft green grass tickling her feet, and Sage felt a slice of heaven had come to earth.

"Remember the first time I asked if I could come courtin'?" Charles propped himself on one arm and placed his hand on her mountainous stomach.

"Every minute of it. I was ordering sugar and coffee from the general store while Mama looked at yard goods, and you were asking about a rifle." She laughed. "You nearly rubbed the finish off that Winchester."

"But I bought it. You were wearing a blue bonnet and trying to look like you weren't watching me."

Just how did he know she had fought to keep from staring at him? Her childhood friend had grown into a handsome man. "Now, Charles, that's not true. *You* were pretending not to look at *me*."

He shook his head as though she were a naughty child. "You're right about me not being able to keep my eyes off you, but—Oh, I feel her kick. She's a strong one."

"You should feel *him* kick after midnight."

Charles kissed her stomach. "I couldn't remember when you'd

gotten so pretty, and I vowed I wouldn't leave the store until you let me call on you." He shooed away a honeybee buzzing over them. "I turned that rifle over and over in my hands until you and your mama were finished with the storekeep. Sage became . the most beautiful name I'd ever heard."

"No one can say my name like you or make me as happy."

He sat up and stared out at the cottonwoods in the distance; one had seen too many seasons, and its gnarled branches twisted to the sky like a crooked old man. Sage's pet wolf chased a rabbit, and the animal scampered away. Birds serenaded them as though they were the only two people in the world—well, three.

"We'll give our baby a fine life, Sage. You'll be the perfect mama because you're the perfect wife." He turned, and his brow etched into deep lines. "Every day I wake up next to you is a gift from God."

She started to sit up, and he helped her. "I will always remember the things you say to me because my heart says them back to you." She touched his face. "Here I am the size of a buffalo, and you're making me feel pretty. Oh—" Placing a hand on her stomach, she grinned. "He's kicking like he knows we're anxious for him to get here."

"It's a she."

She reached up to run her fingers through his thick, nut-colored hair, and envisioned a son with his papa's green eyes, sparkling like the stars. "He'll be here in about six weeks."

"Boy or a girl, it will be a fine baby. Elizabeth Sage."

"Timothy Charles." She smiled, admiring his broad shoulders. Oh, what a lucky woman she was.

There was a long pause before he spoke again. "I have something to tell you."

Her pulse raced faster than a hummingbird's wings. "Is the news good?" she said, hoping he wasn't leaving again. Those times were so hard to bear.

He caressed her face, gently, as he always did, so she wouldn't feel his calluses. "You can tell your father that after two weeks, we won't need him to help with chores anymore."

Sage held her breath. "You won't be traveling?"

"Nope. I head out three days from now, and I'll be back in less than ten days' time. Then I'm home for you and our baby and all of our babies to come, every day, for the rest of my life. I've sold the ranch up north, and I'm heading there to close the deal. We'll have enough money to buy more land here and maybe some cattle too."

She wrapped her arms around his neck and kissed him long and hard. He smelled like the outdoors, and she loved it. Loved him. At times her feelings frightened her, as though she didn't deserve Charles and his affections. Tears slipped down her face.

"I think you're pleased," he whispered.

"Very pleased."

"It's about time I ran this ranch myself and became a respectable husband and papa. Your father's right. I leave you alone much too often and depend on him to oversee the place." He laughed. "Who knows? Now he might learn to like me."

Having Charles and Papa enjoy each other's company would be next to perfect. Her tears flowed like a rushing stream—a steady occurrence of late, with the baby growing inside her. "You are more than I could ever ask for. We'll work this land together and raise a fine family."

His gaze grew intense, as though he had something more he wanted to say but couldn't bring himself to speak.

Had he and Papa argued again? "What is it?"

He shook his head. "A man has no right to be this happy."

"Or a woman." She heard his stomach growl. "I think we need to head back home so I can finish supper. Can't have my husband starving."

He kissed her nose, each cheek, and her lips. "There, I just had dessert first."

Charles whistled for Wolf to join them, then pulled her to

her feet. The gray and white female bounded toward them. Sage patted the animal's head, and Charles laughed. Her pet wolf was the talk of neighboring ranches, but Sage had tamed her. Just like Charles had tamed some of Sage's wildness but not her spirit.

Hand in hand they walked the mile back to their ranch. While Charles fed the livestock, Sage checked on a fork-tender beef roast that had been simmering most of the afternoon, along with potatoes, onions, and green beans. She rolled out biscuits and added another log to the fire before baking them. For a moment, she stole a whimsical glance at the cradle Papa had built and the tiny quilt Mama had stitched. Baby clothes draped over the side. Soon. Very soon.

Grasping the vegetable basket, she hurried outside for fresh tomatoes. From the shade of a juniper, she squinted into the sun and saw men riding near the west pasture and the creek that wound through the ranch.

"We got company," she said to Charles, who was pumping water into the cattle trough.

He caught a glimpse of the men and snatched up his rifle from where it leaned against the trough. "Sage, get inside the house. Now! Fetch your rifle and be ready to use it."

As clumsy as she felt with the weight of the baby, Sage raced to the porch, up the three steps, and inside the house. The tone of his voice had shaken her. He'd never used it before.

He knows who they are.

The loaded Winchester rested in the corner nearest the door. The moment she wrapped her fingers around the metal barrel, the gravity of Charles's warning sent an icy chill up her spine. Who were those men? Or was Charles simply being cautious?

She glanced out the open door toward the riders. Charles had moved into the shadow of the barn, his rifle resting against his shoulder. She closed the door just enough to see outside and shoot.

The four men were a dirty lot, but that wasn't anything unusual.

"Stop right there," Charles said. Wolf growled, and Charles didn't hush her.

"Not until we get what we came for," one of the men said. "We know it's here."

"There's nothing on this ranch that belongs to you. Consider yourself warned. There's more than one rifle fixed on you."

"Liar. Ain't no one here but you and your Injun woman. We came to get what's owed to us, and we ain't leavin' until we have it. We can tear this place apart with or without your say-so."

"This is your last chance," Charles said. "Get off my land."

"When we have our money and you're dead."

"Kill me and you'll have more trouble than you ever thought."

Sage held her breath, straining to listen to every word. She wanted to shout at Charles to give them whatever they wanted. And why did they want him dead? All she and Charles had of value was livestock. The men could have driven them off and been gone.

Before she could further contemplate the situation, a shot rang out, and Charles fell backward. Sage gasped and rushed onto the porch. Another shot, and Wolf sprawled out beside Charles. Something seized her—a mixture of fury and panic. She stumbled down the steps, tripping in her awkwardness.

"Charles!" He didn't move, no matter how loudly she screamed his name. Blood poured from his chest and spilled onto the ground. The men laughed, and she stared up at them, memorizing each grimy face.

The one who had shot Charles pointed his rifle at her. "Tell us where the money is or you can join him."

"We don't have any money. Take the cattle and horses."

"I won't ask again."

She stared into his face, memorizing the dark, curly hair and hollow, wide-set eyes. With Charles's body at her feet, revenge rose in her spirit. She raised the rifle, but too late. He fired.

Two

With the sound of the wind whistling through the branches of the pines, Sage searched for the right words to tell Tall Elk good-bye. The rugged life in the Rockies with the Ute had suited her well. For two years she'd stayed with her mother's people. It was to them she had fled for answers when her parents could not soothe her grief, when Charles and her stillborn son lay in cold, dark graves and the law refused to help her find the killers.

"Stay with me," Tall Elk said. "I can provide for you." For the first time, his stoic exterior slipped to reveal his feelings, the emotions she'd sensed for months but could not return.

"I can't. I have to find them."

For a second she saw the anguish in his dark eyes. Then it vanished, for he understood her need for vengeance. He was above all a Ute warrior. "You've learned well."

"I'm grateful for all you've taught me. Without your help, I would not be able to find the men who killed Charles."

"When it's finished, will you return?"

She didn't want to hurt him or fill him with false hope. "I can't promise you. But if our spirits are to be as one, we shall be together."

Tall Elk handed her the reins of a spotted mare, one of his many gifts to her. "May you find the answers to the questions that cause your unrest." He stared at Hawk perched on her leather-clad arm. "Keep her well," he said to the bird. "In a vision, I saw you as her protector."

Sage's body had healed, but the knowledge that the killers ran free hardened her heart. Her empty arms and the scars on her left shoulder were a constant reminder of what had been ripped from her life.

She now knew how to track down the killers.

Someday justice would be served.

THREE

Colorado Rockies
July, 1882

While other women tended their babies, Sage tracked down outlaws. When winter winds chilled her to the bone and heavy rains soaked her in the dead of night, she thought about a home with a roof and a crackling fire. When desert sands stung her eyes, and rattlesnakes struck at her heels, she longed for comfort and a friend. When murderous men swore no one could catch them, she cleaned her rifle and saddled her horse. Sage had chosen the life of a bounty hunter to track down the men who turned her dreams into a nightmare.

But the days were lonely, and the nights brought back memories of a happier time. Some days she liked to dwell on those precious moments with Charles, and other times they were too hard. She had to keep her mind on the present—always looking for the men who killed Charles and their baby boy.

Sage swung down from the saddle, every nerve taut with her effort to discriminate between nature and man's presence. Her well-worn boots crunched against a brush-laden trail. A twig snapped. A young doe sprang from behind a spruce and disappeared into a thicket as the obnoxious call of a raven rang from the treetops, capturing her attention.

The sweetness of pine and cedar mixed with the freshness of an approaching Rocky Mountain rain alerted her to the storm brewing in the distance. She bent down to the narrow path winding around the mountain to examine the tracks of Aiden Mc-Caw's horse. The animal had thrown a shoe, forcing the outlaw to slow his pace. Good.

Aiden had passed by less than two hours before. He wouldn't be hard to catch, and soon she'd have him. Unless he intended to ambush her on the trail ahead. She glanced up at Hawk circling above and motioned for the bird to join her. More than one man had tried to shoot her red-tailed companion with the idea that killing one equated to stopping the other. A notion that held more truth than she cared to admit. The magnificent bird swooped low on his broad wings and planted his talons firmly onto the shoulder of her leather coat. In the July sun, she'd considered removing the outer garment, but a steadily graying sky across the western ridge of mountains had brought on a sudden chill.

With her finger resting on her Winchester's trigger, she stared up to the mountain's higher elevation. Unpredictable weather was a hazard for those who chased an outlaw over the Rockies. But if Aiden made it over the tall peaks and found safety, another man could lose his life. Another woman could become a widow, and another child could become fatherless.

She'd been in Denver, sorting through wanted posters at the sheriff's office to see if any of the faces matched Charles's killer, when a wire came through that Aiden McCaw had shot and killed an unarmed rancher in the Rocky Falls area. He and his gang of brothers had raided throughout Colorado, Kansas, and Nebraska for several years, sometimes hiding out in the Rockies and other times making their way to the hideouts along the Old Outlaw Trail until lawmen grew tired of the pursuit. She'd wired Marshal Parker Timmons in Rocky Falls that she would bring in the outlaw. And Sage always kept her word.

She lowered the rifle and lifted her binoculars to peer toward the tree line. A chestnut horse and its rider picked their way through the aspens. He wore a black hat with an eagle feather, and he had red hair. That was her man.

"Hawk, we almost have him," she said above a whisper and stroked his soft feathers. "One less killer for folks to contend with." She studied Aiden a bit more—the way he twisted in the saddle and how he rode with his left hand on his rifle. Aiden McCaw was known as one smart outlaw, which caused her to wonder why tracking him had been so easy.

She remembered another trail over higher ground that took a little more surefootedness but would allow her to cut him off at a lower elevation. She preferred surprising an outlaw to trailing him and possibly being led into a trap.

Sage mounted her Indian pony and rode upward and around a wall of mottled gray granite. The summer storm moved closer with blue-black clouds, while temperatures steadily dropped. Thunder rumbled in the distance, like a grizzly's stomach after a long winter.

She swung her pony to the far right. A waterfall roared its power and gushed over centuries-old rocks, drowning out any other sounds, including her horse's steps. Through her binoculars, she saw Aiden had stopped his descent from where she planned to intercept him. Perhaps he was looking for shelter from the impending weather. She scanned the area, behind trees, boulders, and brush to make certain this wasn't a trap. Assured that the man rode alone, she rode upward and made her way to the lower pass before him and hid behind a boulder. When Aiden rode into view, she aimed her rifle and rode onto the trail.

"Aiden McCaw, drop your weapons, then raise your hands."

He slowly lifted his hands above his head, but his rifle still lay across his saddle. Scars of age and violence creased his bearded face, and his eyes bore the souls of those he'd murdered.

"I said drop your rifle."

He scowled, and the weapon hit the ground.

"Now, with your right hand, slowly reach for your pistol and toss it this way."

He spat a chaw of tobacco from a mouthful of rotten teeth. His eyes narrowed, and the pistol fell. "You're going to regret this, Sage Morrow."

He knows me. Perhaps so since she'd worked as a bounty hunter for a few years. "I don't think so. You've just met a worse storm than the one brewing above us."

She rode closer, keeping an eye on Aiden, knowing he could flip a knife with deadly aim. Most likely he kept it in his left boot.

"What are you pinning on me?"

"The marshal in Rocky Falls accused you of killing a rancher. I'm sure justice will be served. This isn't the first time you've killed."

"So the law sent a woman?"

The hair on the back of Sage's neck bristled. "He figured it was an easy job."

Aiden's rock-hard face twitched, and he studied the predator bird on her shoulder.

"Hold out your hands."

Aiden slowly obliged. One word from her, and Hawk would attack the man, and if Aiden knew her name, he knew her well-trained bird. She reached over and wrapped a rope several times around his wrists before securing his horse's reins and stripping him of his remaining weapons. He smelled worse than a pen of pigs.

"How many are behind you?" he said.

She could handle the likes of him and worse. "I work alone."

Lightning slashed through an aspen, and the ground trembled. The chestnut jumped, but Sage held firmly to the reins of both horses. Without another word, she dug her heels into the side of her horse and headed down the narrow mountainside. A blast of chilling air sent bits of debris stinging into her face.

"Where're we goin'?" Aiden shouted above the turmoil at their heels.

"You're going to jail until a trial for murder, and I'm collecting the bounty."

"You got the wrong man."

How many times had she heard that? "Tell your story to the judge."

"You'll be dead before I stand before any judge. You've been set up," Aiden said. "Mark my words."

Sage bit back a terse remark. The less she talked to a wanted man, the better she liked it. She didn't want to listen to their vulgar speech or hear their excuses for breaking the law. Someday, she'd leave this life behind and start all over. But not yet. Not until she found the men who'd murdered Charles.

M arshal Parker Timmons couldn't tolerate lazy people, especially when it was a lazy deputy and that lazy deputy happened to be his older brother.

"Frank, you have a job to do, and sitting here drinking coffee in the office isn't what the people of this town expect."

Frank rubbed the top of his head, minus any hair. "Little brother, you're already talking like a politician."

"Which means everything I do is for the betterment of those I represent. Now get to work." Parker nearly added a few more words that the town's preacher could have outlined his next sermon on, but he swallowed his anger. God and Parker had come to an agreement about his temper, and having the Lord in charge of his life meant living right. Even when it came to Frank and his—

"I'll check on things at the livery." Frank scraped his chair across the wooden floor.

Parker sensed ire rising from the walls of his stomach. The saloon was on the way to the livery, and his brother had a constant hankering for whiskey. Unfortunately, it was destroying Frank and his family. "I just came from there. I'd rather you pay a call on Mrs. Felter, see if she remembers anything else about what happened to her husband."

"I thought you'd already talked to her."

"I have, but she might have remembered something. See if there's anything she and those children need."

Frank frowned. "That's a woman's job—or a preacher's."

Parker glanced away, remembering a time when he might have said the same thing. "What if Mrs. Felter and her children were Leah and your sons?"

Frank picked up his hat and plopped it on his head. "All right. For once, I agree with you. And I 'spect you'd go to your grave after the man who sent me to mine."

"That's right. We've got to look at what happens to folks as personal."

Frank nodded. "I'm trying, little brother." He left the office, closing the door behind him. Parker glanced around the dusty room and settled into the chair his brother had just vacated, glad of the breeze that puffed through the open window. He reached for a stack of paperwork that needed to go to the governor's office.

When the sun had cast its shadows west and Frank hadn't returned, Parker stuffed a burlap sack full of frustration and regret and walked to the saloon. No doubt his brother was there, and this time Parker would have to fire him. It didn't matter that Frank was his older brother. The good people of Rocky Falls needed a deputy they could depend on.

The closer Parker stomped to the saloon, the more his anger bubbled. Certain he heard Frank's voice among the drunks, he threw open the door to the popular stain in town where some men tried to forget life's problems. His gaze swept around the hazy room, where the distinct odor of unwashed bodies mingled with the sweet perfume of the women who worked there.

Frank wasn't posed at his regular corner on the right side of the bar. Neither was he holding a losing hand of cards at the gambling tables where he too often threw away what his family needed to live on. Leah did the best she could to rear their kids and raise a garden in Colorado's short growing season, and the older boys looked after the ranch, but Frank didn't know the meaning of *responsibility*. Seemed like he expected Parker to pitch in and help. Oh, he talked big when he was facing hard times, which was why Parker had given him a job as deputy. Until now.

"Frank ain't here," the bartender said before Parker stated his business. "Ain't seen him all day."

After thanking the man, Parker took a minute to assess where his brother could be, finally deciding that Frank must have finished late at the Felter ranch and ridden on home. They'd talk in the morning. Sure would be a blessing to Leah if her husband had taken to heart what Parker had tried to show him. She needed a husband who took care of his family proper.

By the time Parker caught sight of his ranch and the smoke curling from the chimney of his cabin, darkness had set in. His stomach growled, and he didn't care what Duncan had cooked for supper. He was hungry enough to eat a fence post.

Home. Only one bedroom, but he'd built the place himself, and the sight of it always made him feel good. He'd tripled his original 160-acre homestead along the St. Vrain River and was negotiating to purchase more land. Forty-five acres of one of the homesteads had limestone, and thirty other acres had red sandstone. He saw a future in the nearby stone quarries and the likelihood of the railroad making its way to Rocky Falls; both circumstances promised to make his hard work and sacrifice worthwhile.

After feeding his gelding, he stepped into his cabin. From the stone fireplace, the aroma of beef and beans greeted him. Someday he'd buy a decent cookstove.

"Evenin', Boss," Duncan said. "Just about to head to the bunkhouse. I was beginning to think you'd spent the night in town." He rose from a chair, his weathered face reflecting the years of working outside.

"Didn't mean to be this late." Parker made his way to the fireplace and lifted the lid of a cast-iron pot. "Everybody's eaten?"

"All but you. Let me get you a plate." Duncan lifted a plate from a shelf above the table while Parker dipped into a bucket of drinking water.

"Did the horses get shod?"

"Yep."

Parker took the plate laden with tender beef and beans and a generous hunk of cornbread. "Your boss doesn't pay you enough to foreman this ranch and cook too."

Duncan grinned. "I've been meaning to bring that up with him." He poured two cups of coffee and placed one in front of Parker before sliding into a chair with the other. "Any luck bringing in Aiden McCaw?"

"Not yet. Got a bounty hunter headed this way — Sage Morrow."

Duncan whistled. "The woman? Wonder what she's like."

"I'm about to find out. My guess is she's mean and hard. Doesn't really matter as long as the McCaws are stopped." Parker thought about Oden Felter. They'd been friends for over ten years. He didn't deserve to die with a bullet in his chest because of two dollars.

"You're the man to bring him in, not a bounty hunter."

Parker stabbed his fork into the beef. "But I can't do it all. I need help. And the locals are fearful of the McCaws' reputation."

Duncan took a gulp of his coffee. "Yeah, but if they aren't brought in, folks will blame you." He shook his head. The two had talked of little else for almost a week. "Sent a couple of the hands to drive the cattle to the summer pasture." He stood. "I'll leave you to your supper. I'm turning in."

Duncan seemed to sense when Parker had things on his mind. The problems with the McCaws had made him unsociable. And tonight the situation with Frank refused to let him be. Hard to figure out why two brothers turned out so differently. Both had gone through the war fighting for Virginia and the South, coming out with memories that were better forgotten. Both had come home to learn their father had died of consumption the same day Lee surrendered to Grant at Appomattox.

But whatever Frank had seen and possibly done had scarred him. He returned home midway through the war and stayed long enough for Leah to get with child, but by the time John was born, Frank had left again to resume fighting. When the war ended, Frank came back with a bent toward drinking that grew steadily worse. He never stated what he saw or what he did. When he decided to move his family to Colorado territory, Parker came too. The war had destroyed much of the spirit of the Virginians, and he wanted to be a part of the country's healing and growth. Lately, Frank, too, talked more about shaking the past's hold. Maybe Parker's concern was for nothing. After all, Frank said he was trying.

Tomorrow was another day, and Parker needed some sleep. He blew out the lantern and crawled into bed.

When he thought about it, he'd learned some memorable things from Frank—like how to laugh when the road got rough. His brother loved music and could make a fiddle sing. And Frank loved Leah and their five sons. Seemed like that ought to be enough to make a man go straight, work his ranch, and provide for his family. John ran the ranch like a man and did a good job, but he needed his pa to show him how to be a man. All those boys needed that. Instead, Frank demonstrated how not to live. For the most part, Parker felt like he'd become Frank's daddy. Hard to love an older brother like a man should when he neglected his family.

Someone banged on the door.

"Uncle Parker."

John? Startled, Parker threw back the tattered quilt and grabbed his britches. "I'm coming. Is something wrong?"

"Yes, sir. Pa's been shot." John's voice cracked.

Parker flipped his suspenders over his shoulders and flung open the door. In the dark, all he could make out was the young man's figure. "How bad, son?"

John sucked in a breath, steadied himself. "He's dead. Shot in the chest. Somebody dumped him on our porch."

FOUR

Sage rode through the sunbathed streets of Rocky Falls, leading Aiden's horse. Not a soul was in sight, which caused her to ready her rifle and scrutinize rooftops and the corners of buildings. The journey down from the mountains, along the Fall River, through Estes Park, and southeast to Rocky Falls had taken three days of hard riding, and her body had long since stumbled into exhaustion. Sleep never came to her when she was bringing in a man. She'd rested at night while Aiden slept, but Aiden's threats, like those of so many men before him, kept her awake with one hand wrapped around the barrel of her rifle and the other hand on her Colt. Once she turned him over to the custody of the local marshal, she'd sleep for two days to recover.

Her fear of succumbing to the pressures of a weary body was her darkest foe, but it was during those sleepless nights that she allowed her mind to slip back to the days when she and Charles were first married, when she carried his child and the world looked sparkling and new. So often she imagined that other widows survived their bleak moments with the same golden memories.

Now, as they rode on through the middle of town, she lifted her face to the cloudless sky. The warmth and the dazzling afternoon sunlight were an indulgence after being drenched to the bone in the chilling summer rains. She could almost taste a decent meal — one that promised more flavor than jerky.

"I'm thirsty," Aiden said.

"My canteen's empty," she said. "You drank it all a few miles back. I'll get you water once you're behind bars."

"For a bounty hunter, you take care of me real nice. Won't help though."

Sage ignored the greasy outlaw. After three days of his threats, she was good at it.

"This is only the start of your troubles," he continued as she pulled the horses to a halt in front of the marshal's office. "You best be ready."

Sage had heard enough. "You're wrong, Aiden. This is the end for you, and now I'm able to rid myself of your less-than-tolerable company."

He leaned on his saddle horn. "Don't understand why a pretty gal like you would want to be a bounty hunter. You must have loved your no-account husband more than he was worth."

Sage bit her tongue. No point letting him get to her. With the mood she was in, he might not make it to jail without a few bullet holes. After she'd left Tall Elk in the mountains not far from here, she'd let it be known that she was after Charles's killers. Aiden wasn't the first to needle her with such taunts.

"You didn't even know his right name," he said. "Unless he filled you in on the company he was keepin' and how he kept money in his pocket."

She choked back another remark and more than a little emotion. This was new. How could Aiden know anything about Charles?

"Cat got your tongue? The Ute blood flowing through your veins must run thin, or you'd be carving out my heart."

Sage stroked Hawk to calm herself. She'd contemplate how much Aiden knew about Charles later. Still holding onto both horses' reins, she dismounted. Relief eased her tired muscles, but not the headache wrapping its demons across the back of her skull. The first thing she intended to do after finding a place to stay for a few days was to eat a hot meal and brew some of the willow bark in her saddlebag.

Aiden spit at her feet. "I say, for an Injun, you ain't got much of a fightin' spirit."

"I suggest you keep your remarks to yourself. With all the murdering you and your gang have done, someone might pull the trigger to save a judge the job of sentencing you to hang."

"You ain't gonna shoot me. You and the hawk bring your men in alive so you get all of the bounty."

Sage eyed him with more disgust than she normally revealed. "There's always a first time."

A note nailed to the marshal's door caught her attention. "Get down."

With his tied wrists, he swung his leg over the saddle and dismounted slowly, but he was still light on his feet, like a mountain cat—and just as deadly. Aiden snickered. "Looks like he left you a love note."

She glared at him and gestured with her rifle at the steps leading to the boardwalk. He chuckled before sitting on the wooden planks. Most bounty hunters would have brought him in slung over his saddle instead of riding it. But she believed killing a wanted man for the bounty put her as low as the outlaws. With one eye on Aiden, she read the note.

Gone to a funeral. Be back midafternoon.—*Marshal Parker Timmons*

Judging from the location of the sun, they'd have about an hour's wait. "The marshal's at a funeral," she said. "I bet that puts him in a fine mood."

"He'll be in a worse one soon enough. This town's about to make their undertaker a rich man."

"Why's that? You still think your brothers are going to spring you?"

Aiden's face hardened. "You and the people in this town are

going to regret ever being born. My brothers won't let anything stand in the way of getting me out of here."

Sage had read enough men to tell the difference between a liar and a man who bluffed to save his life. And she believed Aiden's every word. She'd need to stay in Rocky Falls until things settled down. It wasn't what she wanted, but if trouble was riding on her heels, she planned to face it head-on. "Since you're so free with your threats, why don't you fill me in on your brothers' plans?"

His raspy laugh could have been heard all over town. Come to think of it, the town was pretty empty. Whoever had died must have been an important person—or well loved.

"Now why would I want to tell you the plan? That would curdle the milk for sure. It's a surprise for you and the marshal."

Hawk must have sensed her apprehension because he ruffled his feathers. "Easy, fella. We're all right." The proud bird slowly relaxed, but she knew he'd tear into Aiden the moment she gave the word. "I've heard enough, Aiden. Hawk isn't as patient as I am."

He turned toward the mountains as though gauging when the rest of the gang would show up for his rescue. Perhaps she was simply too tired and weak to make sense of him.

Nearly an hour later, a tall man walked down the street and made his way toward her and Aiden. His confident stride and erect shoulders indicated he was a man of purpose, possibly the marshal. Others walked in pairs or threes to the various businesses—a feed store, livery, a saloon and hotel above it, an undertaker, blacksmith, newspaper and telegraph, and general store. As the man walked closer, his marshal's badge caught a sun ray. The shiny star caused acid to rise to the top of her throat. She swallowed hard. Lawmen. Most of them were arrogant and looked down on who she was and what she did. In her opinion, a bounty hunter made their job easier. Of course, some bounty hunters weren't much better than the outlaws. So maybe those marshals had a right to their opinion. But that didn't mean she had to like them, especially the ones who were too frightened to go after killers themselves.

"Are you Marshal Timmons?" she said.

"Yes, ma'am. How can I help you?" His light blue gaze trailed to Hawk, then to Aiden McCaw, still sitting on the boardwalk. His face hardened. "You must be Sage Morrow. Sorry I wasn't here. I've been to a funeral."

Did he think she couldn't read? "I saw the note." She stuck out her hand.

He shook it, his grip firm and strong. "Parker Timmons." Not a smile creased his face. "I see you have Aiden McCaw. Appreciate you bringing him in. Folks here are real upset with the killings." He studied Aiden. Hatred, like shafts of fire, emanated from his eyes.

"I understand. That's his horse." She pointed to the office door, where she'd propped his rifle and pistol. "Those are his guns."

Parker nodded. "Let's get him inside. Did he give you much trouble?"

"Not much." Did Timmons think she'd own up to fearing a wanted man? Truth was, she was afraid of every one of them, but she'd made a vow the day she buried Charles. "You might want to keep your eyes open while he's a guest here. He's made lots of threats about his gang springing him."

"I'm a little shorthanded right now. But I'll make do until his trial. He could have been bluffing."

"Maybe. Don't you have a deputy?"

"I did." Lines raked across his forehead. "We just buried him."

This town had been hit hard. "I'm sorry to hear that. Did he have family?"

"Yes, ma'am. He was my brother."

Instantly her heart softened to the marshal's grief. She hoped the brother had died of natural causes and not foul play. "What happened?"

"He was murdered. Just before he died, he told his oldest son that it was the McCaws. No doubt Aiden's brothers. They've stolen and murdered their last. At least this one has."

FIVE

Parker sucked in a breath to control his anger against Aiden McCaw. The murdering outlaw's gang had killed his brother and a friend. For the first time since he'd been elected marshal, he wished the accused were dead. And he'd like nothing better than to pull the trigger. He took a step toward the outlaw.

"Stand up, and don't give me an excuse to kill you. I'm not the only one who wants to see you dead. This town didn't take too lightly to having Felter and their deputy shot. They might want revenge. And I'm in no mood to stop them. In fact, I might offer my rope."

"I ain't scared." Aiden stood and sneered. "Won't be here long enough to enjoy your hospitality."

Parker opened the door to the marshal's office and shoved Aiden inside. "The cell's open. Get inside."

He wanted to turn his gun on him. Slam his fist into his face ... again and again. But he couldn't. His insides tightened. He'd sworn to uphold the law, not bury himself in revenge. He slammed the cell door shut, then turned his attention to the woman before him, the female bounty hunter who had a reputation that sounded more like a legend. Her dark hair and high cheekbones gave away her Ute blood, and she had eyes the color of rich, dark earth. She stood shoulder to shoulder with him, and Parker was a tall man.

"Will you be in town for a few days until your money arrives?"

"I will." She stroked the hawk on her shoulder, a formidable bird. "I need to get some rest." She paused for a moment as though considering something. "I'd like to help you guard Aiden until his trial, make sure his threats don't follow through—since you don't have a deputy."

"I plan to stay here tonight to keep an eye on him." Parker hadn't ever depended on a woman before, and he doubted he ever would. Even a female bounty hunter. And the stories behind her name couldn't possibly be true ... However, she had brought in Aiden McCaw. "I'll talk to a couple of locals. Maybe deputize them. Seems like his brothers would have cut him loose while you were riding through the mountains."

She tossed a glance at Aiden, who had lain down on the straw-filled mattress. "My thoughts too. It all was a bit too easy." She gave the hawk a smile resembling the affection a mother gave her child. "I'll be at the hotel for a few hours, then I'll be back. Sorry to hear about your brother. Did he leave a wife and children?"

Parker appreciated her concern, another part of her reputation. "Frank and Leah have five sons."

She frowned and compassion clouded her face, as though she'd seen too many widows and fatherless children. "They're in for hard times." She took a breath, exhaustion clearly evident. "When the bounty money arrives, I'd like to give her and Mrs. Felter some of it."

The stories about Sage Morrow weren't all made up. She *was* sympathetic to those who'd been hurt by outlaws. Strange woman. Strange personality for a bounty hunter who toted a hawk for a pet. "That would be very generous of you. I'll be sure to pass on your comfort. They all are grieving."

Sage nodded. "Thank you. I'll not be taking up any more of your afternoon." She hesitated, and the deep brown of her eyes penetrated his. "Unless you need me."

"He won't be asking you for help until tomorrow." Aiden spit foul-smelling tobacco through the bars. "And you ain't slept in three nights. Looks to me like you won't be fit to help nary a body."

"Is he always this mouthy?" Parker said. If the outlaw couldn't keep his mouth shut, he might not live through the night.

Sage walked to the cell and anchored her hands on the Colts at her slender hips. "It took all my will not to break my vow to keep all my prisoners alive to stand trial."

"He wouldn't have been as lucky with me." Retribution continued to race through his veins. Aiden was a murderous cutthroat. *Lord, I'm not honoring You.* Anguish over Frank's death hit him hard again.

"I understand."

Parker had a wagonload of things to tend to, one of which was Leah and the children. But he couldn't leave the prisoner alone. Neither did he have a candidate to guard Aiden.

Sage took a deep breath. "Who's with your sister-in-law?"

"She's at the parsonage with the preacher and his wife."

"If you need to check on her, I'll stay here."

Parker's insides jolted, as if he'd stepped barefoot into an icy mountain stream. What dealings he'd had with bounty hunters had been less than pleasant. They couldn't get their money and get out of town fast enough. They didn't like people, and they sure didn't care about anyone hurting over bad times.

"Ma'am, thank you for your kind offer, but I can't ask any more of you."

"Yes, you can." She made her way to his untidy desk, strewn with a newspaper from Denver, a tin coffee mug, and wanted posters—one of them sporting Aiden McCaw's ugly face. Easing down onto the chair, she urged the hawk to step onto the desk. "Go ahead and take care of your family. I can spend a few more hours with Aiden."

He hesitated, stunned to find himself about to accept her offer. "One hour would help." The plight of his family must have numbed his senses. "Are you always this helpful to marshals and sheriffs?"

She lifted sleep-deprived eyes. "My heart goes out to those

affected by lawless men. But I don't like many lawmen. Never have. Don't like politicians either. There may be a few good ones out there, but I haven't met any."

Parker bristled. "Why not?" After Leah crying on his shoulder for the past two days and trying to comfort his nephews with his own grief weighing on his shoulders, he didn't have any more emotional control. "Officials are elected by the people. If some are corrupt, whose fault is that?" Anger now threatened to grab hold of his tongue. "I plan to enter politics, and I'm proud of it."

A cold, impassionate glare met his reproach. "My personal experience, Marshal Timmons. I'm sure you conduct your business with the utmost of integrity."

The sarcasm cut to the bone, but he chose to keep any more tidbits of information to himself. Her attitude put the two of them on equal ground. He didn't have much use for money-hungry bounty hunters. Even those who appeared to be decent human beings.

He'd see to Leah and the boys and be back in a half hour.

Sage regretted her spiteful words the moment Marshal Timmons left his office. Granted, exhaustion had lit a flame in her body, but that wasn't an excuse to insult a man on the same day he buried his brother. She'd been around scoundrels for so long that she'd begun to sound like one. This afternoon, she acted like one too. Forcing her tired legs to stand, she hurried to the door and outside onto the street.

"Marshal Timmons?" she called.

He stopped in his tracks and slowly turned to face her, red-faced and wearing the lines of a man weathered by grief and responsibility. Sage swallowed her pride.

"I apologize for my remarks. I was rude and unfeeling, not at all considerate of your loss."

He hesitated for a moment, leaving her more uncomfortable

with each breath. "I reckon if that's the way you feel, you should be able to speak your mind."

"Some things are better left unsaid. You don't deserve my remarks on the day you bury your brother and tend to his widow and family."

Marshal Timmons retraced his steps. She'd seen more handsome men, but rarely did she see a man whose eyes spoke for his heart. Eyes the color of a robin's egg. "Back in Virginia, my mother's father raised sheep. Folks disliked him because of what he did, not because of who he was. Cattle ranchers spit on him, poisoned his watering holes, and used his flocks for target practice. Even in church his pew was known as the stinking sheep row. After twenty years, the preacher still didn't know my grandfather's first name at his funeral."

She had that bit of chagrin coming, so she said nothing. Never mind that she could have told a similar story about folk judging bounty hunters or those who had Indian blood running through their veins.

He studied her a moment and continued on his way.

Back inside the marshal's office, Aiden's laughter echoed around the room, scraping at her nerves and interrupting her thoughts about a marshal whose grandfather was a sheepherder. Charles had despised sheep, called them wooly worms.

"What's so funny?" she said before sitting down.

"Oh, I'm thinkin' how all of this is playing right into our hands."

Aiden's life span was rapidly decreasing. "Why don't you tell me all about it?"

"And ruin the fun? Besides, you and Marshal Timmons will find out soon enough. I've planned for a long time to get the two of you together. Looks like my patience has paid off."

Sage sank into the chair. "I'd like to know what you're going to do. After all, there's only me and the marshal here to protect the town."

"Ain't that nice."

"And I'm too tired to be much use."

He laughed again, a deep-throated growl that reminded her of a mountain cat before it leaped on its prey.

Let him think she was too worn out to make sensible conversation. "How many of you are there?"

"Depends on how many of my brothers show up."

Sage closed her eyes and kept her mind busy with questions laid out like a trap. "Rumor is the McCaw gang boasts eight brothers."

"Could be."

She needed the real count. "Are all of them as mean as you?"

"The other four are meaner."

Only five, then. Still, the odds curdled her stomach. "I'm not worried. If they want you so badly, they can have you. I caught you once. I can find you again."

"But you're smart enough to know I let you catch me. Wouldn't you like to know why?"

Sage kept her eyes tightly closed and leaned back in the chair. The more he revealed, the better she and Parker's chances were. "Let me guess. You want to make an example of bounty hunters."

"If that was the case, you'd be dead back on the trail. Why don't you and the marshal figure it out and let me know?"

Weariness settled on her like the evening shadows creeping across the mountains at sunset. And along with the desire to sleep twenty-four hours came a yearning for her bounty-hunting days to be over. Soon she'd find the men who killed Charles. But she didn't even know their names. *Fight the sleep.* She needed to contend with Aiden. "Why don't you just tell me what this is all about?"

"Nope. And I ain't answering any more of your questions either."

"Why? We're just discussing your problem and mine."

"Just like ol' Charlie, ain't you? He had a way of talkin' friendly like too."

The blood through Sage's veins rushed faster than flood waters. He'd mentioned Charles's name too many times. "You must have known Charles pretty well."

"Not well enough."

She ached to learn more, but she could see Aiden was tiring of their game. "Since he's been gone for seven years, what's the harm in telling me? My husband didn't stay home much. Never said where he'd been or where he was going."

"Maybe you should've asked, and he wouldn't have ended up dead."

"You could tell—"

"Ask all you want, Mrs. Morrow. I'm fresh out of words, 'specially for an Injun bounty hunter."

Six

As Parker walked through town to the parsonage, where Leah and her sons had been invited to stay the night, he searched for the right words to comfort them in their loss. Preacher Waller and his wife could, no doubt, consol the grieving family far better than he could, yet Parker believed it was his responsibility to look after his sister-in-law, even if he himself were struggling to see a purpose in God's taking Frank. Had God simply grown tired of trying to shape him into a proper husband and father? Could Parker have done or said anything to change what happened?

And, most of all, *why* did Aiden's brothers kill Frank? What was Frank doing the night he died?

Questions and no answers, and it all fueled his fury. Not since the war had he felt such anger — anger at the situation, anger that he had no answers, and anger that he hadn't been able to see what was coming and stop it.

But through his rage, memories of his brother came unbidden — not the drinking or the gambling or the laziness, but the good things. The way Frank could always make folks laugh. His fingers flying on the strings of his fiddle. Memory after memory from boyhood times to a few weeks ago caused Parker to chuckle. Then the mirth changed to tears. Grief. What a stalking predator.

Parker stood at the front door of the parsonage and hesitated before knocking. He had no more idea what to say to Leah than he'd had when he left his office. Yet, in the end, what good were words? Her husband — his brother — had been murdered, and

Parker intended to track down the killers. He didn't care how long it took.

The reminder of his responsibilities made him wish for once that he could get on his horse and corral the whole gang. An impossible job without a posse. Vengeance was God's, so the Scripture said. But Parker had seen enough bloodshed from the McCaw gang to want them to pay. How did a God-fearing man come to terms with it all? He wanted the whole gang in his jail and sentenced to hang.

He knocked, and Preacher Waller answered the door. Some days he liked the preacher, and other days he barely tolerated the fire-and-brimstone sermons that reared up in most of his conversations. But whatever Parker's feelings for the man, today Preacher Waller and his wife helped the Timmons family hold up in the midst of a tragedy.

"Come on in, Parker. Leah and the boys are in the parlor." Preacher Waller filled the doorway, a mountain of a man, and Parker followed him into the small crowded room. As a youth, Waller was more trouble than he was worth. Fighting and drinking like a mad man. Now he often brought condemnation to the whole town. "I do say, Frank Timmons met his maker as a drunk and sluggard. The coals are burning hot in hell tonight."

Ire rose in Parker's gut. He grabbed Waller by the shirt collar. "My brother knew the Lord. Just because his weakness was strong drink doesn't mean he didn't love the Lord or his family. And you aren't the one to decide his future."

Preacher Waller raised his fist. "Ephesians 5:18 says, 'And be not drunk with wine, wherein is excess.'"

The parlor hushed. Leah stared at Preacher Waller, her eyes filled with tears.

Parker released him before he vented all of his feelings on one man. "You could have left that remark alone. Have a little compassion on Frank's wife and children."

Preacher Waller's round face reddened to the shade of a ripe tomato. "I shall never stop speaking the truth."

Parker glared at him. "Maybe you should spend more time reading Scripture about love." Before Preacher Waller could throw him out of the parsonage, Leah made her way to Parker's side and looped her arm into his.

"Let's talk on the front porch," she said.

Parker took a breath and escorted her outside. He'd come to comfort her, and she'd been forced to rescue him. Turning his mind back to the needs of her family, he vowed none of them would ever do without, just like he had from the beginning. There was no one else to help her. The rest of his and Frank's siblings lived in Virginia, where their mother lived.

"What can I do?" he said when they had settled on the front porch.

"We'll be fine," she said. "I want to take my sons home after church tomorrow. Life goes on, and so does the work to keep us alive."

She offered a faint smile, and he saw glimpses of the girl of so many years ago. "Pray for us. We all need wisdom and strength."

Parker nodded. In a few days, he would persuade Leah to sell their land and move onto his ranch. He'd move into the bunkhouse with his foreman so everything would look proper, and he'd build a bigger house for Leah and the boys. She'd most likely agree, and the arrangements would make it easier for him to keep an eye on them. Times weren't easy for anyone, and tomorrow and the next day would bring increasing difficulties for a widow and five boys. The hope that had once kept Parker believing God would change things for Frank's family had dried up like his brother's flow of blood.

The door opened, and John stepped out to join them on the porch. "Uncle Parker, I'd like a few words with you if that's all right."

Moving toward the door, Leah squeezed John's arm before leaving the two alone.

The young man lifted his shoulders and stared at the church. "I want to take my pa's place." He pulled himself up to his nearly six-foot height. "Deputize me. There were more than one set of horse tracks leading up to the porch that night."

Parker peered into John's face. A shadow of a beard sprouted, but eighteen years didn't make a man. Neither did bitterness and revenge.

"Son, your job is to take care of your mama and your brothers. I could put your pa's badge on your chest, but what would your mama do without you? I'll find the rest of the gang. Aiden's in jail, and it won't be long before the rest will be there too. The best thing you can do for your pa is what you're doing right now, holding on to that sweet lady who is fighting the tears for your sake."

John's chin quivered, and he swallowed hard. "An eye for an eye and a tooth for a tooth. You weren't the one who saw him draw his last breath or gasp as he said, 'McCaw.'"

"That's right, son. But we're called to live in ... peace whenever possible." Parker almost said "forgiveness," but he thought twice about asking John to forgive when his pa's body was mere hours in the grave. Right now Parker wasn't able to forgive either. Anger controlled everything about him, a seething fury at the injustice of his brother's death.

"You heard what the preacher said about pa. It might be true, but he has no right to speak about him that way. I can't believe God has a man like him as a preacher any more than I can believe the McCaws should run free." The boy shook with uncontrollable emotions.

Parker couldn't talk any sense into him until he calmed down. "We'll talk after you take your ma home tomorrow."

"We aren't spending the night here after what he just said.

I'm the man of the house now. If you won't deputize me, then I'll take out after them myself."

"Another death in the family would destroy your ma. I understand how you feel, but out of respect for her, please let me handle this."

"Maybe for today."

"Let's keep talking about this. You've done a man's job since you were ten years old, and now you have a heavier burden."

John stiffened. "I'm going back to the cemetery for a while. Tell Mama I'll be back to take her home."

Parker watched him until he disappeared behind the church. An angry man often didn't have a lick of sense, especially one who wasn't full grown. Parker said his good-byes to Preacher Waller and his missus and then promised Leah he'd check on her at church tomorrow. The business of Aiden McCaw in the town's jail needed his attention.

On his way back to relieve Sage, he stopped at the general store and wired the proper authorities in Denver notification of Aiden McCaw's presence in his jail and a request to send Morrow's bounty. A US Marshal would arrive in a few days to deliver Sage's money. The sooner Sage received her due, the sooner he'd be rid of her. Something about the woman bothered him. Maybe it was the way she spoke her mind. Or maybe it was because she had the guts to bring in a hardened man like Aiden McCaw. She didn't appear to need a man for anything, and that was against nature. Or maybe it was the hawk and its piercing eyes. He'd heard many stories of how Sage Morrow searched the state for the men who had murdered her husband. How the part-Ute woman learned how to track and survive in the wild. He'd even heard she knew how to talk to animals and make a man do whatever she wanted. What was he supposed to believe? For certain he wanted her out of town.

Parker opened the door to his office. Sage was already on her feet with her Colt drawn.

"Whoa, I'm the marshal. Shoot me, and you'll have a real problem."

Her eyes darkened, and with sleep threatening to take over, she looked more than a bit menacing. Her hand slipped to her side. "Aiden insists on the same thing."

Parker glanced at the prisoner and cringed at the ear-piercing snore. "Did he give you any problems?"

"Said he needed the outhouse, but I told him he could use the chamber pot. That way, you could empty it."

His favorite chore as a marshal. "Thanks. Ah, I sent a wire for a US Marshal to take Aiden in and bring your money." He paused. She did look real tired. "I appreciate your staying while I looked in on Leah and the boys."

"I was glad to do it." She tossed a look at Aiden, whose mouth was gaping open like a fish. "Can we step outside?"

Parker led the way. His only desire was to placate the woman and get her out of his hair. Thank goodness she left the hawk on his desk. Outside, she rested her hat atop dark hair that hung straight to her waist and was tied with a piece of leather. He hadn't noticed how shiny black it was before.

"He said a few things I ought to pass on," she said. "Often it's hard to tell when a liar's telling the truth, but he added your name to mine in his list of threats. He claimed he and his gang have plans for both of us. Does that make any sense to you?"

Parker listened, measuring every word. "Because he's in my jail?"

"I thought you might be able to explain his cocky attitude. With your brother killed and all, I thought you could add a little light to Aiden's claims. I wondered if you and your brother had found their hideout."

"I have no answers. Only questions. The only thing Frank said before he died was the word *McCaw*. Anything else?"

"He said there were five of them total." She yawned. "I'm

gathering up my belongings and heading to the livery and hotel. You can find me there. But I'll be back after a few hours of sleep."

Don't forget your hawk. "Don't worry about me. Get a good night's sleep, and I'll talk to you tomorrow. I'll ask him a few questions myself."

She slipped her hand into an elbow-length leather glove for the hawk. They walked back inside, and the squeak of the door didn't arouse Aiden in the slightest. She coaxed the bird onto her arm.

"How's your sister-in-law faring?" Sage said.

"With the folks clearing out of the parsonage, she finally shed the necessary tears. I want to help her, and I will, but the ache in her heart will take time."

"It gets easier, but you never forget."

For a moment, Parker had forgotten about Sage's being a widow.

"Your story about sheep reminded me of how too many folks judge others without the facts."

So she'd listened, and her Ute blood was most likely a source of harsh talk. "I learned a lot from my granddad. He told stories that showed folks how to live right. My father was a cattleman, and I followed in his steps. But granddad's life lessons about sheep are still there."

"Were you named after him?"

"Yes, ma'am. How did you guess? It's Parker Moses Timmons."

"Moses was a leader." She reached out and shook his hand, then whirled around and left without another word. Strange woman. Peculiar. Strong. And easy to look at.

SEVEN

Aiden eyed Marshal Timmons hunched over his desk, reading papers and writing on some of them. A pot of fresh coffee stayed warm on the woodstove. Smelled good, but the good marshal had refused to give him a hot cup of it earlier. 'Course, his brothers had killed Parker's brother, according to the plan. Seemed rather ironic ... considerin'. Until then, he'd bide his time until sprung from jail.

A newspaper lay on the far corner of the desk, but since Aiden could barely read, all he could make out was *Denver*. He hoped the front page was about the McCaws. All of Timmons's fancy reading and writing was a joke. He should have never stuck his nose in the McCaw gang's business.

Timmons had lit a lantern a few moments ago, and the glow sent shadows bouncing off the walls. Those weren't the only shadows that would be waiting once darkness settled in and the people of Rocky Falls slept.

He'd hated being trussed up like a pig while Sage led him down from the mountains. Downright humiliating. He'd give her credit, though. She and that hawk held their own in a man's world. The Ute had done a good job teaching her how to track and shoot. Rumor was she could throw a fair knife and speak their language. She was more respectable than most, giving him plenty of water and food in the morning and evening. He hid his smile at her consideration. Why, she'd even given him privacy when nature called. Didn't know of a single bounty hunter who cared about a man's private needs. Or who was as pretty. Feisty too. But he'd use her reputation to play into his hand. All aces.

Until two years ago, Aiden believed Charles and Sage Morrow had taken their secrets to their graves. Then he learned she hadn't died when Charles met his end. He chuckled. What Sage didn't know was the hunter had become the hunted.

Fools. Sage and Parker had waited too long. Why did they act like they'd never met? Must be for his benefit. But he was a smart man.

EIGHT

After a hot bath and a real plate of tough roast pork, onions, and potatoes, all floating in grease except for the bullet-hard biscuit, Sage fell asleep with a stomachache just as the sounds from the saloon escalated into obnoxious comments. The owner of the hotel and saloon hadn't been pleased about Hawk, but she'd assured the man that the bird would be in her care. To show her sincerity, she paid for three nights in advance — including the meals before she'd sampled the cook's food. From the looks of some of the patrons, Hawk could have taught them a few lessons in civility and self-control.

The customers wielded guns and knives with gusto, and those were the women. A stall at the livery might have been cleaner and safer than her upstairs room. Sage lifted the window and propped it with the chamber pot to freshen the air and so Hawk could come and go as he pleased.

Sage intended to sleep until midnight, then check on Timmons and Aiden at the jail. With the shouting, raucous laughter, and the steady clinking of glasses downstairs, she had little hope of actual sleep, but the moment her head touched the pillow, she succumbed.

Hours later, as sunlight streamed through the window, Sage's mind slowly adjusted to where she was and how hard she'd slept. Her senses that normally kept her alert had faded when she stretched out on a real bed. Her eyelids slowly fluttered open, and she glanced out the window. Judging from the sun, she must have slept well past noon. Feeling for her pocket watch on the floor, she saw the time read 2:35. How had she slept past the church bells with the open window?

Sage should have been up many hours ago, yet her aching body hesitated to make a move toward the day. Her headache and stomachache had disappeared, and all she needed to do for the next week was relax until her money arrived . . .

She startled. *Aiden McCaw and his men.* The threats made to Marshal Timmons rang through her mind like a clanging bell. A curse fell from her lips, something that rarely happened, just in case God was listening and sent a bolt of lightning in retribution. Although she'd cast God out of her heart, she still knew where He lived. Throwing back the tattered quilt, Sage grabbed her boots and strapped on her Colts.

She glanced at Hawk on the windowsill. "I may have gotten a man killed because I slept so long." The leather glove slipped over her hand and up above her elbow, and the bird took his position.

She rushed down the stairs, pausing only when a portly woman whose face had as many wrinkles as a plowed field asked if she'd slept well and wanted breakfast.

"Possibly later," she said without taking the time to thank her. "I need to check on a matter first." Her manners needed mending. Older folks needed to be treated with respect. She stopped at the door and noted a couple of fresh blood stains on the floor. She must have slept through the sounds of the fight. "Thank you, ma'am. I am quite rested."

The woman smiled, and her entire face lit up. "When you get back, let's sit down to a good meal. And I apologize for the pig slop you got for supper last night. One of the girls wanted to cook—or let's say she wanted to try. She needs some cooking lessons before I give up my kitchen again."

"I appreciate the invitation." Sage hurried out the door, hoping Aiden had been bluffing about his brothers springing him from jail.

The town looked deserted except for a man leaning against

the door of the saloon. Or maybe the door of the saloon was holding him up. No doubt everyone else was at home in commemoration of the Sabbath. Her parents had observed the day without fail. Once she stepped off the boardwalk and into the muddy street, she ran toward the marshal's office.

She knocked. "Marshal Timmons?"

No answer.

She turned the knob and stepped inside. Quiet. Too quiet. The cell door stood open. Foul-smelling Aiden had vacated, leaving nothing in his wake but a chipmunk scampering across the floor. Her gaze swept the room, dreading what she might find. Marshal Timmons lay face down on the other side of his desk with his head near the wood stove.

"Oh, no."

Not a sound. Not a muscle stirred. Sage touched his neck and felt a faint pulse. *He's alive.* The town didn't need to lose another good man. Blood splatter decorated the wooden floor, but not enough to be a gunshot or a knife wound. This was her fault. She should have been more alert. She should have stayed there with him. Sage swallowed hard. *I told him I'd be back after a few hours of sleep.* Guilt slid through her veins.

She gingerly turned him to his side, and he moaned. A huge lump with the imprints of the stove legs marred the right side of his head. His right eye had swollen shut in a deep shade of purple, and his mouth was split open. There was the source of the blood.

"Marshal Timmons, can you speak to me?"

He mumbled something, and she blew out a breath. "I'm so sorry. I should have stayed here last night instead of sleeping at the hotel."

His left eye cracked open, then closed.

"I'll get you some water and clean you up." All she found was cold, stale coffee in a mug. Hard to clean blood and dirt with that, and she needed to see how seriously he'd been hurt.

"McCaw gang," he managed, and dragged his tongue across

his cracked and bleeding lips. He desperately needed water. "They were inside before I knew what happened."

"You were outnumbered. Can you tell me how badly you're hurt?"

He took in a ragged breath. "I think my ribs might be broke."

"I'm so sorry. Do you have a wife or someone I need to contact?"

"Do I look like a family man?"

He was disagreeable, but she imagined his head felt like it would explode. "I'll get some water at the hotel and be right back." She studied him for a moment. Every hurt and innocent man seemed to take on Charles's characteristics.

"Don't leave."

She sat back on the floor and lowered Hawk beside her. "I'm listening. But let me remind you that you need tending."

He seemed to muster the strength to speak. "They were disappointed you weren't here."

Was that supposed to make her feel any better about leaving him to the mercy of wanted men? "What did they say?"

"We'll … talk about it later."

"Is this beating their calling card?"

"Maybe." His chest lifted, and he grimaced. His left hand covered his right ribs. They probably were broken. At least he wasn't spitting blood.

"Do you have a doctor in town?"

"Not yet."

Confused, she peered closer to examine his face. "You don't have a doctor, or you don't want me to fetch one?"

"The latter."

"There's nothing you can do but have a doctor look at your wounds. We can figure this out afterward."

Parker slowly nodded. From the lines across his forehead, he hurt powerfully bad. "I'm not dying. I'll know when that's happening. Aiden's men dared us … to come after them."

She remembered Aiden's comments. "I'm not surprised, but I don't know why. Do you?"

"Other than increasing their reputation by killing a bounty hunter and a marshal at the same time? But that doesn't make any sense either. I'm not a man of notoriety, but you have a good reputation for bringing in wanted men."

"Other bounty hunters have brought in more. Parker, please rest until I'm able to bring back help for you."

He closed his eyes. "Aiden said you owed him something and I knew what it was."

How could she have something belonging to Aiden? And she'd just met Parker Timmons yesterday. *He did want me to find him. Why?* "I have no idea what he's talking about." Too bad she couldn't bring in his whole gang, but Aiden was the only one who had tracks for her to follow.

"He ... he said you'd say that."

Frustration had a way of bringing out the worst in her. "Tell me where the doctor lives, and we'll talk about this when you're bandaged up. I don't like leaving you alone, but I don't have a choice."

"What time is it?"

"After three. Why?"

"If Doc isn't at home, he's probably at church." Parker tried to raise his head, but a moan escaped his lips. "A picnic's been scheduled for a long time—that and afternoon preaching."

Once Timmons gave her directions, she let Hawk loose to hunt. She walked briskly down the street, counting the number of businesses and houses according to Parker's directions. Rocky Falls looked pleasant enough, built on a slope with junipers and cottonwoods to shade the folks. Today the town looked peaceful, despite the tragedy caused by the McCaw gang.

No one responded to her knock at the doctor's house, a tidy little place with a whitewashed fence, which gave her little choice but to stop by the church.

No one was outside on the church grounds, which meant she'd have to look for the doctor inside. Sage opened the door during a prayer. How appropriate was that? Goodness knew, with the McCaws running rampant, the marshal and the whole town needed someone to come to their aid. The preacher, a wide-shouldered man who looked more like a blacksmith than a man of God, eyed her suspiciously.

She remembered the Colts strapped at her waist.

Parker hurt in places he didn't know existed. Not since his horse was spooked by a mountain cat and threw him into the side of a boulder had he ached so much that dying looked appealing. He needed to be cleaned up, not tended to like an invalid. Getting the doc made about as much sense as Aiden's riddles of the night before. In fact, he'd get up and show Sage Morrow that a little beating never stopped Parker Timmons. After filling his head and gut with determination, Parker attempted to sit. A stab of invisible fire burned through his chest, and a groan escaped his lips. The last time he'd broken ribs he was twelve years old and fell out of a tree in Virginia. Come to think of it, he'd been pitched around most of his life. But his tolerance for pain had fallen once he hit the back side of thirty. Age had a way of catching up to a man, and what did he have to show for it, except a keen desire to represent the people of this fine state of Colorado?

He closed his eyes and allowed his thoughts to retrace last night's jailbreak. The gang had jumped him sometime after midnight, and he had no idea how many of them there were. Four distinct voices had filled the night, and far too many fists had been driven into his body.

"We ain't killin' you," Aiden had said. "This is a warnin'. You and Sage have something we want. The two of you come alone. Never no mind where, 'cause we're making sure you follow us. If you have any ideas about riding with a posse, forget it. You'll understand later."

In the haze of pain, maybe he'd heard wrong. What could Sage and he have that Aiden wanted? Until recently, most of Parker's knowledge of the McCaw gang came from the wanted posters and newspapers. Now and then they kicked up trouble around the Rocky Falls area, but folks here didn't have much to steal, and none of the miners had made any large strikes. Parker's arrests were mostly locals, not outlaws—greedy men who allowed whiskey and selfishness to rule their choices and their fists.

He remembered something else Aiden said: "Your brother made a stupid mistake. I'd like to think you're the smarter one."

The McCaws *had* killed Frank. If his head hadn't hurt so badly, he'd have tried to focus on what wasn't said. How could he and Sage ride into the mountains after them when they didn't know what Aiden wanted or which way to head? He could trail with the best of them, and Sage had advanced skills from her Indian ways. What mistake had his brother made? And what linked Frank, Sage, Parker, and the McCaws? Too much to think on when his whole body was bruised.

Parker fought to stay awake in an effort to think through the previous night. But every time he wrapped his mind around a possibility, his senses numbed, and he began to float away. He needed to talk to Sage about her connection with the McCaws. The thought of Frank bringing this misfortune on his family needled at him too. With all of Frank's problems, getting involved in an outlaw gang didn't fit. Money never meant much to Frank. He enjoyed good times like fishing and hunting and a bottle of whiskey. Gambling ... had Frank gotten himself into trouble by owing what he couldn't pay? Parker shook his head. His brother had his faults, but lowering to associating with outlaws to pay a gambling debt wasn't one of them.

As soon as he rested a little, he'd get this situation figured out. Until then, he'd pray for guidance ... and his ribs.

Parker struggled to open his eyes. He heard his name being called and tried to respond, but he felt like he'd been dropped into a well and didn't have a rope to climb out. Surfacing and having a doctor poke around on his body didn't sit well either.

"Parker, this is Doc Slader. Can you hear me?"

He could hear, just couldn't speak.

"Listen, son. I need for you to wake up."

The familiar voice urging him to crawl to the top made the ascent a little easier, until Parker finally opened an eye. The other one refused to budge.

"Good," the doctor said. "You look awful, but I believe you'll live."

Right now he didn't know which was worse, dying or living. "Think ... I have a broken rib." It hurt to talk.

"Miss Sage here made mention of that. I'm going to feel around a bit to see for myself." The moment Doc Slader touched Parker's side, agony seared his whole body. "Yes, sir, a few broken ribs, all right."

"I missed church. Should have been there for Leah and the children."

"You would have been sitting by yourself. She wasn't there either."

Leah must have been sick. She never missed church. "I'll ride out to see her later."

Doc shook his head.

"What's wrong?" Parker didn't like the frown on Doc's face. All he needed was a little sleep, and he'd be his normal self.

"You're not going anywhere all beaten and bruised like the town drunk. But you should know Leah's boy Davis is missing."

Parker tried to pull himself up, but the pain blinded him. "What do you mean? Where did he go?"

"Went to get water for his mother this morning and didn't return."

Misery swept through Parker, a deep sorrow that he couldn't put into words. "Did Davis fall in the river?" The river flowing through Leah's ranch didn't have a fast current, yet Davis could have lost his balance, hit his head.

"Don't think so. The bucket was on the bank, full of water, and John found horse tracks nearby."

You'll understand later. Aiden's words came back to Parker like a bad penny. Taking Davis ensured them of Sage and Parker's riding alone. "Where's John now?"

"He took off with Frank's rifle to follow the tracks."

NINE

Sage sat at Parker's bedside at Doctor Slader's house. The doctor had been called to the home of a rancher who'd been kicked by a horse and would probably be gone for hours. Mrs. Slader had her hands full with nine boys to look after. The thought of it made Sage's head spin. Then again, maybe someday she'd meet a man who'd want a dozen boys.

Sage kept a damp cloth on Parker's forehead and studied him for fever. Even if he was a lawman—and she'd met only a few she liked—she still hated for an innocent man to endure a beating. And although exhaustion had been the reason she slept through the gang's jailbreak, she still felt responsible. The old familiar restlessness nipped at her heels, the longing to do all she could to make the country a safe place to live. Common sense told her it was impossible, and her heart reminded her she wasn't God. But she well knew the pain of devastation and the tug of revenge.

She grasped every opportunity to talk to the injured man about Aiden's escape. Perhaps she shouldn't prod him, except unanswered questions threatened to burst from her brain.

"Parker, can you hear me?" Leah Timmons sat on the edge of a chair, proper like, the way a lady sat. The way Sage used to sit. A little self-consciously, she shifted and stiffened her back as Leah dabbed a lace-edged handkerchief under each eye. The woman was tiny, too small to carry such a heavy load of widowhood with children to rear.

"Give me an hour, Leah," he whispered. "I'll get Davis and

John found and back home to you. Don't worry. They couldn't have gone far."

I doubt if you get out of bed for two days, Sage thought.

Leah blinked back the tears. "I know this is selfish, but you are the one person I can depend on. Oh, Parker, I'm so scared. Don't die on me too." A southern accent laced her words.

"I'm too ornery to die. All I need is a few hours to get my wits back."

Leah stood and laid a hand on Parker's shoulder. Sage pitied the distraught woman, who had every reason to be upset — her husband was dead, her youngest son was missing, and her oldest son had taken off with his pa's rifle to find his little brother. It all added up to anguish of the worst kind.

"I'll go after your boys in the morning," Sage said. "If it wasn't so close to dark, I'd go now. I'll track them down and get them back to you as quickly as I can."

"I keep praying for God to protect my family. But troubles keep happening." Leah sniffed back a sob and shook her head as though to chase away her tears. Strawberry blonde hair curled around her face, and freckles dotted her nose and cheeks. Both characteristics gave the impression of Leah being a mere girl, but her girlish days were gone. She turned to Sage. "What if John or Davis runs into the McCaws or a bear or mountain lion? What if the McCaws took them?"

As a child, when Sage's parents had taken her to church, she heard the sermons expounding on Romans 8:28 and James's call to patience and perseverance. She hadn't appreciated folks repeating them during her own tragedies, and she wasn't about to heap them on Leah. "I don't have any answers for you, but I'll do my best."

Leah took a deep breath. "When Frank died, I thought my worries would be about putting food on the table, not losing my John and Davis and even Parker. I ... I know you're a smart woman and know ways to track down people. But can you really find my boys?"

Sage swallowed the emotion rising in her throat. Given a choice, she'd gladly rear a dozen children instead of looking for Charles's killer. But Tall Elk had taught her how to read trails like a scout, and she'd use every skill within her power to find Leah's sons. "I promise you I will not stop looking until I find them."

"Bless you, dear Sage. You've given me hope." Tears flooded Leah's eyes, and Sage blinked to stop her own. She'd given up on ever having female friends when she was a girl. Good Christian women forbade their daughters to have anything to do with Sage, never mind that Sage's mother had abandoned the gods of the Ute to worship the white man's God. But at this moment, Sage didn't care what Leah's beliefs were about Indians. What mattered was getting those boys back to their mother.

Sage had planned to give Leah and Mrs. Felter most of the bounty from Aiden's capture, but now that he was on the loose again, she couldn't lay claim to any money. "Why don't you go home and be with your other sons? I'm sure they're missing you."

"You're probably right. One of my younger boys cried when I told him I was coming into town. I couldn't bring myself to tell him about Parker being hurt." Leah's large brown eyes gave her a look of innocence, which contrasted with how much she'd seen of the harshness of life.

Sage wrapped her arm around Leah's shoulder. "Your children need you. I'll leave at dawn. I—"

"Not without me." Parker's raspy voice sounded weak. He had a little more color, but he'd be of little use with his constant pain in catching each breath.

"You can't ride in your condition," Sage said. "Besides, you'll slow me down."

"Watch me." His chest lifted and lowered. "My ribs are wrapped, and I've slept most of the day."

"I think you were unconscious most of the day," Sage said.

"Still asleep."

"Hawk and I work better alone," she said, but she shrugged. No point arguing with Parker. She didn't want to mention her suspicions that Aiden might have those boys or that they might be harmed if she wasted time, and odds were he'd sleep right through her departure in the morning.

He said nothing, only stared at the ceiling as Leah said her good-byes and left.

"What are you thinking?" Sage said.

He frowned, and his distorted face resembled a walnut. "The same thing you are. That the McCaws most likely have Davis and probably John too." He swallowed hard. "And I'm hoping those boys are still alive."

A knock at the door interrupted Sage's thoughts. "Come in."

Mrs. Slader stepped in, a tall thin woman with a kind face. "I found this on the front porch." She held out a folded piece of yellowed paper. "One of the boys said a man rode by and put it there. It has Miss Morrow's name on it."

Sage took the note, angst rising as to the sender. "Thank you. Did he recognize the man?"

"It was my middle boy who brought it to me. I asked him, but he said it wasn't anyone he knew."

"Thank you." Sage unfolded the note. *We've got both boys. You and the marshal come alone if you want the boys alive.* She couldn't let Mrs. Slader know the contents. If Leah found out, she might not be able to handle the news.

Mrs. Slader nodded at Parker. "You're looking better, Marshal, but you need a few days in bed." Without waiting for a response, she slipped back out the door and left Parker and Sage alone.

Sage waved the note. "Unfortunately, our suspicions were right. The McCaws have Davis and John. We're to come alone if we want them alive." She walked to the window and looked out at mountains to the west. "I have no idea what connects you, me, Charles, and possibly your brother to the McCaws, but we need to figure it out soon. They want us to follow, so the trail will be easy for me to pick up."

Silence clung to the air while she watched a couple of the Slader boys wrestle in the street.

"The only connection I see is we're all working to keep the likes of him and his gang away from law-abiding people," Parker said. "Aiden McCaw is a smart man, real smart, and he's manipulated his brothers since the war to get what he wants."

"I've heard they were a part of Quantrill's Raiders during the war and then set out along the same path afterward."

"I heard the same thing," Parker said. "We know he won't hesitate to carry out his threat. I just wish I knew what he wanted."

For the next hour Parker slept, and Sage thought a lot about Charles and their relationship. Some of her musings were about Aiden's continued talk about her husband, the man she loved beyond reason, the man who'd left her alone for weeks at a time. Uncertainties about Charles's loyalties and a possible association with the McCaw gang clawed at her heart. The man who'd said he owned a second ranch in Colorado, but didn't. His killers insisted he had their money. Could he have neglected to tell her about other things too?

If voicing those shadowed memories helped put the McCaw gang behind bars and find those two boys, then she'd tell Parker all she could remember. Even if it meant she learned Charles wasn't a man of integrity.

Deep in thought, she slowly realized Parker was awake and staring at her. "Aiden mentioned Charles, my deceased husband, on more than one occasion, like he knew him."

"Wasn't he killed several years ago?"

"Seven. No one ever found who did it. I've searched wanted posters and descriptions of outlaws for years, but it is as though the men disappeared. But I'll never forget what they looked like, especially the man who killed Charles." She stared into Parker's eyes. "Aiden McCaw wasn't with them. No redheaded man rode onto our ranch that day, but the rest of his gang could have been involved. I've no idea of the physical features of Aiden's brothers." The more she remembered about Charles and the day he died, the more the scars of her heart cut deeper.

"I've heard of your search for his killers."

"Aiden said Charles wasn't his right name. How can that be? Charles and I grew up in the same area. I knew him from the time we were children. But if Aiden thinks he is someone else, it may have something to do with what's going on. He says he knows who killed Charles, and it's caused me to think he might have ordered it. He also knew Charles spent a good deal of time away from our ranch."

Parker stared at her, obviously mulling over what she'd said. "Where did he go?"

Sage held her breath, her mind weighing how much more she could tell without emotions overcoming her. "He told me he had a second ranch in northeast Colorado, and he was often gone to check on it. After his death, I contacted the land office and learned he didn't own any land there. He'd lied to me."

"Did you ever ask to go with him when he traveled to this ranch?"

"I did, but he thought it wasn't a good idea."

The look on Parker's face was the same look that other folks gave her when she explained why she stayed home. Papa asked to go with him once, but Charles refused. "We lived in southern Colorado and raised cattle on a small ranch." An inner voice urged her to continue. All she could think of was the bereaved look on Leah's face and the thought of what the McCaws might do to her sons. "Charles had a wandering spirit. I knew it when we married, but his ways didn't matter. I knew how to take care of the ranch, and we had a neighboring boy and Papa to help when the work got to be too much for me."

"I've known a few men who couldn't handle being tied down." Parker's voice sounded gentle, coaxing her on.

"He said he liked the wilds, to hunt and breathe in free air. And he loved northern Colorado. He always apologized when he rode off ..." The suspicions that she'd carried for years surfaced again. *Was I a fool then to believe every word he said?*

"Excuse me for asking this, but do you think he ran with a gang of outlaws?"

He'd spoken what she'd feared, and it sounded viler than in her thoughts. "I don't know. I've been confused for so long about the things he kept from me." She took a deep breath to gain control. The more she expressed her deep-rooted fears, the harder it became. "His killer said Charles had money that belonged to them. The men went through our cabin and tore it apart. Look, Parker, I was young, naïve, and I loved a man who was different from anyone I knew. As children, we fished together and talked about all kinds of things. He didn't ridicule my Ute blood or make me feel less than a human being."

"No need to get upset. I'm just trying—" A stab of pain must have taken his breath. A moment later he attempted to speak again. "I'm just trying to make sense of our dilemma." He paused. "We don't know each other well, and—"

"We don't like each other much either."

He smiled, the first time all day. "I'll grant you that one, but we've been thrown into an icy river headed for a waterfall."

"One of us has to find a way to reach the bank."

"So what else are you thinking?" Parker said.

Sage wondered if Davis and John were still alive. The quiet streets of Rocky Falls didn't need any more bloodshed or missing children. She'd never spoken this freely to anyone about Charles, not even to Tall Elk or her parents. "Papa never liked Charles. He said a man who stayed away from his wife was up to no good. He and Mama didn't grieve for him."

"I'm sorry." Parker's words were spoken softly, as if he understood a little of what she'd gone through.

She stared out the window to where Hawk circled above.

Sometimes she thought she'd given all of her love to the bird ... a predator who welcomed her affections. "After I learned that Charles had lied to me about owning another ranch, I searched wanted posters for a picture or a description of him." She paused and remembered her relief in knowing he wasn't an outlaw. "When I found nothing and I could not get the local sheriff to help me find his killers, I decided the only way justice could be served was for me to find the killers and bring them in. That's when I traveled into the Rockies to search out some of my Ute people who still lived there. I needed to learn their ways."

"If I'm hearing right," Parker said, "then you're having second thoughts about Charles. He might have been involved with the McCaw gang—or a rival one."

"And he may have gone to his grave with the knowledge of what his killers wanted." She swung back to him, suddenly feeling a kinship to a man she'd otherwise dislike. "But I haven't figured out where you might fit in, or your brother."

"Frank could have walked into something unaware."

"Or he'd become involved."

Parker pressed his lips tightly together. Finally he took another deep breath. "I'd sure hate to think my brother had turned outlaw. But he did have a problem with drinking and gambling."

"Desperate situations breed desperate people." She watched how he reacted to her comment with the understanding that the truth about those a person loves can be the most difficult to bear. She should know because the truth about Charles might be the most difficult pain of all.

"My grandfather used to talk about sheep being one of the dumbest animals on the face of the earth. They don't have a lick of sense, which is why Frank and I sometimes helped to keep close watch on them. They'd get stuck in thorny bushes, fall into places where they had no business going, and stand beside a hungry wolf. I've seen my grandfather break a sheep's leg so it would stop wandering, but sometimes it went back to its old habits."

"Are you talking about your brother?" she said, her stomach churning with the implications. "Or Charles?"

"Maybe both. What did Charles look like?"

How did she describe the man of her heart? "He had hair the color of pecans and eyes as green as a mountain lake. Average build. Seldom raised his voice." She pulled a pocket watch from her britches. It had belonged to Charles, and she'd slipped a picture of both of them into it. "This was taken right after we were married."

Parker stared at the picture, then shook his head. "Never knew a man who looked like that. Doesn't matter. I'm riding with you in the morning."

"You'll hold me up with those broken ribs."

"Let's get one thing straight here, Sage. I'm the marshal of this town. My brother's dead, along with another friend, and my nephews are missing. I've been threatened and beaten. The Mc-Caws aren't getting any more of a head start on me than they already have. And we already know they're watching the town and will know when we leave. The note said for both of us to come. We don't know what they want from us, but I'm a praying man, and God has the answers. I believe He'll show us the trail and give us what we need to know."

Sage's eyes narrowed. He'd spoken a mouthful, like a speech. What chance did those boys have with a battered marshal who believed God would ride with them?

After Sage left, Parker talked to God long and hard about his family and his town. The US Marshal was due in a week with bounty money that Sage would never see unless she brought in Aiden McCaw again. An extra gun would help even the odds, but he and Sage had to ride alone. They'd be riding into a trap, and he knew it. But what choice did they have with Davis's and John's lives in the pendulum?

Deep in his belly, he realized Aiden wouldn't think twice about killing either one of those boys. How could Leah survive one more nightmare? The thought sickened him, made him mad enough to kill Aiden McCaw with his bare hands, a feeling that had grown inside him until he burned with hate, like a fire he couldn't douse.

Parker needed to figure out how to outwit a man who boasted of watching his and Sage's every move. So far that man had been successful. Did one of McCaw's people walk the streets of Rocky Falls? From the sounds and the goings-on in the saloon every night, he could name five men and two of the women working the saloon who were candidates to fit that description.

It was possible Widow Bess might have overheard some talk. She was a decent woman, the only bit of goodness at the saloon and hotel. Every line in her face was pure wisdom. Rumor was if she didn't stop trying to pull the girls out of the evening's profits, she wouldn't have a job.

The truth of a matter had a way of sinking its teeth into a person whether he was ready to handle it or not. One of the Mc-Caws had killed Frank and left a fine woman as a widow. Although there were mountains of frustration and disappointment in many areas of his personal life, Parker had always wanted the best for his brother. Even when it meant giving up Leah.

Parker met Leah when they were fifteen years old in Virginia. Frank, older and oozing charm, won her away from him, and they married just before the two young men enlisted in the Civil War. Both brothers were sure the war would be won in a month and they'd return to their parents' modest farm, three younger sisters, and Leah as heroes. Instead it drew out four long years. All during the intense fighting, Parker regretted not standing up to Frank for Leah, but years had passed since he'd thought of her like he did when he was a naïve boy. He exchanged his tender love for the role of a brother-in-law and an uncle. Too often his role brought him to Frank and Leah's doorstep to help John with work on the ranch. Now Parker simply felt an obligation to his brother's widow to do all he could to help her in her plight.

*My mind's wandering when I have more important things
to do.*

Parker wished he knew what the McCaws wanted. For sure a
swap lay ahead. Since Aiden hadn't indicated what to bring, the
exchange had to be some kind of information. But what? A chest
full of gold made more sense than this. If Aiden merely wanted
Sage and him dead, then he'd have taken care of Parker the previous night and killed Sage while she was in the mountains on
his trail.

*Lord, looks like we're riding into a death trap with no choice
in the matter.* And he'd be riding with a woman. God knew how
he felt about a female slowing him down. Most women couldn't
take the rugged mountains. Take his mother, for example. After
Parker and Frank's father died, their mama tried living in Colorado. But when the weather dropped below freezing and stayed
there, she caught the next train back to Virginia. And even Leah
had stayed in Rocky Falls only because of Frank.

Then again, Sage Morrow didn't strike him as most women.
Sage wasn't a delicate creature who'd be a burden. She was strong
and resourceful. It amazed him that she'd survived the many
times she'd set out to bring in a wanted man. She set foot in areas
that most women shuddered at the thought of. Those were tales,
but Parker now believed they held a lot of truth. The image of the
defenseless woman who needed a man to protect her ended when
he met Sage Morrow.

Glancing out the window to where the sunset streaked across
the horizon in slowly deepening orange tones, Parker realized
he had to make himself get out of bed. Only a fool would wait till
morning to try to move. He breathed in and out several times to
brace himself for the pain ahead. But he had to tolerate the agony
in order to build up his strength. He gritted his teeth and sat up.
Tears filled his eyes, and they had nothing to do with his family.
Reaching over to grab the back of a chair, he forced himself to
stand. One step at a time. He could do it. He had to.

TEN

Darkness shrouded the hotel room as Sage allowed the events of the day to wash over her. For certain she wanted to leave in the morning before sunrise — without Parker. He needed to mend instead of chase his nephews and the outlaws. In the shape he was in, he'd get them both killed. She'd deal with the snakes of the McCaw gang in her own way.

Bess, the woman who worked the registration desk of the hotel and saloon and who had invited Sage to eat with her, had given Sage directions to Leah's ranch. From there she'd follow the McCaws' trail. Finding those children was her priority. Once those boys were safe, she'd deal with Aiden and whatever he wanted. The hours spent running down the gang would provide time to figure out what the outlaw alluded to — and if Charles had been involved with the wrong people. The thought of her husband riding with outlaws sliced through her heart. Surely it couldn't be true ... but the suspicions stacked against him. Perhaps learning the truth now equaled finding his killers.

The sorrow in Leah's eyes haunted her. Enough problems faced children growing into adults without outlaws using them for target practice — and the McCaws would do that very thing. Sage's parents had lost five children before her birth, and they still grieved each small body. The time had come to pay Mama and Papa a visit, and she would do so after business ended in Rocky Falls. Long ago she'd forgiven them for not liking Charles; they all needed each other. Would they recognize their daughter

in the bounty hunter? They'd worked so hard to calm her wildness and mold her into a white woman. Mama, with all of her
Ute blood, believed the ways of the white man were the ways
of the future. She taught Sage about her Indian heritage, and
Papa taught her about the white. But always the emphasis was
on embracing the white man's mannerisms and their God. Sage
didn't understand their insistence. Or maybe she didn't want to
understand them.

Sage heard a knock outside her door. Gripping the Colt tied
to her right side and eying Hawk, she took a step to the door.
"Who's there?"

"Parker."

Had he gone mad? She unlatched the door to find the marshal leaning against the door. From the looks of his drawn features, the pain drained his strength. He needed another dose of
medicine—the kind that would make him sleep and heal.

"I'm in the next room." He stood as straight as his weak legs
would allow. At least he appeared to do so, no doubt in an attempt to look tough. "I checked into the hotel a few minutes ago.
Wouldn't want you to leave without me in the morning."

She crossed her arms over her chest. "Are you drunk or just
plain crazy?"

"I'm not a drinking man, and I'm sane. Thank you for your
caring questions. I have a couple of things to discuss with you if
you have a few minutes."

She gestured him inside. Thoughts of the impropriety of having a man in her room vanished from her conscience when she
remembered she stayed in a hotel that rented rooms by the hour.
Not that it made much difference. Most folks judged her morals
once they learned she'd convinced a Ute to teach her how to track
and survive in the wilderness for the purpose of hunting wanted
men. "Are your intentions honorable?"

He smiled, sort of lopsided. "Don't have any money on me."

"Then you're probably at the right room. The girls down the

hall have a man slip a gold piece under the door." She laughed at the pitiful sight of him.

She motioned for him to sit on the bed while she stood. The tiny room smelled of those who had come and gone for reasons she cared not to think about. Sort of embarrassing, especially with Parker sitting there.

"I've been rummaging through my brain for what Aiden wants from us, and I have some questions," he said.

If this was about Charles, she might not be able to answer. "All right. I may have a few for you too."

He sat straight up. Breathing had to be easier in that position. "Aiden's claim about your husband not telling you his rightful name is pestering me. You said you grew up in the same area. So you knew his family?"

She'd camped on this earlier today while Parker enjoyed the benefits of laudanum. "They lived near the same town as I did."

"How did they take his death? I mean, were they shocked?"

"They passed on shortly before we married. Charles inherited their ranch. I remember they were not happy with his frequent trips."

"Then he couldn't have lied to you about his name."

"Not at all." But something Papa said echoed in her mind. *You made a big mistake, daughter. Lovin' a man despite his faults is a good thing, but you loved him without any sense. Now he's dead, and he might have had a wife somewhere else.*

"How did he pay for his trips away from home?"

Parker had edged dangerously close to sticking his nose too deep into her affairs. But wouldn't she do the same? "I'm not sure."

"Then it wasn't from your ranch?"

Parker and Papa had a lot in common. She'd learned how to read folks since those days. "He never took much money with him."

He nodded, digesting her answers like bad food. "Did he take provisions?"

"Very little."

"Did he say where he was going?"

"Only to his ranch in northern Colorado."

"Did he mention friends there?"

The truth about Charles not owning a second ranch had come pounding at the door of her heart. "No."

"So he was a loner type?"

"Pretty much."

"Did he bring you gifts when he returned?"

She remembered a broach and ribbons for her hair. "Sometimes."

"Expensive ones?"

"Not really. Parker, your questions remind me of a fancy lawyer." She gathered her emotions with an understanding that he needed those answers just like she did in order to outwit the McCaws. "Until today, I never considered him being an outlaw. He was gentle and kind, a good man. But ..." She withdrew into the black cave of doubts. "I've been around enough men to know Charles could have been another man when he wasn't with me."

"Do you remember anything at all that could help us?"

"He could have been connected with Aiden or another gang. I don't know why we were shot, except for the money the men claimed he had."

Parker raised a brow. "Whoa. Back up. You were shot too? I hadn't heard that before. My source said you shot two of them before they rode away."

She felt her spunk rising to the occasion. "You could consider asking folks for themselves about matters instead of relying on gossip and newspapers."

"You're right, and I apologize. So he died, and you survived."

"Right." She blinked to keep the tears away. "We were left for dead. My father found us."

He slowly stood from her bed. The man had to be in horrible pain. "I'm truly sorry for your loss, Mrs. Morrow. Guess you and I have had our share of sorrow, but life is a mixture of bad times and good. I think that is what forms us into the people we are today."

She liked the way he formed his words. "Is that another lesson about life from your grandfather?"

He grinned. "No, it's one of my own."

"I'll remember it—just the way you spoke it."

An awkward silence hung between them, and she didn't recall feeling this uneasy for many a year.

"Is there anything else I should know?" Parker said.

"I can't think of anything right now. But I'd sure like to know what you and I have that makes Aiden willing to risk his neck, kill more people, and abduct two boys. It has to be money and revenge, but for what? I'm alive, but I'm not supposed to be, which may or may not be related to his game. He allowed me to catch him and set up an escape to lure both of us into the mountains after them. All carefully thought out. Outlaws are smart. Most of them are smarter than those who take out after them without a plan. That's you and me, Parker. We're doing a stupid thing going after Aiden and playing into his hand. But we don't have a choice with your nephews' lives at stake." She pressed her lips together. With Parker, she had a tendency to speak before thinking through her words. "What connects you to me or Charles?"

"I was hoping you might provide a clue to that answer."

She refused to feel defeated—or foolish. "If I had an idea, I'd have already been gone."

He reached for the doorknob, his face pale and rigid. "You've taught me a valuable lesson tonight. Don't rely on hearsay. Search for the truth. Good evenin', ma'am. Thanks for taking the time to answer personal questions. I'll be ready at dawn."

Sage respected Parker's determination and admired his tenacity. He'd demonstrated his integrity and strength in the midst of crisis. Yet he'd still find her gone when he struggled to crawl out of bed in the morning.

An hour before intense shades of yellow and purple would swirl across the eastern sky, Sage strapped on her gun belt, made sure her weapons were loaded, and carried her boots and Winchester down the creaky hotel steps. She didn't worry about Hawk; he always found her. The only noises from residents were the deep snores that had the potential to arouse the dead.

In the blackness, she opened the door and sat on the boardwalk to tug on her boots. A near hole was working its way through the top of the right boot, and the heel on the left had been replaced twice. She planned to purchase a new pair after she brought in Aiden. Of course, she promised herself the same the last time she brought in an outlaw. But she'd given most of the bounty to the wife and children of the murdered man. The money she did use took care of basic needs in her ongoing search for Charles's killers.

Sage pulled her trouser leg down over her left boot, then sat for a moment, hunched on the steps of the boardwalk like an old beggar woman. For seven years the hunt had taken precedence, but now a new craving threatened to overtake her need for revenge: her desperate need for the truth about her husband.

She heard footsteps behind her and swung around with her hand on her Colt.

"Slow down, Sage."

She recognized the gravelly voice of the woman who had registered her for a room and prepared last night's supper. "Goodness, Miss Bess. You ought to be more careful. Startling someone in the dark could get you hurt."

"Oh, I've been told that before. I heard you come down the stairs and wondered if you'd like a fresh cup of coffee."

The woman was a saint. "Thanks. You must have read my mind."

"Can't remember if I introduced myself proper. The older I get, the more I forget." She held out a mug of coffee. It smelled better than a field of wildflowers.

"My papa always says that the best way to get to know someone is over a cup of coffee." Sage inhaled the fresh aroma and took a sip. "This smells wonderful, ma'am."

"For a bounty hunter, you certainly talk proper. Like a lady."

Sage laughed. "I was born a woman. I chose to be a bounty hunter."

"What about breakfast before you head out?" Bess sat beside her on the boardwalk. "I have some biscuits and ham left from yesterday morning. In fact, I have them right here. I imagine jerky gets old when you're trailing somebody."

"Yes, ma'am, it does. I'd be happy to take something to eat." Sounded like Bess understood her habits. Sage had seen how the woman treated the soiled doves, calling them "honey" and treating them like they were respected women. Perhaps her kindness extended honestly to a woman bounty hunter who was part Ute. "Maybe when this is all over, I can enjoy another one of your fine meals here at the hotel."

"Glad to help." Bess handed Sage a small cloth bundle, then slapped her ample knees and stood. "I'll be praying you find those boys without trouble. Leah doesn't need to bury any more of her family."

Strange for a woman who worked with the worst of the town's men and women to mention praying. "I'll do my best."

"Where's your hawk?"

Sage heard the fearfulness in Bess's voice. "He's most likely watching us from the windowsill until I call for him. He looks menacing, but he obeys me."

"Obedience for all of us is an important thing. When we have that meal together, we can sit and talk. I'd like to get to know a woman who puts aside a woman's role for a hard job like bounty hunting."

A friend was a rarity Sage hadn't ever enjoyed. But a friend equated to trust, and she'd never been able to inspire that trait in anyone other than her parents and Charles. "Maybe we can."

Bess held up a finger. "Don't leave yet." She stepped back into the building, leaving Sage a little warmer and not just because of the coffee. A moment later, she returned with a lit lantern. "You can leave it with the livery boy, and I'll fetch it later."

Sage thanked her and stepped into the inky blackness with the lantern to light the way. Last night she'd assigned the livery boy the job of keeping an eye on her pony, saddle, mule, and provisions, and told him to sleep in a nearby stall until she arrived this morning.

As much as she'd needed another solid night's sleep, dreams of Charles had kept her awake. In the past, nightmares reliving the shooting brought the tragedy to the surface. Other times, peaceful ideals of the life they could have shared together brought tears and a renewal of her vow to find his killer. Oh, for a home again. Bess had observed much in their brief encounters. Sage hadn't completely given up the mannerisms of a proper white woman, perhaps because of some deep understanding that she was just as much white as she was Ute.

Last night, Charles spoke in her dreams about forgiving him. Her nighttime visitation had become a confusing mixture of memories and a vague reality that ended abruptly, as though the dream's meaning was to enlighten her for the days ahead. The quest to find the truth would gnaw at her until it was laid out raw. Until it was, she'd not give in to the nagging doubts that plagued her. He'd been a good man. She simply hadn't learned the whole story—yet. Charles's words from the past echoed around her as they had in her dream, pointing to a good reason not to believe he'd run with an outlaw gang.

"A man has two choices in this life, Sage," he'd said. "He can take the path of his own selfishness or take the path of God's heart."

Sage remembered the event vividly as it tiptoed across her mind. They'd been married but ten months.

"Race you to the creek," she'd said.

"But you'd have to win." He tossed her a teasing glance, his green eyes sparkling and dancing.

Oh, how she loved him, the way he held her, the way he looked at her. No matter that his wandering ways left her alone on many nights. She'd take what he could give. "My horse is faster."

"Winning is everything except when the journey is more important than the end," he said.

In truth, she'd spurred on her mare, and he'd still reached the creek before her. They'd laughed, enjoying the time together. Two glorious weeks later, he left again for a month.

Now, as she recalled the previous night's dreams, a shiver raced up her arms, a mixture of early-morning temperatures and the vividness of her dreams. As the years passed, she'd begun to ache less for Charles. Could those feelings be wrong?

Mama said the day would come when she'd be ready to reach out to another man. Every time she saw a family together, she longed for her own. She remembered her stillborn son and the bullet that brought on his premature birth, and the desire for revenge took another strangling hold. If she couldn't have Charles, what was left of life? She'd go to her grave loving him.

Her dresses and cotton chemises were packed in a cedar trunk in southern Colorado, and her grandmother's dishes on her father's side were there too. But the thankfulness she'd given to God on her wedding day lay buried in more than one grave.

The livery loomed before her, and she pushed her grief aside. Opening the door, she stepped inside and shielded her eyes as her meek lantern light flooded the stable. No, not her flame only. A man held up a lighted lantern. Sage startled at the sight of Marshal Timmons with the stable boy.

"'Mornin', Sage. Just like you, I figured the earlier we left town, the better off we'd be. Lucky for us, I know these mountains."

ELEVEN

Three hours later, after riding as hard as they dared while following the outlaws' trail through the foothills of the Rockies, Sage gazed up at the white-tipped mountains. Early morning often lured her to the lofty peaks with cloudless blue skies and breathtaking heights. Some resembled stone pine cones, while others were covered in green and brown, with silver patches of snow. In the distance, huge sheets of ice blanketed the sides of jagged gray peaks, while pine and cedar hugged the slopes below. The landscape in between the mountains and the valleys, from rushing waterfalls to huge boulders rolled into place by non-human hands, was nature's way of inviting others to enjoy the beauty but warning them of its dangers.

Not far from there was the land once occupied by many Arapahoe and Ute Indians, and in some places their trails shot far above the tree line. At times she could almost see and smell the curling smoke of a Ute campfire and hear their language in the air. Sage's mother had told her that *Ute* meant "Land of the Sun," and her people practiced a religion that revered animals. Perhaps within that ancient faith was the source of her way with creatures of all kinds.

Tall Elk had introduced her to the beauty and reverence of the Rockies, the land where he wanted to share his life with her, the land belonging to his people for thousands of years. But since miners had infringed on that land, fighting between the Indians and white men had forced most of the Indians onto reservations near Durango and in Utah. A few, Tall Elk among them, lived west of Rocky Falls in remote areas not yet coveted by the whites, but they, too, would soon be banished to the reservations or die defending their way of life. Tall Elk would have loved her and taken care of her, but it was wrong to use a man to forget the past—as wrong as it was for the whites to take Indian land.

A male mourning dove had serenaded Parker and Sage for the past few minutes with his *coowaah, cooo, coo, coo*. She understood the woeful song. It had become her heart's cry.

Parker had fared much better with his injuries than she anticipated. He rode straight and tall, although his face held the grim stance of pain. Admirable. She respected him for it.

"I sure wish John hadn't proceeded with his plans," Parker said, breaking the silence between them.

"I agree. But you and I know the pull of revenge." She blew out an exasperated breath. "They probably have someone following us as well as those ahead."

He reined in his horse and swung a leg over the saddle. She followed his lead, both of them examining the horse tracks they had followed for miles.

"Looks like John headed northwest. I imagine he rode right behind them. Especially since they didn't attempt to conceal their trail."

She bent to smell the freshest prints. As she and Parker had surmised, John was a full day ahead of them. Somewhere between here and farther along the trail, the McCaws had seized him. If he'd been angry and left to find those who killed his father, would he lose logic and try to fight the whole gang? Would Davis cry out? Aggravating Aiden's men would shorten the likelihood of the child staying alive. She despised questions with no answers.

"How old is Davis?"

"He turned four in April."

Her breath caught in her throat, and it had nothing to do

with the thin air and everything to do with the son she'd lost. "Is he a strong little boy?"

Parker tossed her a curious look. "Yes. Smart, too. He loves John. Looks up to him like a father. And John has done a good job with him. Calls Davis his 'little man.' I know what you're thinking. Davis won't be whining and carrying on."

"Sounds like John's a mature young man."

"I thought so until he made mention of going after Frank's killers. At the parsonage, when I went to check on Leah, he wanted me to deputize him. A lot of good my talk did."

Sage understood John's need to bring the McCaw gang to justice. She studied the peaks in the distance, not stating the obvious about what the McCaws could do to the older boy. "Is there a northeast passage I can take? I'm not as familiar with this section of the Rockies."

Parker pointed beyond the meadow. "Right through there. Steep in some areas — too steep to ride. There are three lakes on that upper range. The middle lake will take you down the other side."

"The only way I can see for us to get an advantage is to force them to split up." She peered up toward where Parker indicated. "We're after them, and they're after us."

"Makes me wonder who's confused."

"Unfortunately, it's us. If one of us can locate their campsite, we have a better chance of rescuing those boys. Perhaps tomorrow we should take separate trails."

"I like that idea," he said. "One of us could follow John, and the other veer onto a path that might confuse them for a while. We could plan to meet somewhere and hopefully have an edge on them."

She walked to her pony and lifted the canteen from her saddle bags. "Are you feeling well enough to climb those mountains?"

"Yes, ma'am." He chuckled. "My mama lives in Virginia. I don't need one here."

That man could be purely aggravating. "Very funny." Yet he and Charles had similar personalities. They could have been friends, and his supposed ranch was in this area. "Are you sure you never met Charles?"

"Yes, real sure. I'd have remembered."

"But Aiden said Charles didn't use his right name. I should have asked him what name he called my husband." She took a swallow of water. "Trying to figure out what Aiden is after makes me feel dimwitted, stupid."

"Sage, you're far from stupid. From what I've seen, you're a whole lot smarter than many men I've known."

His words made her feel strangely uncomfortable. Parker had a habit of doing that. "I had a good teacher."

"I heard you spent a year with the Ute. Of course, that's hearsay, and I need to get my facts straight from you."

She smiled, then swung up onto her saddle and waited while he did the same. "You heard correctly, except it was two and a half years. Tall Elk is a Ute from my mother's tribe. Right now most of the Ute in Colorado are on a reservation. Tall Elk and some of the others refused the order to live there and stayed in the Rockies. I found them in the mountains to the west."

"Was it hard, or had your mother prepared you for Indian life?"

She let her mind wander to those first few weeks among the Ute. "It was extremely difficult. Until then, I was half-Ute, living in a white man's world."

"Any regrets?"

"Not at all. He taught me valuable lessons about living in the wilds, defending myself, and tracking. But Charles taught me how to shoot a rifle and use both hands with my Colts." She patted the neck of her pony. "I guess that's another reason for me to suspect he wasn't the man I thought I married. He was an excellent marksman."

"Do you plan to go back to the Ute?"

She sat up straight on her pony and thought of the ranch she'd left behind and of Tall Elk. "Parker, I have no idea where I belong anymore."

"I hope you find the answers you're looking for."

Sage observed the man beside her. He meant what he said, which revealed a compassionate side of him, unlike a lot of other men. "For a lawman who has his sights on politics, you're not such a bad character."

Parker touched the brim of his hat. "I'll take that as a compliment."

The next morning, the two followed John's trail to the base of the mountain where the McCaws had made their ascent. Parker studied every rock and tree, anticipating one of the gang to ride out. A glance at Sage told him she was just as alert. Both of them rode with their hands on their rifles and their nerves tuned to a change in the wind. A grove of aspen trees scarred by elk and mule deer that ate the bark during the lean winter months caused him to ride cautiously through the shadows.

Sage reined in her pony. "A black bear," she whispered and pointed to the left of them. "And two cubs."

The she-bear rose up and roared her displeasure. Parker's horse spooked, and he held on to keep his seat. He didn't want to break another rib or get mauled by an angry mama bear. Neither did he want to waste a shot that would echo around the valley and give attention to their location.

Parker and Sage backed up their horses, giving the bear ample room to go wherever she chose. The bear stopped and watched them but didn't advance. After several moments, she disappeared up the mountainside, with her cubs scurrying behind her.

"I was ready to send her to bear heaven if I had to," Sage said. "But I hated to leave her cubs behind to fend for themselves and bring the McCaws down on us. Next time we might not be as lucky."

"I prayed."

"I used to do that a lot until I realized God doesn't care."

Parker didn't respond. Anger rode with him every time he thought about Oden Felter, Frank, and his missing nephews. Someday he and God needed to talk about what happened. But even with the fire of revenge burning in his soul, Parker couldn't abandon God—not completely.

When they found John and Davis and figured out how to get Aiden back to jail, Parker hoped he could initiate forgiveness on his part and hopefully encourage Sage to do the same. That seemed like a long time off. Like him, Sage had faced tragedy, and most folks would say she had good reason to discard God. She carried a heavy load of sorrow, and only God could lift it from her shoulders, just as only God could lift his burden. Problem was, neither one of them wanted to give up the anger and revenge.

Right now Parker refused to think about his nephews being dead. He shoved the horror of it away and continued climbing the path John had taken.

"We have more problems." She pointed east.

He'd seen the gathering gray clouds, and those clouds might bring rain that would wash away not only John's tracks but the McCaws'. The scent of pine and cedar heightened with the sudden chill. The Rockies had seen rain nearly every day, and streams and lakes were gushing over their banks. Getting drenched didn't bother Parker, but he had a high respect for lightning. He had seen too many men and animals fried up like Sunday chicken to allow himself to be caught in the open with a bolt of power that equaled a cannon ball. He and Sage urged their horses faster along the men's trail, with the steadily graying clouds at their heels. As he'd expected, John's tracks led up the northern ridge of the mountain. Fifty feet more and a melee of tracks blotted out the original trail. They'd found where the McCaws had latched on to John.

"At least we know we're on the right trail." Sage glanced at the blue-black sky. "Can you get us to a shelter before the storm hits?" She untied a slicker rolled up behind her saddle. A flash of light and a crack of thunder hastened their desire to find someplace dry.

"I can. It's up this path, the way the gang climbed." He pulled his oiled duster close to his body and clamped down his hat.

"I'll follow and backtrack later so we can still split up."

Parker circled a piece of rock that jutted out over the path and climbed farther up through trees and brush. For the next several feet, he listened to the crashing thunder and held his breath each time the lightning flashed. The wind bent trees in homage to nature and tossed small debris at the riders. A grown man shouldn't be fearful of nature, but he didn't have to tell anyone that the blinding light shook him to the core. His horse screamed and reared, and a tree crashed across the trail in front of him. He held the reins firm, while pain raced through his ribs.

"Hold on, Parker," Sage called.

And he did—even if a woman told him to. Twice today his chestnut gelding had been spooked. If his horse went over the cliff, then he'd go with it. The gelding stumbled. Sure didn't make him look like a rough-and-tough mountain man. Sage jumped from her mount and grabbed his horse's bridle. After a few seconds, the horse calmed. Parker had heard she had a peculiar way with animals and birds—another legend, but it appeared true.

Rain began to fall in torrents, but the thunder and lightning subsided. Both horses picked their way over the rocks and mud-soaked earth. Cold rain ran down his back despite his slicker.

Holding his arm against his broken ribs, Parker dismounted to survey the path ahead and another fallen tree. Sage stood beside him. He expected no less from her. With water dripping from her hat and hair, she looked ... well ... pretty. "Once we clear out some of these loose branches, we can lead the horses over this," he said.

"I'll get my rope. My pony's strong."

Parker took in a painful breath and realized that what he'd once resented about Sage, he now appreciated. The two were equal—despite his cracked ribs—working together for a common purpose. And, more than that, he liked being with her.

The rain slowed, and in its place came a mist that screened the mountains, making it impossible to tell where the sky ended and the mountains began. Sometimes truth was like that.

"Look," he began, as he shifted to ease the agony in his side. "I'm sorry that I'm so useless."

"Never mind. We both came to do a job." She tied the rope to her saddle horn, then deftly wrapped the other end around a thick limb.

Parker watched her with the pony. It was as though she were talking to the animal. The hawk rode on the saddle. Curious. The pony backed up and slowly pulled the limb from the path.

"Did the Ute teach you how to communicate with birds and animals?"

She laughed. "No. It's a gift I was born with." She guided the pony's steps. "I've had some unusual pets in my days. Even had a mountain cat until my papa forced me to let it loose." She paused. "In truth, it followed me to school and frightened the other children and the teacher."

A woman with a bent toward predatory animals. That had to mean something. "I heard rumors about a wolf."

"You heard right. One reason Charles didn't fret when he was gone was my pet wolf. I raised her from a pup. At times even Charles was afraid of her, but she wasn't around him long enough for the two to make good friends."

"Where is the wolf now?"

"The same men who shot me and Charles killed her."

Sage had lost plenty in her day. "Talk to me about Charles," he said. "I had to have met him for Aiden to deem me so important."

"Maybe not." She heaved against a branch, and he reached to

help her. "This all could be about something Aiden wants you to do. Could be something political." A rush of wings announced the hawk's departure.

He'd ponder on her suggestion for a while. He'd made it known he was interested in representing folks in Denver, but the election was months away. "The only thing he could want from me is a way to get his hands on land and cattle. Surely he wouldn't think I'd appoint him to a political position."

"He has John and Davis, and one of his brothers killed your brother."

Parker's insides twisted. "It won't come to that. I'll have him and his murdering brothers locked up and awaiting sentence by the time I take office ... if I take office."

"Who knows? He might want to build a huge resort for rich folks to come and spend money. Or he might want prime timber land to build a sawmill or a stone quarry. After all these years, the McCaws might want to settle down. The outlaw life has to be taxing on a man—always on the run, dodging bullets, and the nightmares of what they've done. What else does Rocky Falls have to offer?"

"There's sandstone and limestone quarries in the area. I own some interest in those. Nothing but hard work for an honest man."

"Which brings us back to your first conclusion of him wanting political favors."

"Getting inside their heads and thinking like they do is the only way to beat them at their own game." Parker realized the fog had diminished. He glanced about. "Where's Hawk?"

"Hopefully looking for the McCaws."

"I heard a hawk can see a mouse a mile away. But how does he tell you what he sees?"

She shook her head, and a smile stayed fixed on her lips. "He doesn't. Neither do I speak bird language. I'm just a woman who likes birds and animals, and they like me." She straightened. "His usual habit is to find other humans and fly back to me. If I can see from whence he came, then I have a good idea where other folks might be."

He wiped the moisture from his face. "Next you're going to tell me you talked to the mama bear."

"I might have." He could see she was attempting to hide a laugh. "I told her you'd taste better than me."

"Thanks. Next time I'll talk to her. Seriously, I did notice your pony didn't get spooked with the bear or the lightning."

She glanced away from him. "That's part of the gift. Never met a horse I couldn't ride. But I wouldn't go betting on me out-talking a mama bear who's worried about her cubs."

What an interesting woman. "Did one of your parents have the same gift?"

"You sure ask a lot of questions."

"That's the only way I know how to find answers."

She paused as though thinking through his question. "My Ute grandmother had the way."

Suddenly Parker wished they were riding these mountains for pleasure instead of trailing outlaws. He found himself actually enjoying their conversation. It helped him keep his mind off the pain. "Hawk is what makes me curious."

She peered up at the sky before tugging on another limb. "Hawk and I understand each other. He's fiercely protective, and I love him for it."

A pang of jealously settled on Parker, and a strange sensation filled him, warming and chilling him at the same time. What he wouldn't give for a woman to love him like Sage loved Hawk. A woman as beautiful and strong as Sage Morrow.

How sad she'd lost everything the day she and Charles were shot. Most women would have moved back with their parents or taken up school teaching. "You're a remarkable woman, Sage Morrow. Can't think of anyone right now I'd rather get soaked or chase outlaws with."

She tossed him a strange look, as though she didn't know what to make of him … or herself. "Thanks. Parker?"

"Yes, ma'am."

"About your fear of thunder and lightning. If it's time for life to leave you, it doesn't matter if you're in a storm or walking across the street in Rocky Falls."

How degrading for her to see his fear. "That noticeable, huh?"

She tilted her head. "I'll not tell. Wouldn't want you to lose any votes. Might want to talk to God about those fears. They'll get the best of you if you don't find a way to overcome them."

"Yes, ma'am." A strange remark from a woman who shied away from God.

She nodded and gathered up a handful of brush. "How do you tend cattle in the open?"

"I always had a place marked out where I could herd them and hide. Another point you don't have to tell. My foreman figured it out a long time ago. Teases me about it now and then."

"I'll keep quiet. Might need a favor some day." She grinned at him, and, in spite of his embarrassment, he found himself smiling back.

When the fallen tree was clear enough for the horses to step over, Sage mounted her pony. "I'm heading back down."

"I know you're used to riding hard and alone, but be careful. I'll meet you where the trail comes to a fork and figure out what to do from there. One of us is going to run into the McCaws."

"Yes, sir. And, Parker, you're not so bad for a lawman."

A mighty fine compliment indeed.

TWELVE

Sage rode her pony down the trail to the foot of the mountain, then set out again on an alternate trail. The gang would need to split to follow them, making it easier for Parker and Sage to defend themselves and find the boys. The clouds passed by and the sun warmed the earth. She pulled off her slicker and rolled it tightly while studying the terrain. Hawk circled above. He'd called to her once she'd begun her descent, but she couldn't tell if he'd spotted the boys. Sure would be easier if the bird could talk. He'd be better company than the men she brought in for bounty. However, she didn't mind Parker.

She whistled for Hawk, mimicking his high-pitched shriek and warble. He swept down from the west in a flight of grace that no man could ever duplicate. Hawk flew onto her outstretched arm, a symbol of power, fierce and magnificent. She often wondered how she'd been able to tame his stalwart heart. Or perhaps she hadn't subdued him at all, but he'd merely granted her his companionship.

When she was a child, Sage's school friends had been wary of her when she had no fear of wild dogs. Later she was told to keep her wildcat and wolf away from civilized folks. Mama claimed her mother had shared in the same peculiarity, experiencing no qualms about befriending a bear. Sage left those furry animals alone, not wanting to know if they found her a threat. Whatever the reason for her kinship to animals and birds, she saw it as a blessing.

Tall Elk had found the baby hawk struggling on the ground

after his mother pushed him from the nest. The Indian presented the bird to Sage during a time when she often could not speak for the anguish embedded in her heart. Tall Elk recognized her innate ability to communicate with animals and encouraged her to seek out what her uniqueness meant. But he didn't realize she no more understood her gift than she understood the ways of nature. He believed the hawk would protect her and help her heart heal, and he'd been right. Sage was grateful for the bird's devotion, for it softened her grief to care for him. When she decided to hunt down those who had destroyed her life, Hawk had become a natural part of that quest.

"So are the McCaws west of here with Leah's boys?" she whispered to Hawk and stroked his variegated plumage.

Once on the alternate trail, she urged the pony to climb higher, winding around rocks and boulders and enjoying the sun on her face. For the most part, July temperatures kept the mountains fairly mild except for the storms, high winds, and the unpredictable snow of the higher elevations. Sage remembered Parker's high respect for lightning. More people were killed by lightning bolts in the Rockies than by wild animals. Everyone was afraid of something, and some folks were afraid of a lot of things. She wished her own fears were as easily defined. Right now the demon nipping at her heels was that Charles had been running with outlaws.

The pony stepped over bitterbrush and red-berried currants, with golden asters and light blue columbines scattered like jewels along the rocky path. After a time, she ceased admiring the wildflowers and concentrated on reaching the next small plateau, where she would be able to look out to the valley below. When she reached it, Hawk stirred and lifted his wings to soar into the treetops.

"Are we close?" she said, as though he understood. Perhaps he did.

She climbed higher until they reached a lake covered in lily pads. Brown and rainbow trout darted through the water while tall pine reflected in the shimmering pool. Tall Elk had instilled in her a reverence for the quiet beauty of nature, something she'd taken for granted in the past. Marrying him wouldn't have been an unhappy life ... just empty. Even here in all of nature's beauty, her soul longed to be filled. The love of a good man or the laughter of a child might erase the tears and heartache, but she was afraid to give her heart away. That made fear number two.

Parker feared lightning. Sage feared the years ahead would be scarred with loneliness. Fear number three. Guess she had more concerns than she thought.

A half mile higher, she came upon a deep green lake, larger than the previous and bordered by rocks and boulders as though carved from a giant rock bowl. She dismounted and tethered her pony to an aspen beside a patch of pink wildflowers. The rest of the way would be on foot.

Hawk flapped his massive wings and soared to a tall tree limb. Sage's instincts and Hawk's actions led her to believe she was heading in the right direction. Taking a long drink of water, she swung the canteen over her shoulder and grabbed her rifle. She'd reached the fork where Parker indicated they should meet. So where was he? He knew the area better than she did. Impatient, she chose to continue upward to where she could get a better view of the mountains.

Another half mile up, she came to a glistening emerald lake with a sparse growth of trees against a cloudless sky. In the distance, blue-gray cliffs saluted the heavens, stealing away her breath. A sense of awe for the untamed and wild filled her. Hawk circled above her, hopefully guiding her to where she'd find Leah's sons.

Sage scrambled up a rock and peered over the top. Directly below, a waterfall cascaded into a chasm, its air-filled water churning white and crashing against the rocks. She pulled binoculars from inside her jacket and scanned the area.

Searching the surrounding mountains' height and depth, she

peered into trees and brush for signs of the boys or the McCaws. Hawk had helped her locate humans before, and he could again. A breath caught in her throat. On a rock platform above a stream northwest of where she lay sat Aiden McCaw and his men. She focused on each man, and the images from the past took form. Her stomach tightened.

As vividly as if it were yesterday, she recalled the day strangers rode up to the house and demanded Charles give them their money. There were four of them then, and those four were in her sights now. One man stood out from the others—the one with dark curly hair and wide-set dark eyes who had killed Charles and shot her, sending her into early labor that killed their baby. Her search was ended, the object of her vengeance found. She'd sworn to kill them, but she'd do her best to bring Aiden and his brothers in alive.

Sage tore her attention from the nightmarish faces and searched for Leah's sons. She let out a sigh. *There they are ... alive.* The older boy was tied with his hands behind his back, and the younger one sat at his feet. Closer scrutiny showed Davis's hands were tied too. She scanned the area for a way to rescue them. The McCaws had chosen a fortress-like position. Clever. The wind would be cold at night, but the strategic location made rescue look impossible. A narrow path led straight up to their campsite, easy for them to guard. The only other way was to scale a cliff.

She peered through the binoculars to find Parker. Glancing around the surrounding area, she noticed some movement back down the mountain across from her. He stood behind a cluster of cedars on the far ridge, his binoculars positioned over his eyes. His horse was tied to a tree behind him. No doubt the physical exertion had forced him to stop before reaching their agreed upon site. Sage motioned to Hawk and pointed the bird toward Parker.

"Let him know I see him," she whispered, and yanked a button from her shirt. Placing it in Hawk's talons, she sent the bird toward Parker.

Hawk flew directly to him and screeched. Parker glanced up. Hopefully he'd recognize the red plumage. The bird dipped low. Through the binoculars, Sage watched Parker drop to the ground and examine something, then slip it into his shirt pocket. *Good.* Hawk had released the button. Now Parker needed to stay there until she arrived.

She scooted down from the rock and made her way back to where she'd tethered her pony. If Parker would stay among the cedars, she could loop around and reach him in a short while. She started to tremble under the weight of finding the boys and the man who had so long shadowed her mind, like Satan himself. All these years she'd thought of nothing but finding him and those who'd ridden with him, but now she had to choose between her hatred and Leah's sons.

Parker had been involved in many different strategies to bring down an enemy—from his teenage years wearing the gray in the war to his job as a marshal. But he'd never taken orders from a woman who used a hawk as a carrier pigeon.

And yet he hid in a thicket of cedars for a woman bounty hunter and her hawk while the lives of his nephews were threatened by the dangers of the wild and an outlaw gang. She must have learned where they were to send Hawk with a button. A bit of damaged pride rested in that knowledge. He should be the one scouting the mountains for John and Davis instead of gasping for breath with his sides on fire and waiting for her to appear.

The past few days had been a flurry—from Frank's murder to the beating he'd received at the hands of McCaw's gang to Leah's missing boys. In the middle of this was a strange bounty hunter who had the face of an angel and the reputation of a devil with mystic powers. Hidden within her tragedies was the truth about the connection Sage, Charles, and Parker had to the

McCaws. One truth had already surfaced: he longed to get to know a woman called Sage.

A twig snapped behind him, and he whirled around, his finger resting on the trigger of his rifle.

"Easy, Parker." Sage's soft voice reminded him of quaking aspen leaves, a taste of exquisite beauty amidst a breeze. Her slender figure emerged from the cedars. "I thought if I made a little noise, you wouldn't be so quick to shoot me."

"You don't know me." He should have laughed, but instead frustration took control. *He* should be passing on needed information to her.

"I found the McCaws and your nephews."

His optimism slid up a notch, and he shoved away his pride. "Are they all right?"

"From what I could see." Her face clouded. "Their hands are tied, but other than that they look fine. You can't see them from here."

He didn't like the look on her face. "What are you not telling me?"

"There's only one narrow trail up to where they're camped, and two McCaws are guarding it."

He hadn't trampled these mountains to hear rescuing John and Davis was impossible. "Show me where they're at. There has to be another way to get to them."

"There is."

His aggravation escalated. How could a woman delight and vex him at the same time? "How?"

"The only other way is to scale the rocky crags behind them, about seventy-five feet up."

"We brought extra rope." He attempted to ignore the pain in his chest. "I'll climb it tonight and hope the stars are out. I can rescue them."

Sage shook her head. "You can't make your way up the cliff with broken ribs."

Parker sensed the heat rising up his neck. "John and Davis are my brother's sons. They're my responsibility. I'm not a crippled old man."

Her face softened. "I know all about who you are, how you run a clean town and how folks respect you. But right now you aren't physically able to free those boys." She stepped closer. "Killing yourself doesn't help them either. Leah would end up losing all of you. And we already know what Aiden is capable of doing. I can make the climb."

"What would you have me do while you risk your neck? Nothing?"

"You can watch the ledge and cover me when John needs to climb down to safety."

Only one thing was worse than a man being wrong, and that was when a woman was right. "Sage, I'm a man. You doing all the work isn't right. I can't let you scale those rocks."

"Yes, you can. And I will. I've got a stake in this too."

Why did this woman talk in riddles? "How do you figure?"

"I recognized Aiden's brothers as the men who killed Charles. I saw the man who pulled the trigger." Sage took a breath and gripped her rifle. "Leah's youngest son is a reminder of my own son who lost his life that day." Pain crested in her eyes. "The men who killed Charles and shot me didn't care I was with child. We were nothing to them. I *need* to make sure John and Davis are safely returned to Leah. Then I will deal with the McCaw gang."

The stories behind her giving bounty to widows and orphans made more sense. Anger again rose for what the McCaws had done—would continue to do if someone didn't stop them. The murdering brutes. "I'm real sorry. The McCaws have ravaged this part of the country for too many years and must be stopped." Parker understood the torment searing her face. He'd seen agony beyond human comprehension during the war. Tragedies shaped the strongest of men, and Sage had not been spared. She was right. He'd be useless in an attempt to reach those boys when it took all of his strength to move and breathe. He had no choice but to swallow his pride — one more time.

Parker trusted a God who would scale the rocks before Sage lifted a foot onto the first foothold.

THIRTEEN

Sage spent most of the late afternoon studying the sun-bleached rock that led up the steep incline to the McCaws' campsite. She memorized every crack and fissure for a possible foothold, calculating her steps and trying not to think about snakes. Two thirds of the way up, she noted a sharp ledge that looked large enough for her to stand on. That could offer a brief reprieve for herself, but she'd need to lower the boys all the way down to Parker. Peering through her binoculars to the top of the cliff, she found a projection of rock directly above the ledge, to which she could tie the rope and lower the boys.

From a distance, the ascent looked nearly impossible, but standing on the ground and planning each step eased her mind. Tall Elk had taught her how to scale rock, and she could make it to the top. The problem was in getting those boys back down. Davis was young. Would he understand that he couldn't cry out? Falling rock could wake the McCaws, and they'd open fire. Unlike Parker, she didn't want any bright stars, and the moon would be a slice of unwanted light.

Parker stood wide-legged with his arms crossed and his hat slanted over his eyes. He was a good man; she'd decided that when he took the beating and refused to stay behind. They worked well together, and to her surprise, she actually liked him. Sincerity and warmth brimmed in his eyes, blue as a robin's egg, and she saw a strong desire in him to help others. He was pleasing to look at, too, with light brown hair and a handlebar mustache, and the lines across his brow gave him the distinction of a man who had experienced hardships. Colorado needed men like Parker Timmons to govern and form policies for the betterment of many and not just a few. She hoped he did well.

They'd stayed concealed in the shadows all afternoon and talked little while making preparations for later on in the night. Once the boys were safe, they would ride Sage's pony down a different trail than she and Parker planned to take in case the McCaws discovered they were missing before morning. Sage and Parker planned to take an easier trail on his horse, causing the outlaws to think they were the boys. Parker said John was skilled in traveling the mountains, and by the time dawn lit the sky, the two would be well on their way to Rocky Falls. Parker had already made sure there was jerky in the saddlebag and water in the canteens.

Sage observed him pacing and fidgeting while waiting for the sun to set. He chewed on a weed and rechecked the mule, horses, and ropes. He cleaned his rifle and loaded it while taking frequent glances up the cliff. A weasel studied them from the trees, no doubt thinking humans were peculiar creatures. And Parker waited. Sage pitied him for the anguish that must be tearing through his soul.

She motioned for him to sit beside her on a rock. "Have you tried praying?" she whispered.

"I haven't stopped." Curiosity etched his face. "Strange thing for you to ask."

"I never said I didn't believe in God. My problem is what He allowed to happen to my family."

"Maybe we're not supposed to know the reason."

If she hadn't been forced to whisper, her voice would be rising by now. "When innocent people are killed, it's wrong."

"I agree, but it's not God's fault. The McCaws chose to murder." He moistened his lips. "I'm one to talk, when I'd like nothing better than to blow a hole right through every one of them.

But I still know the truth from God's perspective, even though it's not what I want to hear right now."

She turned from his scrutiny. This conversation wasn't what she intended. "Yes, it is God's fault. A God who's in control of everything and supposedly loves the world shouldn't allow murder."

"I'm sure Eve felt the same way about Cain and Abel."

His response irritated her. The last thing she wanted was to discuss God. Mama and Papa already tried until they gave up.

"Sage." Parker placed his hand on her arm.

She jerked back. "Don't ever do that again." No man had touched her since Charles. It made her feel like Parker was attempting to betray Charles's memory.

"I'm sorry." He stood. His shoulders lifted and fell. "I sure would hate to see a fine woman go through life filled with hate and bitterness when she didn't have to."

"I'm better off than most," she said through clenched teeth.

"Are you?"

They didn't speak any more for the next hour. Birds sang, and a pleasant breeze bathed her face. But a lump formed in her throat, stealing her concentration from what needed to be done. Anger would not serve her in the midst of trouble. It caused good men to make bad choices, and bad men to pull out knives and guns.

Darkness finally crept around them, and it comforted her. Parker had touched her physically and, if she were honest, emotionally. There, she'd admitted it. Later on she'd deal with why everything about the man both bothered and attracted her.

"It's time," she whispered to the man in the darkness. "The ones who'll take the second watch should be asleep."

Parker nodded. "This time tomorrow, we'll be much closer to Rocky Falls and in better spirits."

She hoped so. Tonight's meal of hard biscuits and cold smoked ham had satisfied the hunger, while her mind whirled with what lay ahead. "And not arguing about God."

"I'd rather you see Him in me." His words were soft, barely audible, and as intimate as a kiss. For a moment she wished she still believed in God enough to ask for restoration. No, she was simply afraid and not confident of her own skill.

Glancing up the steep rock with far too many stars to light the way, Sage knew her endeavor could take her life and those precious boys. If there was a God, she hoped He would cast His favor on John and Davis. "I'll be back."

"Sage Morrow, you have no idea how difficult it is to have you go after those boys when it should be me."

She was inwardly amused at his confession, but she understood his regrets. It had to be hard for a man to allow a woman to lead the way.

"I know. I can hear it in your voice. Whatever happens, those boys come first. Make sure they are safe."

"I will." He took a breath, and she knew it pained him. "I'll make this up to you somehow ... and I'll be praying."

"I promised Leah I would do all I could to bring her sons back safely." She paused while a haze of other dangerous moments of her life swept past her. Parker Timmons had integrity, and she would not discount it. "I appreciate your prayers."

FOURTEEN

Aiden finished the last of his bitter coffee and listened to the fire crackle and spit. Hard to get comfortable in the mountains. The moment the sun went down, the thin air turned cold, mirroring his black soul and causing him to ache all over. He chuckled at his own description, priding himself on a reputation that caused grown men to cower and women to weep. An icy wind chilled his back, and he stretched out his hands to warm them over the fire. He stared up at the blue-black sky filled with hundreds of candle-like flickers. Back before the war, when he had a family in Mississippi, they'd all sit on the front porch and count the stars as they lit up the night. He'd tell stories until past the time to go to bed. Those days were gone, along with his wife and three sons, who were all too weak to fight cholera with nothing in their bellies — thanks to the Yankees. Why think about them? He couldn't bring them back, but he could take what was owed to him and help his brothers finally have what rightfully belonged to them.

His gaze settled on Parker's nephews. Fine-looking boys, but he'd not hesitate to kill them like his brothers had done their pa. The stupid man had found their campsite and attempted to make an arrest. The older boy wasn't much smarter than his pa, thinking he could rescue the little one all by himself. Aiden kicked at a burning log. He'd let Parker and Sage think he'd swap the two kids for the money. Then he'd get rid of all of them.

Quincy and Rex guarded the only trail up to the campsite while Jeb and Mitch lay by the fire. At midnight, they'd change places. Aiden wasn't known for his patience, but he'd learned over the years to devise fail-proof plans that brought him the advantage of waiting until the time was right to strike. He'd take over at dawn until midmorning, giving his brothers time to rest and eat.

The only man who had ever outsmarted him was Charles Morrow—or whatever his name was. He'd never talked about a wife. In fact, he'd never said where he'd come from, which was why they'd followed him after their last job in Denver. No wonder he kept Sage hid. She was easy to look at, but why marry an Indian?

"They won't try anything tonight," Jeb called out to those guarding the rocky path. Aiden snorted. The youngest of the brothers, Jeb was a fool to think Sage and Parker were sleeping. Parker had been beat-up bad, but he was tough and not about to lay low for long.

"I don't trust either one of them." Aiden sensed the temperature falling, and he grabbed an army blanket. "They won't bring a posse, but they sure will do their best to rescue these boys. Maybe even tonight."

"Suit yourself," Jeb said. "I'm getting some sleep before I have to take over guard duty. Tomorrow is when it'll all come together. Parker looked real bad when we left him." He stared into the flames licking up at the night sky and set his hat over his face.

"We ain't dealing with somebody stupid," Aiden muttered. "We have an Injun bounty hunter and a marshal who's out for blood."

"You're getting old, big brother." Jeb laughed. "They bleed and die just like the rest of 'em."

"Not until I get what I want."

FIFTEEN

Sage couldn't waste any more time talking. She slipped off her boots and socks and into moccasins to make the climb. Slipping the rope over her head and under her arm, she began her climb up to Leah's sons. Hawk had disappeared, but if she needed him, he'd be but a wingspan away. Still, what could Hawk do if the McCaws opened fire?

With each secure footing, the peak looked less ominous. Starlight glistened off the rock like silver sprinkles, and a quarter moon cast a faint light, though fast-moving clouds approached from the southeast. Beauty could be so menacing. She gripped the rough indentations and pulled herself up to the next level. At times she closed her eyes and imagined the rock formation as she had seen it from the ground. Ten feet, twenty, forty, and then a rock platform. But in the dark, she couldn't find the ledge.

She reached up to another hold and climbed higher. Her foot slipped. She grasped onto the rock with her fingers while her feet dangled in empty air. A scream died in her throat. She swung her legs back to the cliff, and her foot found a crack to balance her body. The crack widened to a platform. *The ledge.* She pulled herself onto the rock platform and rested for a moment, hugging it like it was her mother, willing her heart not to burst from her chest.

Holding her breath, she felt her way along the ledge until she had a firm hold on the rock above her and climbed higher. She dragged her body up, each step bringing her closer to the top edge. *Thank You.* Her simple prayer startled her. She must have been around Parker too long.

With renewed confidence, Sage yanked her knife from her belt and held it between her teeth. No more surprises. If a McCaw waited at the top, she'd have a weapon.

When her fingers reached the peak, Sage fought the urge to peer down, even if all she saw was blackness. She trembled and sucked in a breath to steady her nerves before raising herself high enough to see what awaited her. The rock projection that she'd seen below appeared to aim straight up to the sky like an arrowhead. It was larger than she originally thought and provided space for her to hide between the cliff and the McCaws. She could tie the rope around it and hope she had enough length to lower the boys to where Parker could help them.

Firelight lit three sleeping men and two boys. The other two McCaws must be guarding the trail. She swung her feet over the top and crawled to hide behind the rock. After tying the rope around it, she crawled to the boys.

With the stealth she'd learned from Tall Elk's careful instruction, she slipped her knife between the ropes binding John. He opened his eyes. She touched his lips, and he lay still.

Davis was more of a concern, as he was more likely to be afraid. She'd have to gag him, but she'd rather frighten the little boy than have him cry out and expose all of them. It took but an instant to wrap her bandana around Davis's little mouth. He started to squirm, but John touched his arm, instantly calming him. She cut his bonds and kissed his little cheek, thinking of Timothy in the grave beside Charles's. Shaking off the unfathomable grief, she carried the child to the cliff edge. Glancing back, she saw John snatch up a rifle from one of the sleeping men before crawling to join her.

She wrapped the rope securely around Davis's waist. "Hold onto the rope very tightly," she whispered. "Don't let go. I'm going to lower you to the ground where your Uncle Parker is waiting. Use your feet to walk down the rock."

John and Sage lay on their bellies and slowly allowed the rope to drop Davis to safety. How good the dark night hid the dangers.

Parker tugged on the rope below, signaling Davis had made it to the bottom. Just as Parker had said, John knew what to do in his descent. She allowed a few minutes for him to get several feet down the cliff before she grabbed the rope and followed. When she reached the ledge, she rested and waited for Parker to tug from below that it was safe for her to continue down.

Below, a scraping sound tore the silence, followed by a clatter of rocks bouncing against the wall and crashing to the cliff's foot. More fell, and in the darkness it sounded like a boulder cutting loose and tumbling down to where Parker and Davis waited.

"The boys are gone," one of the men above shouted.

"How'd they get away?" Another one cursed. "My rifle's gone."

Sage hoped John didn't hesitate to keep scurrying down the rope. He and Davis needed every precious moment to get away. Her mind screamed for him to hurry before the McCaws figured out what had happened.

Aiden cursed. "They snuck right past, you fools!"

If the McCaws attempted to come after them from the top, they didn't have a ready-made route for pursuing. While she waited for John to finish the climb, she studied the upper cliff and hoped none of them shone a torch to see where she clung to the rock face. *I promised Leah.*

"Find their tracks and get after them," Aiden called. "I'm goin' around to make sure they didn't come up the cliff."

The rope tugged from below. Sage pulled out her knife and cut it. She could make it back down on her own. And if one of the gang chose to come after her, he'd find his descent ended at the ledge.

That's when one of the McCaws decided to fire his rifle from the top. The reports exploded and echoed, bouncing from one rock to another. Sage hugged the cliff side, hoping the boys and Parker were safe.

A force slammed against her body, and a stab of white-hot pain pierced her side.

O nce the rocks ceased to roll down the side of the cliff, Parker heard the commotion from the men above. He tucked Davis safely away from the falling debris and watched John shimmy down the last fifteen feet of rope. Where was Sage?

As if in answer, the rope slid down the cliff, landing like a heap of vipers at his feet.

Then the rifle fire began.

Parker forced himself to hustle the boys into the shelter of the cedars, Sage's words echoing in his head, *Whatever happens, those boys come first.*

"Get your little brother on that pony," he said to John. "You two take off down this mountain and don't look back. Take the rougher trail—you know the one we take when we're going huntin'. Ride all night and tomorrow and keep going until you get to Rocky Falls. Don't stop for anything, and don't hesitate to use that rifle. Once you're at Rocky Falls, go to the preacher's. Tell him I said to ride out to your mama's place and tell her you're all right, but don't let anyone else know you're in town."

"Yes, sir." John pulled himself into the saddle and reached for Davis to sit behind him. Raindrops began to splatter the ground. "I'll see you at Preacher Waller's. Thanks, Uncle Parker."

Parker listened to the pony pick its way down the path. Once the sound diminished, he turned his eyes to the inky blackness above him, where he heard Sage inching her way down.

"Sage, you all right?"

"Not exactly." Her breathing was labored. "I've got a hole in my right side."

An image of Frank's body slammed against Parker's mind. He refused to lose another person to the McCaws. He reached up to help her down, being careful not to touch her wound and trying to ignore his cracked ribs. "How bad?" His hands felt the slimy blood along her right thigh.

"I think ... hope it went all the way through."

The idea of digging out a bullet filled him with apprehension. "We'll get you back to Doc Slader's."

"The boys?" Her voice had grown weaker in only a few seconds.

"They're gone. John can be trusted to get both of them home." He lifted her into his arms, and her weight sent daggers along his ribs. He blinked, fighting dizziness and his own agony.

"I'm not going far." Her breathing grew shallow. "Please, leave me somewhere. This—"

Sage's body fell limp in his arms, and he stumbled to the ground, pain searing his chest and sides. He struggled with the blackness threatening to overtake him. "Sage," he whispered. When she didn't respond, he felt for a pulse. It was there. *Thank You. Help me get her to safety. And keep the boys safe.*

Parker found the strength to lay her body on the rock-and-earth floor. He made his way to his horse and the pack mule to get a blanket. Where could he take her in this condition to treat her wound and keep her away from the McCaws? For that matter, how could he get her on his horse? Dear God in heaven, he couldn't even carry her with his busted ribs.

There was a way; he simply hadn't thought of it yet. A travois would have worked well, but there wasn't time. And he didn't want to toss her over his horse like a sack of feed—or a dead man. Besides, she might bleed to death in the process, or they'd walk into the McCaws' path. What could he do? It wouldn't take long for the McCaws to surround the area and finish off both of them. *Think!*

Parker remembered a clump of brush several feet from the foot of the cliff. He could move her there, then lead the horse and mule down from the path, take another trail up behind the brush, and reach her from the rear of where she lay. All of that in the dark. But it wasn't impossible. He had many of these trails memorized, and he understood if God was in this, He'd be the guide.

Sixteen

Parker placed his hand over Sage's mouth to suppress her moans. Aiden's men were combing the area, and Parker thought he could hear their hearts beat — or maybe it was death stalking Sage.

"They've done left," one of the men said. He held up a lantern, and Parker hunched low into the brush over Sage's bleeding body. Hawk rested beside both of them. The bird was a strange source of comfort in the essence of danger.

"I see the tracks of their mounts," the man said with the lantern. "Looks to me like the Indian pony left before the mule and horse."

"Makes sense if one of 'em was shot," Aiden said. "Let me have that lantern."

Parker held his breath.

"I see blood. Since her horse is ahead of the others, my guess it's Sage. I must have shot her when she climbed down the rock. Parker wouldn't have had the strength to scale it after the beaten'. He'd send her on and bring the boys."

"We could have got one of those kids," a brother said.

Aiden laughed. "I like that too."

"One of them wounded will slow all of 'em," another man said. "We'll have them in no time."

The lantern swung Parker's way, and he huddled lower over Sage's body, fearing he might hurt her. "Never can tell with Parker and Sage. My guess is he's taken whoever's wounded someplace where he can bandage 'em up and wait till daylight."

He swore a streak that would make the worst of characters at the Rocky Falls saloon blush. "Let's get going. I want all of them found. Parker and Sage won't hold out on us if we're torturing one of those kids."

"Why don't we wait 'til sunup?"

"Jeb, you're too lazy to ever 'mount to anything but shoveling manure," Aiden roared. "We're talking about two people who know what they're doing. And that hawk is more human than bird. Probably the devil himself."

If that bird were supernatural, he'd most likely be more kin to an angel.

At least Parker and Sage's hiding place bought them a little time.

Then again, Parker hoped the McCaws' conversation wasn't a trick to have him expose their whereabouts.

Amidst the grumblings about heading down the mountain in the dark, the gang mounted their horses and stole out into the night like the snakes they were. Once assured they were gone, he removed his hand from Sage's mouth and lifted the blanket packed against her side. It was soaked with blood, and it would be at least three hours until the sun rose over the horizon. Her breathing came in shallow gasps. He felt around him for mud to pack her side ...

Sage fought for consciousness through a mantle of blackness and fire. The agony in her side felt like someone had pressed a branding iron to her body. Memories of the gunshot that had nearly killed her years before surfaced, and she attempted to focus on what had happened this time. Leah's sons ... had they gotten away? And Parker ... had he been hurt too? She remembered his broken ribs and how easily any of the McCaws could have overcome him. Opening her eyes might hold a merit of danger —for if she'd been taken captive, they would increase her suffering. The torture would be worse than what she felt now. This way, she could listen to what was going on.

She heard nothing, but she sensed the presence of someone or something. Flashes of the preceding night faded in and out. Charles ... an outlaw? Where was she? Her mind gradually surfaced, and she recalled the climb up the cliff to snatch Leah's sons from the McCaw gang ... and the perilous descent with a bullet hole in her side. What had happened to Parker? Her nose detected an unusual yet familiar scent. Herbs. Willow-bark tea? Someone pressed a warm poultice against her side. Perhaps one made from aspen bark. Yes, someone was treating her wounds.

The McCaws would not tend to her wounds.

Moistening her lips, she chanced opening her eyes. In the distance, she saw the pink and purple of sunrise as if a blessing had graced her. And probably so since she was alive. Sage blinked and saw Parker kneeling over her, his face etched with concern.

"Mornin'," he said.

She forced a smile, but even that hurt. "Am I going to live?"

"I think so. You're one fighting lady."

"Thanks." She mustered more strength. "Parker?"

"Hush. Don't try to talk. The boys got away last night. I believe they'll make it." His voice sounded soft, gentle.

Thank You. Goodness, had she prayed again? She turned her head slightly to see Hawk. A rabbit lay in front of his talons.

"He brought breakfast." Parker laughed lightly. "We've both kept vigil."

Eating didn't appeal to her at the moment. She edged toward blackness, welcoming it, embracing it.

"I've two kinds of tea here — one made from willow bark and another from yarrow. Both should help with the healing and the pain. It's ready whenever you are." He raised a tin mug.

Dare she fight peaceful unconsciousness?

"This will taste real bad, but it will help. I carry them with me just in case. Comes from doctoring cattle and cattle hands."

He placed his hand under her head. "Take a deep breath, 'cause lifting your head is going to hurt."

What about his ribs? She'd do her best. "I'm ... a bad patient." The first sip was horrible, just as Parker claimed. The Ute had instructed her in the way of healing plants, tree bark, and sap. She'd been forced to taste them then, and Parker had brewed the same. "Thanks."

"You'd have done the same for me."

Yes, she would have. "You risked your life." Oh, how it hurt to talk.

"Rest while you can. As soon as you're able, we need to get out of here."

She tried to lift her hand to help tip the mug, but it seemed like her arms were tied to her. Dying sounded like a good idea, but she was too stubborn to give in that easily. "As soon as I sleep a little ... we can go."

"We'll try—"

She didn't hear another word. As much as she fought to stay awake, her eyes closed, and she drifted to a safe place that held no pain or memories or doubts.

SEVENTEEN

Parker had never seen such grit in a woman, and most men didn't measure up to Sage's courage. He wondered how many people would doubt his story of how she scaled a cliff to rescue John and Davis. But the boys knew, and they'd never forget her daring feat—and her sacrifice. Silently, he thanked God for all those years of taking care of cattle, learning about the medicinal qualities of plants and herbs. Sage had a strong chance of surviving. And he wanted her to live, even if his reasons were selfish. This woman had affected him like no other before, and he wanted to know her better. In fact, he didn't think he could ever grow tired of hearing her talk and laugh. And now, more than anything he'd ever desired before, he wanted to help take away the pain embedded in her soul. But Parker was smart enough to realize that before he could help her move past the shattered areas of her past, he'd have to come to terms with his own hate and bitterness for the McCaws. Anger had controlled him, led him blind since Oden and Frank's murders. The fury had to stop soon, for now what angered him controlled him.

Seems like his life had been one uphill climb after another. During a thunderstorm in the mountains he realized the need for God in his life. When a friend was killed, he realized the importance of upholding the law.

While she slept, he studied her face, smooth, with no hint of pain, and admired her beauty. He could look at her for a long time—flawless skin and high cheekbones were clear markings of her Indian heritage, and she had the longest eyelashes he'd ever seen. He touched her cheek, then stroked her black hair where blood had coated the ends. Charles Morrow should never have gotten himself killed and lost this woman.

Soon Parker needed to wake her for the journey ahead. The McCaws would return to where the boys had been rescued once they realized John and Davis had made it down the mountain. The gang would be relentless in their pursuit, and Parker had no desire to take on all five of them singlehandedly. But Sage's care was more important. The mule was packed, and his horse was saddled. He pulled out his pocket watch and decided he could give her another fifteen minutes. God had carried her this far, and Parker could only pray He would hold her tightly during the rough trek ahead.

"Hawk, are we ready for this?" He stared at the magnificent bird, noting its formidable stance and aggressive nature. Many times in the past, he'd shot hawks for sport. Now he stood together with one in devotion to a woman.

Fifteen minutes later, Parker clamped his teeth into his lower lip and hoisted Sage onto his horse's saddle. She clung to the saddle horn, then leaned over it while a soft moan broke through her labored breathing.

"Sage, this is going to be rough," he said. "But I'll do my best to get you back to town and to Doc Slader's." Then he wondered if he should have tied her to the saddle. But that seemed even crueler than what he'd already done.

When she didn't respond or perhaps couldn't, he grabbed his horse's reins and the mule's, then walked beside Sage. Hawk flew above them as though he led the way. This wouldn't be the first time that Parker wished he had the eyes of a hawk.

The way down the mountain would be long, especially when he had to take an alternate route to avoid running into the Mc-Caws. He tried not to think about John and Davis, but apprehension still crept in. With the boys' head start, they should have ridden around the Moraine Valley and be well on their way to Rocky

Falls. But nothing would stop the McCaws from riding into town and bullying the folks there into giving them what they wanted.

Perhaps he was cutting the folks of Rocky Falls short. Before he left, Parker had searched for a deputy to leave in charge. But none of the other men in town would agree to wear a deputy's badge since Frank was killed, so he had no choice but to put Preacher Waller in charge. All of the townsfolk except the preacher feared what the McCaws might do. Waller was a crack shot, and even though Parker didn't approve of the preacher's methods of browbeating his congregation, the man would stand up to a dozen outlaws.

As the hours drifted by, Parker stuck to little-used trails with plenty of tree cover. He kept one eye on Sage to make sure she didn't topple from the horse. She hadn't spoken for the past two hours, and Parker hesitated to initiate any conversation. He could only imagine the pain tearing through her body—pain that robbed her of much-needed strength.

Several times Parker stopped to check on her. She teetered between unconsciousness and torment-filled reality. The bleeding had slowed, but she was so weak that it alarmed him.

Early this morning, she'd drunk another mug of the willow-bark tea and then vomited it up. He'd wiped off her mouth, and she'd asked for another cup. Her determination was what kept her alive, and each time he viewed her courage, his respect for her increased. Leah needed a heavy portion of Sage's guts for what lay ahead in raising those boys. And if Parker's mother had developed an ounce of Sage's strength, she might not have deserted them for the comforts of Virginia.

Parker remembered a time when he believed he'd never care for a woman again. Leah's rejection had cut deep. But he was a boy then, and now he was a man. In a few short days, his manner of looking at life had changed, and all because of one woman. This didn't change his responsibilities as marshal or his political inclinations or how he felt about taking care of Leah and the boys. The possibility of adding Sage to the wagonload of his life made it all seem easier, sweeter. He stared into her face and wondered what it would be like to have a woman like her in his life. Maybe when the McCaws were behind bars, he and Sage could be more than friends. He'd like to court her and do things proper.

He hoped she felt the same.

Any other time, he'd have been mesmerized by the mountains, seemingly formed by some sleeping giant who breathed in and out to form the peaks. Today they were one more obstacle to cross. Sage whimpered, and he stopped the animals.

"Are you doing all right, Sage?" He brushed aside her black hair to see her face. Her eyes were closed. "Can you say anything to let me know you hear me?"

Nothing greeted him. This didn't look good. Hawk's long shrill screech caused him to search the steadily darkening sky for the bird. For a long while, he'd flown overhead, then he disappeared into the treetops. Too bad the bird couldn't talk and tell him if the McCaws were close by.

He gently shifted Sage on the saddle, knowing his every touch had to be agony.

Late afternoon rays of sun cast a golden light from the west, even as the clouds directly above let loose in another downpour. Too wet to appreciate the beauty of the silver drops touched by sunlight, Parker picked up his pace. Tucked into a dark shadow of the canyon ahead was a cave that Parker and Frank had stumbled upon years ago. Hidden behind a wall of brush, it offered a refuge for Sage to rest.

"We're about there." He breathed a prayer that she could hear him. "This cave will be dry, and I don't think many folks know about it."

Sage didn't respond.

When he spotted the cave's entrance, he stopped the horse and mule and tied the animals to a tree. Working his way up a steep path, he sensed the pangs of hunger getting the best of him. The rabbit that Hawk had brought this morning had been tied to the mule. Maybe he could get Sage to eat a little.

A mountain cat screamed, and Parker jumped. Right above him at the mouth of the cave, a female sounded her displeasure. He raised his rifle and began to back down. Firing a shot would be like ringing a dinner bell for the McCaws.

"Easy, girl," he said. "You can have your cave. We'll find someplace else."

It looked like another night in the open. Lightning flashed across the sky, and in the distance, thunder rumbled.

Sage woke to the sound of splattering rain against an overhead rock. She couldn't see a thing but a small flickering flame, but when she attempted to move, she felt plenty. She felt more alert—more alive than dead. "Parker ... where are we?"

"Taking cover from a storm." We'll rest here tonight and continue on at daybreak." The mellow tone of his voice told her they were safe even if Parker didn't like storms. The poor man had enough problems without her wound adding to his burden.

"I'm still alive."

He chuckled. "I think you're too stubborn to die." He sighed. "You are one strong woman, Sage."

"I don't feel very strong."

"Strength isn't always measured physically. I've got rabbit here waiting for you."

"Not now." The idea of eating didn't settle well. "Do you have any more tea?"

"Yes, ma'am. Right here waiting on you." He slipped his hand under her head and lifted her enough to take a sip. "Nice and easy so you can keep it down."

She forced herself to drink a little. "Thanks." When she glanced down, she saw she was wearing his blue chambray shirt. Hers must be covered in blood. That meant he'd dressed her. The thought troubled her, then she discarded her qualms. Parker had taken good care of her.

"You remind me of a dog my granddad once had," he said.

That sounded real complimentary, but she didn't have the energy to question him or protest his choice of words.

"She was the best sheepdog he ever owned. Kept the coyotes and other predators from the flock. Never seemed to get tired. She knew how to herd the sheep toward watering holes and on to where the grass was tender. Then one day a copperhead got her. She did her job until she dropped. That's when I saw the snakebite. I tended to her when the rest of the family gave up."

"So she recovered?"

"Yeah. She was real loyal to me after that."

Sage closed her eyes. "Are you thinking I'm going to be real devoted?"

He laughed. "There're two points to my story. One is you're one strong woman, and you don't let the ugly turns of life stop you—like the hole in your side. The other is, I haven't prayed so hard for anyone since that dog nearly died from the snakebite."

Parker's admittance gave her an odd sensation of how close he was to God—Parker counted on Him for *everything*. "I appreciate all you've done. You could have left me up there, and no one would have blamed you for it."

"I would have."

Curiosity about Parker Timmons kept her fighting sleep, although she knew she needed rest to heal. "What makes a man—" She held her breath while a stab of fire ripped through her side and down to her toes. "What makes a man, like your grandfather, choose sheepherding above cattle?"

"My grandmother came from Scotland to Virginia, and her people raised sheep. She brought her love for them here and convinced my granddad he needed to be raising them too."

"Here?"

"No. Virginia. She lives there now close by my mother and aunt."

"What do you like about sheep?" She paused and waited for the agony in her body to diminish. "I . . . I don't mean to be rude. I just don't understand."

"That's quite all right. First of all, I'm a cattleman like my father. Can't see myself raising anything but cattle and horses. Yet I have a tremendous respect for sheepherders. All the way through the Bible, the writers talk about sheep being akin to man. Now sheep are pretty stupid and need someone to look after them, a shepherd. While it humbled me to realize that just like them I needed a God-Shepherd, it also gave me an understanding and admiration for those who tend to them. Most of what I just said came from my granddad's analogy. According to him, the logical part of owning sheep was he could eat them and the wool brought a fair price."

"You eat cattle too, and their hide brings a fair price. Look at the leather coat you're wearing and your saddle."

"I agree." He urged her to take a little more tea. "Like life, we do best where our roots run deep."

"But you left Virginia for Colorado."

"My roots were in Frank and Leah."

She opened her mouth to speak, but his fingers lightly touched her lips. The intimacy reminded her that he had already seen her body, including the scars from another bullet hole. "Hush, Sage. Talking will wear you out, and you need your rest."

Parker made sense—both about her resting and the sheep. Peculiar how he caused her to look at things differently. She liked him. In some ways, he reminded her of Charles. In the good ways. She closed her eyes, and he lowered her head to the ground. Tomorrow would be a better day. It had to be. Right now she just plain hurt all over.

Eighteen

Aiden glared out at the blinding rain that fell in thick gray sheets and splattered on the ground. The water poured off his hat and soaked through his clothes despite his slicker. Anger fused with his hunger for revenge and deepened his hatred for Sage Morrow and Parker Timmons. Twice they'd outwitted him, and their clever tactics served to fuel his vendetta. By the time his brothers picked up a set of Indian pony tracks and realized the boys and Parker and Sage had not met up, they'd lost over two hours. The older boy had been taught real good. He didn't take the easy trail but one that swung out from it. Didn't matter nohow since the gang had lost them, and the rain had washed away their tracks. It would be a lot of work to find those boys again. That didn't mean it couldn't be done, and he was determined enough not to give up.

Likely those boys were holed up somewhere waiting for the rain to pass, and the mud would make their tracks easy to follow when they set out again. He'd make a fine example of those two. Aiden let the worst of his torturing pleasures wash over him. He knew a few tricks of his own to prove to Sage and Parker that he'd never give up on reclaiming his money.

But if the McCaws could find Sage and Parker first, Aiden wouldn't need the kids. "Mitch and Quincy, keep looking for those boys. The rest of us are backtracking to the base of that cliff. Sage and Parker couldn't have disappeared."

"Now?" Jeb's whining had about got the best of Aiden. If he

didn't feel sorry for the poor boy for losing some of his good sense after getting shot in the war, he'd leave him alongside the road.

"You heard me. Quit your bellyachin'."

"The rain's done washed away any signs of their trail. I'm wet and cold. This wind could blow a man off his horse."

Aiden lifted his rifle and pointed it at Jeb. "One of those kids is bound to make a mistake or get tired and hungry before they make it home. Any of the rest of you got a problem with this?" When Mitch, Quincy, and Rex said nothing, Aiden had his answer. "Now get out of here." He stared at Jeb as though daring him to refuse the order.

Jeb started to turn his horse around, then swung back to face Aiden. "We could go to where those kids live and pick 'em up again."

"And put ourselves in the open to get picked off?" Aiden's words slashed through the roar of rain. "Those folks aren't going to take lightly that we nabbed a couple of kids, 'specially since we gunned down their pa. The men of Rocky Falls will have guards stationed around the ranch for sure."

Jeb slowly rode off with Rex. If it was left up to Jeb, they'd all stop looking for the money.

The rain pounded harder, and the trail would get even slicker, but Aiden wasn't about to give up. He'd planned this for a year and a half, and he'd come too far and too long to quit.

NINETEEN

Parker didn't know what he hated more—being delayed by the downpour and risking the McCaws' finding them or exposing Sage to the rain and risking her getting pneumonia.

"Let's go," she whispered.

Her weakened state alarmed him. Just when he thought she was improving, she began to slip. Speaking took more and more effort, and the loss of blood had left her pale and trembling.

"We can't. You won't make it."

"We've ... ridden in rain before."

He glanced at her where she leaned against the back of the overhanging rock sheltering them from the weather. "I refuse to lead you to your grave, and that's exactly what will happen in this weather."

She closed her eyes. "We have to get back to town. Your ... your nephews. Folks depend on you."

"John is near to being a man. I trust him. And Preacher Waller is in charge." Parker refused to change his mind. How could he make a choice that held the potential of killing her?

"You would know for sure if you'd gone with them and left me behind."

He hadn't even considered leaving her to the mercy of Aiden McCaw and his cutthroats. What they would have done to her made his skin crawl. "You're not naïve, Sage. I couldn't leave you to face them like this."

"But the life I've chosen is laced in danger. I'm—" She

seemed to reach deep down for each word, "I'm concerned about those boys too."

"John's capable. He simply needs a little more sense about understanding what he can and can't do." Parker remembered what all he'd seen at John's age. "But I guess he got his rashness honestly. At his age, I'd been fighting with the Virginian Rebs for three years."

"You grew up real fast."

"I did. I thought I'd be a hero or something, and I ended up spending most of my days dodging bullets and trying to stay alive. Nothing noble about that. Something I don't wish on John. He's already seen more than I wanted for him. Can't help but think Aiden views him as a man, which means Aiden has a bullet with John's name on it." Just like his gang sent a bullet through his pa.

Her eyes fluttered open, and her chest lifted and fell. "And what if Aiden is—" She gasped for breath. "Terrorizing the townsfolk?"

"The men there will not let a gang of outlaws take over without a fight. Please don't try to talk anymore."

"A fight"—her eyes closed, as though she couldn't bear the thought—"is what I'm afraid of. They need their marshal. Rocky Falls needs you."

"Hush. I've considered the same things. The McCaws have me worried too. Now that you know his brothers were the ones who killed Charles, I understand why they want you." He brushed her hair from her face before he realized he'd touched her without permission. "You can identify them all and send them to a hanging. But why they want me is a mystery."

"Which ... one has dark curly hair and wide-set eyes?"

"That's Mitch. Vicious mean. Is he the one who shot your husband?"

She nodded. "Now I have a name. Leave me, please. I'm feeling better. I'll be fine. And when I'm up to it, I'll make my way to Rocky Falls."

"Forget it. I won't hear another word." His worries were far too many to contemplate. As much as he trusted God, he also believed God wanted Parker to do his part. Those he loved were in danger's path, and he couldn't be in two places at the same time. But God could.

"I can't leave it alone," she said. "Finding the McCaws is what keeps me alive."

"I understand. They killed my brother and my friend. They nabbed my nephews and shot you ... twice. When I think about all they've done, I burn." He shook his head.

"I've hated them for so long that sometimes I think there is nothing else left inside of me."

"And what happens after they're brought in? What happens after you learn the truth about your husband?"

She peered up at him, her eyes revealing the sorrow more than words. "Sometimes I wonder if knowing the truth will only make the pain worse. Maybe I'll leave this life. Maybe there's nothing else I can do."

He refused to respond to her reasoning because he understood. He'd thought long and hard about Charles Morrow being an outlaw, but Parker saw no reason to bring that up again. Sage would have to come to a reckoning about her late husband. "I believe when the time comes, you'll be able to handle whatever you learn."

"And the connection to you?"

"I still think Aiden may be looking for political favors."

"Could be." She glanced down at her side. "Do you want your shirt back? I can wear my coat."

"I'm fine." Did she have any idea the pain she'd go through in wrestling with his shirt? "You rest now, and we'll talk about what to do when the rain lets up."

She stared out into the sheets of water rolling off the rock and crashing to the ground. "Parker?"

He studied her, knowing exactly what she was about to say. Dragging his hand over his face, he braced himself.

"I want to leave now. I can make it. Both of us have business in town, and it isn't getting done while we watch the rain. I'm stronger."

Not one thing about Sage's reputation was a myth — except no one had ever told him she was strong and gentle at the same time. How her eyes sparkled in the sunlight, and how her hair shone like a raven's wings. Most of all, no one had warned him about how a man could easily fall in love with her.

He'd find a way to fulfill his vow to take care of Leah and her children. He had a town to protect from the McCaws and any other lawbreakers. He had his sights on politics and who knows what else God might put in his path. All of that could be done with Sage. When this was over, he'd convince her to stay with him. Each minute alone with her increased his need for her to be his wife.

But he and Sage weren't going anywhere until the rain stopped.

The clouds finally cleared away just after dawn on Thursday. They set out again, riding slowly, but by evening Sage could barely cling to the saddle. Even after Parker made her another poultice of aspen bark mixed with yarrow, she slept only fitfully.

On Friday the morning sun shone warm and bright, sparkling on leaves and bushes like she envisioned diamonds as Parker led the horse and mule along the trail. He'd taken excellent care of her, but he looked pale. No doubt his ribs were hurting him powerfully bad. He'd tugged on her enough to cause a normal man with broken ribs to pass out. She'd find a way to make this up to him.

When the sun grew hot, Parker helped her shed her coat,

and she nearly fainted. She wouldn't be alive if he hadn't been there to nurse her. That knowledge made her uncomfortable, as though she might one day owe him a favor she couldn't return. Silly woman. First she wanted to repay him for all he'd done, and then she fretted about what he might ask of her. They were a couple of sorry-looking creatures, both hurting and beat up. Good thing they'd be in Rocky Falls in a few hours. She hoped they didn't step into a snake pit. Best she get a few questions answered now.

"We're not riding straight into town, are we?"

"No, we're heading the back way to Preacher Waller's place. I told John to go there instead of home. The preacher's not afraid to use his gun." He chuckled. "He used to spend more time in jail than anyone I know, until the Lord snatched hold of him."

She remembered the preacher who looked like he could handle his own. "Is that how he keeps folks in church?"

"He's been known to visit a few backsliders now and then. All it takes is a wife to complain to him. Trouble is Leah was too embarrassed to ask him for help when Frank threw up behind the barn after a Saturday night drinking. Whiskey had a powerful hold on my brother."

Frank and Parker Timmons sure were different. "What else are you not telling me?"

"Are you reading my mind, Sage? No matter. Frank's gone, and it doesn't matter that he had a few weaknesses. He was murdered, and the killers need to pay."

"Is your preacher the kind of man who comforts the downtrodden?"

Parker thought before he spoke. "Preacher Waller's forgotten what it's like to fall under temptation's sway. I don't want to be one spreading tales and judging others, but in my opinion, Waller preaches too much fire and brimstone and not enough love."

"I believe understanding is the key to helping other folks," Sage said.

"I agree. A person can't help another if he doesn't know what kind of hand's been dealt."

"Maybe your preacher is too ashamed to admit what he did in the past."

Parker glanced up at her and gave a smile. Her insides tingled, taking her by surprise. Now where did those feelings come from? With a deep breath, she twisted to gaze up at the sky. Hawk was flying above them. Faithful friend. A stab of pain followed, and she gripped herself, hoping it wasn't a sign of infection. One more time she was thankful the bullet had gone straight through her flesh and didn't lay embedded in her side.

As they made their way through the foothills before Rocky Falls, both of them were quiet. She knew what bothered them the most was what lay ahead and what Aiden planned next. If the ranting and raving Aiden had done the night he discovered the boys were missing was any indication of his temper, he'd be ready to burn the town and everyone in it.

"Any sign of the McCaws other than the tracks we saw yesterday?"

"No. I don't like that they split up. But John and Davis were way ahead of them."

"Soon we'll know. And then we can figure out our next move."

He shook his head. "The only plans you're going to make are to see Doc Slader. It's a miracle you didn't bleed to death."

Being told she couldn't do something irritated her more than a swarm of angry bees. "I'm on the mend, and I have a job to do. And what about your ribs?"

"Whoa. You're getting better all right. I hear the fight in those words."

"Glad you understand what's at stake here." She needed for him to talk. It took her mind off the intense pain. "Tell me about your ranch."

"I started out with a homestead, but I've added quite a few acres since then. It's a generous slice of heaven. Rolling land with the St. Vrain River flowing right through it, making it easy for the livestock to get water. It's green and pretty. My cabin isn't big, but it's sound. The wind has howled around it for a long time."

"How many acres?"

"A little better than three homestead parcels—five hundred acres."

"Who takes care of it when you're gone?"

"Duncan Riddle, my foreman, and two other hired hands. Duncan's the best man for the job, and he's a good cook, too. I don't worry about a thing when I'm gone."

"That must make life easier."

"It does. When you're feeling better, I'd like to show it to you." He paused. "Ever think about giving up being a bounty hunter? Seems like a mighty lonely way to live."

Sure she did. The dreams she'd once held tightly had been shattered, yet, in fanciful moments, they came alive again when she thought of having a good man—and children. "Sometimes it crosses my mind."

"I bet you've gotten plenty of offers."

"Oh, I have. But mostly from outlaws who thought they could sweet talk me into saving them from facing a judge."

Parker laughed, and once again she enjoyed the low rumble of his mirth. "Any offers from lawmen?"

Her pulse quickened. *What is he asking?* "I don't recall any."

He stopped the horse and the mule and looked up at her. "When this is over, would you consider allowing a city marshal who's wanting to be a politician to come calling?"

Heat flooded her body. She stared into his blue eyes and saw something more frightening than all the outlaws she'd ever brought in.

"Did I insult you?" he said.

"No ... not at all. I'd like for you to think about what you're asking."

"I have."

She thought of Charles and Tall Elk. She considered the dangers she and Parker had faced. "I think it best if you wait until the McCaws are behind bars before we discuss this ... possibility."

"All right." He urged the horse and mule on again. "You know, in all of this, you and I have never fired a shot."

Sage hadn't considered that aspect of the past few days, mostly because she'd been on the receiving end of a gun. "The next time we're out looking for the McCaws, we'll probably use up all the ammunition we have."

"Glad you said 'we.'"

Sage sensed a catch in her throat. Without pondering it, she'd begun to think of Parker as more than a friend. "I figured we both had a stake in bringing them to justice."

Parker pushed his hat back from his forehead. "I have more than one concern in this thing. And you know what I'm talking about. The McCaws could have taken the town hostage. Committed more murders."

She shivered, and it had nothing to do with the pain tearing through her side, leaving her ice cold one minute and burning up the next, but with the thought of more innocent people being killed. Another jab of liquid fire spread through her. She refused to mention it to him, for they were almost to town. Thirty minutes later, she sensed her temperature spiking. Her head swirled, and she closed her eyes to keep from falling off Parker's horse.

TWENTY

P arker stole through the trees behind Rocky Falls' cemetery to the parsonage, where he hoped to find John and Davis—and the town free of the McCaw gang. He'd left Sage several yards back until he made certain they weren't riding into a trap. In the past two hours, her condition had worsened. Fever raged and her wound was inflamed.

Now, with the houses and buildings of Rocky Falls lying just beyond the church and parsonage, Parker wondered what kind of hornet's nest awaited him. He hid behind an occasional tombstone and steadily made his way toward the house. At times, Preacher Waller practiced his sermons in the church, and the shouts had been known to echo around the cemetery. But nothing unusual captured Parker's attention, and that bothered him, especially since Preacher Waller and his wife had four lively children who were known to play in the cemetery. Parker had never understood why the man allowed such disrespectful behavior from his children, but there were a lot of things Parker questioned about the preacher.

Parker slowly made his way to the church in hopes Preacher Waller would be there. At the back door, Parker listened again for sounds of the McCaws. Once assured that the building was empty except for possibly Waller, he opened the door. The town's preacher stood behind the pulpit, his head bowed as he obviously prepared to lift Sunday's sermon to the skies for heavenly approval. The sunlight streaming through the windows gave his bald head a bit of a halo, which hit Parker as rather humorous.

How well he recalled the days when Waller drank, fought, and carried on with the ladies. The saloon had a special table just for him ... and a room reserved upstairs.

Waller whirled around once Parker stepped into the church and closed the door. "Parker, we've been looking for you to show your sorry face ever since the boys made it back."

Leave it to the preacher to hand out compliments. "So they're here and fine?"

"Yes. John made good time. He talked to Culpepper about what happened but not much to me. All I know is that the boys were separated from you and the Morrow woman. That young man needs a lesson in communicatin' with adults."

Parker already understood how John felt about the preacher. "Where are the boys now?"

"They're fine. Myrtice and Leah have all the children across the road picking beans. I thought it best for all of Frank's family to be here at the parsonage."

What a relief. Maybe he should take back some of his less-than-charitable thoughts about the preacher. "Thanks. Any sign of the McCaws?"

"Nothing." He walked toward Parker. "It's been real quiet. 'Course I've been praying God's wrath on them."

For once Parker agreed. "We'd be fools to think they've given up on whatever it is they want."

"I asked John what they wanted, but he acted like he didn't know. Where have you been anyway?" Waller frowned.

"Sage and I ran into some trouble. One of them shot her—a clean shot, but she's in real bad shape and needs Doc Slader's attention. For a while, I thought I'd lose her. Looks like the wound is infected."

Waller shook his head. "Bounty hunter is not a fittin' job for a woman, but I guess it's better than bein' a soiled dove."

The remark ruffled Parker. The preacher didn't know a thing about Sage. "She saved those boys' lives."

Waller's brows narrowed, and he frowned. "John told me the same thing. The only thing he would say. But a woman like that is most likely on God's judgment list."

"A woman like what?" Rage crawled from Parker's heart upward to his neck. He wanted to slam his fist into Waller's jaw. He turned to stare out the window to stop himself from disgracing God's house. One more time Waller had gotten all caught up in his own interpretation of the Bible. "Like I said, she risked her life to get those boys away from the McCaws."

Preacher Waller rubbed his chin. "Don't look good for you two to be alone in them mountains all that time. What about the time alone before she was shot?"

Parker stiffened — maybe it was the lack of sleep, or his broken ribs, or worry about the McCaws planning more murders that made him want to cram those words back down Waller's throat. "I could have brought her back sooner, and you could have preached her funeral."

"I'm just pointing out how it looks to the townsfolk. You don't need gossip flying when you're wanting to win an election."

"If winning an election means I no longer care about people in trouble, then I don't want it." He turned to leave before he spouted a few words God didn't need to hear. "I need to get Sage to the doc's."

"I'll help you take *Miss Morrow* for help. You don't look too good yourself."

Parker swallowed another mouthful of spite ... almost. "I'll get her there *myself.* One of the members of your congregation might see you and think you have a caring bone in your body."

Sage drifted off to sleep with her rifle in one hand and her Colt in the other while Parker scouted out Rocky Falls. *God, if You're listening, please make sure those boys are all right.* Praying wasn't something she did much, but children were this country's legacy, and they deserved protecting. Maybe God would listen this time.

She'd wanted to stay alert, but the torment stirring in her body exhausted her strength. And the heat ... the intense heat ... A rustle in the brush instantly alerted her.

"Don't fire," Parker said. She must have looked pitiful, for compassion filled his face. He dropped to his knees beside her. "Can you make it into town, or do you want me to get a wagon?"

"I made it this far on a horse. The boys?"

"They're fine. Leah and the rest of the children are at Preacher Waller's. And the town's quiet. Too quiet as far as I'm concerned."

She took a breath to steady the pain. "Aiden and his brothers are watching."

"Right. So let's give him something to think about and get you to the doc's." He reached to pick her up. "You're hotter than before. We need to hurry."

She heard something more than concern for her in his voice. Something had put Parker in a surly mood. "What ... happened while you were gone?"

"Nothing."

He was lying, and she surmised broken ribs and a gang of outlaws had nothing to do with it. At the moment, she didn't have the energy to pry it out of him. All of her might went into fighting to stay conscious.

Several minutes later, the two trailed across the pasture beside the cemetery. She concentrated on white-laced wildflowers and black-eyed Susans beneath her to keep from falling off Parker's horse. The crosses and tombstones didn't do a thing to soothe the fears slamming against her brain.

"Uncle Parker." A male voice shouted from the distance.

"Hey, John. Good to see you."

Sage couldn't lift her head.

"What happened to Miss Morrow?" John's voice rang with panic.

How bad am I?

"A bullet got her."

John gasped. "Is she going to be all right? I remember hearing shots fired when Davis and I were leaving. I'm real sorry. Didn't think about either of you getting hit."

"We're on our way to see the doc. She's weak, but she's a fighter."

Sage wanted to acknowledge both of them, but she couldn't bring herself to utter a word. Was Davis with him? *Such a sweet little boy.*

"I'll steady her," John said. "Looks like she's about to fall. I'll never forget how she scaled that cliff to rescue Davis and me."

If she could, she'd thank him. What had happened to make her feel worse? A chattering of excited children exploded around her. Then the sound of women's voices chased them away.

"Parker, why is she wearing your shirt?" A man's voice rang out a few minutes later, and it was too deep to be John's.

"Good question," a woman said with a definite air of disdain. "Doesn't look proper."

"What would you have her wear?" She'd never heard Parker sound so angry. "Her blood-soaked shirt is in my saddlebag burnt with a bullet hole."

"I don't appreciate your raising your voice in the presence of these God-fearing women."

"I don't care what you appreciate. This woman did what none of you would have attempted. So don't give me your high and mighty words about what's proper."

"I'll always remember what Sage did to save my children." Sage recognized Leah's voice. "What can I do?"

"You can pray. John here is going to help me get her to Doc Slader's."

The deep-voiced man spoke again. "That's the last time I fill in as your deputy."

"Don't get me any more riled up, Waller. You best watch the sky. I hear a storm's brewing for hypocrites."

If Sage could utter a word, she'd have told Parker that he had more guts than any man she knew to go up against a man of God.

When this was over and he asked her about calling ... courting, she hoped she could say yes. A part of her really wanted to. But would she ever be right for any man?

Twenty-One

They're back in town, huh?" Aiden watched the goings-on in Rocky Falls through binoculars from a foothill outside of town. Everything looked normal except for Parker's horse and a pack mule tied up outside the doc's house. Aiden watched Parker and the oldest boy of Frank's pull Sage off a horse. The kid carried her inside. He had broader shoulders than most men. Sort of reminded him of Karl at that age.

"What do you see?" Mitch said.

Aiden chuckled. "We must've broke the marshal's ribs. He don't move too fast, and Sage ain't in too good of a shape either."

"That woman must be part cat for the times she should have died. I left her for dead the day I shot her and Charles."

"More like a she-devil." Aiden handed Mitch the binoculars.

"What do you expect for an Injun?"

Aiden spat a brown streak of tobacco toward Rocky Falls. "Weakness don't have to mean a bullet through the heart. All it takes is others thinkin' you're spineless, and then you lose your confidence."

"Like the folks of Rocky Falls believing their marshal is a coward?"

"That's part of it. My plan has lots of parts."

Mitch handed Aiden back the binoculars. "Like you used to do in the war and then after. Big brother, you're one smart outlaw."

"Don't forget it either. And you're not far behind me."

Mitch grinned. "Killing the deputy and taking those kids was a good idea, and it almost worked too. What are you thinkin' we do now?"

"We need to let them sweat by doing nothing for a spell," Aiden said. "We could ride in there and shoot up the place. Or we could demand Parker and Sage meet us outside of town or we'll destroy their town. Or we could watch which way the wind is blowin' and set fire to some timber. But they expect us to raise hell. I'm thinkin' if she's hurt bad then we need to wait until she's better."

"Can't tell us where Charles hid the money if she's dead."

Aiden pulled out his pocket watch. Revenge had ridden with him for a long time, and he didn't intend to lose to a no-account marshal and a near-dead, half-breed woman.

"Are you sure the money's worth all this trouble?"

Fire burned in Aiden's chest with the memory of how things had gone wrong that day. "The money and what's behind it. Our brother's dead because of Charles."

Mitch swore. "He was shot because Jeb didn't have the sense to cover him."

"Jeb's slow, but Charles led them into a trap. You were there. You know what happened."

Mitch nodded. "You're right. Sometimes the mind has a way of losing important facts. The money won't bring Karl back, but it'll help us forget. He would have wanted that."

"You keep thinking about what we lost. Sage has a weakness, and once we figure out what it is, we'll have her right where we want her—and our money."

"And Parker?"

"His brother's grave is still fresh, and he has family to look out for. Hard to think straight when people are depending on you. He could make a few mistakes."

"And you still think those two are planning to take off with our money?"

"I'm positive. Enough time's passed that the law wouldn't be suspicious of 'em. They put up a good front when I was there. Actin' like they didn't know each other." Aiden took another look at the town. "Get me Rex. I have a job for him."

"I'm right here." Rex had walked up behind them unnoticed—one of his good traits that had helped him stay alive during the war and later when they had jobs to do.

Aiden clasped his hand on Rex's shoulder. "Tomorrow I want you to ride into town, friendly like. Register at the hotel but stay clear of the saloon. Then go to church on Sunday. Find out all you can about Parker and Sage. Our gal there should have learned a few more things to pass on. Don't let folks see you with her."

Rex shook his head, but Aiden expected him to refuse. Rex had a mean streak, but he was cunning. "Are you trying to get me killed? Sage will recognize me as one of those who killed her husband. So far I've been lucky."

"She isn't going anywhere from what I've seen. Ride on back Sunday night or Monday morning. Stay out of trouble."

"And you don't think Parker will recognize me either?"

Aiden took a long look at his brother, not ready to lose another one. "Take a bath and get Mitch here to cut your hair—and shave. Right now you look like the devil himself." He lifted his binoculars again. Frank's oldest kid sat on the doc's front porch. "Our own mother won't know you once he's done. No swearin' either."

"And what's my name?"

Aiden wished his brothers could make a few decisions of their own. "Make up something. Tell folks you're a rancher from Texas lookin' for land. Tell 'em you have a wife and kids and want to make sure the area's law abidin'. Tell 'em your wife is lonesome, and you want land where she and the kids can have company. The important thing is to find out all you can about Parker and Sage. We need a little dynamite to blow up their plans to spend our money."

TWENTY-TWO

"S he has fever, and there's infection setting in." Doc Slader dabbed carbolic acid on Sage's wound, which was as brown-red as the laudanum mixed with canary wine and cinnamon sticks used to deaden the pain. He glanced up, his spectacles balancing on the end of his nose. "Good thing you applied a poultice. Without it, she'd have died."

Parker had prayed for her until he had no words left. "Looks like I didn't do a good enough job if it has infection."

"She's alive, Marshal. That counts for a whole lot."

Parker's gaze shifted from the gunshot wound to Sage's pale face. "Is she asleep or unconscious?"

"I gave her enough laudanum to put her to sleep." Doc Slader lifted her body to examine where the bullet had exited from her side. "Hold her for me, will you? I don't see any infection on this side, but I want to treat it just in case."

A soft moan escaped Sage's lips. How much more could she handle and still hold on to life? And to think she'd been shot before by one of those dirty scoundrels. He'd seen the ugly scar on her left shoulder, real close to her heart, and another one on her back. This was one strong woman.

Whenever Parker saw folks suffering, he remembered watching surgeons during the war remove arms and legs while men screamed for God and their mothers. Blood everywhere. Limbs dropped in buckets or on the ground. Guts dumped outside of camp for vultures to feast on. Parker pushed the nightmare aside. He wasn't ready to lose Sage—now or ever. The realization had taken root in the mountains, and each moment intensified his feelings. "I also gave her yarrow tea, but after I saw the willow-bark tea made her bleeding worse, I stopped."

"Good. I'd have done the same." He lifted his head, and the mass of brown and gray hair tied back with a leather strap made him look more like a mountain man than a doctor. "How'd she get shot?"

Parker mulled over how much to tell and whether giving too much information might endanger the doctor. Then again, most of what happened had already spread like gossip on an old woman's tongue. "She rode with me to find Frank's boys. One of the McCaws shot her while she rescued them."

"Heard about the jailbreak and John and Davis going missing." Doc continued to talk as he cleaned the wound, which Parker had come to recognize as his way of working. "I expected Sage Morrow to be hard-looking. The bounty hunters I've seen in the past were as rough as the outlaws they were bringing in. She's a handsome woman. Part Indian I see."

"Ute is what she said." Parker wasn't about to comment any more about Sage's Indian heritage. Some folks had their own prejudices about it, but not Parker. He didn't judge a person by the color of her skin or where she came from.

Preacher Waller and his wife would make sure the town knew about Parker and Sage spending nights in the mountains. Anger snaked through him at the thought of the town's preacher questioning why she wore his shirt. No wonder this part of the country was mostly heathen, with men of God acting no better than the lost souls. Yet who was he to complain? He did his own share of sinning.

Doc stood back and wiped his bloody hands on a soiled cloth. "That's all I can do for now. You might want to tell John how she's doing." He pointed toward the open window behind Parker. "He's been waiting on the porch for a couple of hours. I imagine he's beholden to both of you for rescuing him and his little brother."

Parker had forgotten about John. The more he tried to shelter the boy—and he wasn't a boy but a man—from the evils of the world, the worse things got. Perhaps it was time to be open and honest about what was going on.

He found John sitting in a rocking chair on the front porch. Hawk was nowhere around, but no doubt the bird had his eye on the door.

John slowly rose as Parker approached. He was as tall as his father. "Is Miss Morrow going to be all right?"

Parker clamped a hand on the boy's shoulder. "Doc's treated her, so now we wait and pray."

John offered a grim smile. "I think you'd be a better preacher than Waller. How'd you keep from punching him back there? I sure wanted to."

"Real tempting. But I didn't want to give him anything else to gossip about."

John glanced down the street. "Can I stay with you at the jailhouse instead of going back to the parsonage? I don't mind bunking down in a cell. The mice are better company than the folks at the parsonage."

Parker started to refuse, but John had a good argument. Waller had a way with words. He made sure folks knew what he claimed about the Bible was truth. "I'll talk to your mama."

"I will. No point you heading back there. A fight would really get the preacher riled up—and for sure be the subject of his next sermon."

Smart boy. Leaving Waller in charge while he and Sage searched for John and Davis hadn't been one of Parker's decisions. He needed to find a good replacement for the next time he was gone. Better yet, he needed a reliable and permanent deputy.

"I still want the job as deputy."

Did he read my thoughts? "When you're twenty, John. Things around here have gotten too hot, and I don't want you involved. The best thing you can do for your family is to take care of them."

"I'll ask you again when I'm nineteen."

Parker smiled at his nephew. He had Frank's wit and Leah's persistence. "You're already done with your schooling and running your pa's ranch. Why take on more responsibilities with four younger brothers needing you to show them how to grow into men?"

John nodded, as though digesting Parker's response. "I've taken care of the ranch and looked after Mama and my brothers since I was fourteen. But I'll wait another year to ask you about the deputy's job."

Maybe John would change his mind by then. "That's fair. Have you been checking on your ranch?"

"Every day. Mama isn't happy about it, but there's work to be done. I had the other boys stay here in town. No point risking them getting hurt. I rode out there early this morning and did a few things. At least the cattle are out on the range. So not much needs immediate attention outside of checking on the horses, feeding the chickens, and gathering eggs. Makes me wonder when I'll ever catch up, though." He leaned on one leg like Frank used to do.

John had become a man right before Parker's eyes. But he still wasn't going to take a deputy's badge, not at eighteen. "You're a good man, John. Nearly got yourself and your brother killed, but still a good man."

"Yes, sir. I'll use my head in the future." He trotted down the steps. "Oh, I forgot," John said, pausing on the bottom stair. "Widow Bess stopped by here about a half hour ago. Said she'd be back to check on Miss Morrow this evening." At Parker's nod, he turned and headed down the street toward the parsonage— a place Parker didn't intend to visit for quite a while. He had enough problems. Waller's wife and children needed a heavy dose of pity and prayers. Living with that man had to wear a person down.

Parker's thoughts reverted to the McCaws. Considering Aiden's reputation, the situation would get worse. It still puzzled him as to what he and Sage had that Aiden wanted. It was ridiculous to think Aiden had waited until Sage received a wire from a town where Parker was a marshal to put the two together. That bordered on unrealistic, unless someone in the town worked with Aiden. If that were the case—and Parker didn't have anyone to suspect—Aiden had planned to kill someone near Rocky Falls and have Sage come after him, which brought Sage and Parker together. That, too, was highly unlikely and increased the suspicion that someone in Rocky Falls had been working with the McCaws to make sure the pieces fell into place. Who had Parker talked to before wiring Denver about needing a bounty hunter? He and Frank had discussed it, but no one else. *Frank? Surely not.*

Poor Oden probably hadn't done a thing to aggravate Aiden. He was just unlucky enough to become the murdering gang's bait. Where did Frank fit, unless the McCaws wanted to add a little more wood to the fire by killing Parker's brother? He didn't want to think his brother had been involved, though it was beginning to look that way. When Sage felt better—and she would, for he refused to believe otherwise—they'd talk about what she'd been doing since her husband died to see if they could make some sense of this mess. He'd also take a hard look around town to see if he had an enemy.

Aiden wasn't known for backing down from a fight or giving up, and with Sage and Parker getting the best of him, the gang would make someone pay. Hopefully their revenge didn't mean another dead body.

He slipped back into Doc's where he could sit at Sage's bedside. The day wore on with nothing out of the ordinary going on, which gave Parker time to think. And as in times past, he couldn't remember anything about Charles Morrow.

Doc stopped in to check on Sage around suppertime. When he finished fussing with her bandages, he turned a clinical eye on

Parker. "Go get yourself a good meal and some rest, Parker. You can't do a thing for Miss Sage. It's up to God."

Parker swallowed hard. Hunger had taken root in his stomach for the past several hours. While she slept, he could take the opportunity to send a wire to the sheriff's office in Denver to see if Charles Morrow had ever been linked to the McCaw gang.

Next stop was to see Bess. If anything in town was riding on the wind, she'd know about it.

TWENTY-THREE

When Parker left the telegraph office, he met Bess on the boardwalk outside of the hotel. She had a plate of food covered with a cloth, and he could only hope it was for him.

"I'm on my way to the doc's," she said. "And I thought you might want this."

"Bless you," he said. "I'm starved, but I didn't want to leave Sage any longer than necessary."

The two fell into step. "How is she?"

"Doc's given her enough laudanum to make her sleep for a long time. Infection's set in where she was shot."

"I've been praying for her since she lit out of here the morning you two went after John and Davis."

"Thank you. We needed it. And we were able—" He paused. That wasn't what happened at all. "I should say *Sage* was able to rescue them. But one of the McCaws got even."

"I like her," Bess said. "She's not what I expected from a bounty hunter."

"I agree. She's courageous and strong, but graceful, too. I'll always be grateful for her saving those boys." The words sounded good to his ears and reinforced the direction of his heart. But those matters were private.

"Where are the McCaws now?"

"I wish I knew. This isn't over, Bess. There's—" Again he stopped in mid-sentence.

"What are you not saying?"

"Maybe not enough. Maybe too much. You might even think I'm crazy."

"Parker, what's going on?"

Bess had been the one who'd listened to him when a subject worried him. He could trust her. "In the past, I've asked you to keep things to yourself, and you have. This situation with the Mc-Caws has led me to believe that someone else could be involved in relaying information to them."

She shot him a sharp glance. "Someone in Rocky Falls?"

He breathed out a sigh. "Possibly. Aiden made mention that Sage and I have something he wants. I'm thinking he wanted to trade John and Davis for that something. Neither Sage nor I understand what he's talking about. She and I never met until last week when she brought Aiden in. Nothing links us together. She did discover it was one of the McCaws who shot and killed her husband some years back, and they claimed he owed them money. But I never met the man."

"You want me to keep my eyes and ears open?"

"I do. And, Bess ... Did you trust Frank?"

She moaned her sympathy. "He was a good man who was troubled."

They crossed the street toward the doc's house.

"Parker. What about Frank isn't setting right with you?"

The thought weighed heavy on his heart and mind. "He could have been working with the McCaws, and the thought sours me. Frank was my brother, and despite the whiskey, he was a good man. I know he had his weaknesses, but it will take a sizeable amount of convincing for me to believe he'd sell out Oden Felter and this town to a gang of murderous outlaws."

"What if he got caught up in something he had no control over?"

"I hope not. I pray not. Right now I want to bring his and Oden's killers to justice. Revenge is burning hot inside me. So hot that I don't want to make any mistakes, which is why I needed to talk to you."

She patted his arm, though her brow was knit with concern. "Your words are safe with me. And I'll be looking and listening."

They walked up the porch to Doc's house. Hawk had returned and found a spot on the railing outside the window where Sage rested. Bess shuddered, so Parker stood between her and the bird as he knocked on the door. "You and I have had our share of bad times."

"God's always taken care of us, and I have no reason to doubt Him now."

Parker smiled. He and God weren't on the best of terms right now. Part of his anger was aimed at Him for taking Oden and Frank. The next time he had the McCaws in his sights, things would turn out a little differently.

Parker rubbed his eyes in an effort to rid himself of the sleep vying for his time at Sage's bedside. He'd made his rounds, sent word to Duncan at the ranch that he was still alive, and now he waited for Sage to get better. She hadn't moved or uttered a sound, and when he touched her hot skin, he wondered if she'd ever be cool again. He lit the lantern on the table beside him and studied her pale face. Doc said she was asleep, and her fever needed to break soon. Parker understood what Doc didn't say. If her fever didn't break, she'd die.

Doc had brought in a Bible, but Parker hadn't touched it. Perhaps the doctor had guessed Parker's relationship with God needed mending. He wanted to open the Book, but he didn't. He wanted to be on good terms with God, but he didn't want to let go of the hate. He wanted peace but not at the expense of giving up his stubborn pride.

What matters the most to you?

It had been a long time since he'd heard that whisper. He drew in a breath to steady himself and ponder the answer to the question swelling his mind. The first time he realized the centrality of this question was during the war—fifteen years old and wearing a gray uniform splattered with blood. But not his own. He shook too badly to move, and his heart thumped hard against his chest. Enemy fire had him and another soldier pinned down. The other man, as old as his pa, had a hunk of flesh missing from his leg. Parker lay overtop the injured man as bullets whizzed past them.

"Make a run for it, son," the man said. "Staying behind with me will only get you killed."

Parker gazed out to where their men had taken cover in a grove of oak trees. If he dashed from the brush, he might clear the fire.

"Go on, son." The man's shallow breathing broke his words. "No one would fault you for running."

Parker nearly did. The thought of dying with so much of life ahead of him struck paralyzing fear into his heart. He wondered if his legs would move. Then he heard the question.

What matters the most to you?

What good was living if he left a good man to die? The soldier had a family in Georgia and a plantation that he said was beautiful, especially in spring. He had a son not much younger than Parker. He had little daughters the same age as Parker's sister.

So Parker stayed. Eventually their fellows rallied and drove the enemy back, freeing Parker and his companion from their inadequate shelter.

Parker wished the memory hadn't surfaced to dissuade his vengeance. Every time he thought about Oden and Frank, he wanted to kill every one of the McCaws, as though a scab had been ripped off his heart. But what really mattered the most right now?

Sage.

He didn't need to think twice about it. Parker couldn't bring Oden or Frank back, but he could pray for Sage's healing with a clean heart. There lay the problem, and there lay the solution. If Parker wanted God to listen to his prayers, then he needed to tear down the wall dividing them. Forgiving the outlaws was impossible alone. Not even a consideration. Parker rubbed his face again. He had no choice.

TWENTY-FOUR

Sage wished she could wake up without any pain. In fact, she wanted to wake up with a clear mind and remember where she was and how she got there. Most of her thoughts drifted in and out, leaving her confused and disoriented. There was one exception: she'd finally found out who had murdered Charles and their baby. She should feel relief. Instead, more questions twisted at her heart and mind. How did Charles know the gang? The idea of him riding with outlaws made her physically ill. Had the McCaws found the money they were looking for that day? If not, were they still looking for it? The truth had to surface. For seven years she'd thought of nothing but finding the men who had destroyed her family. But truth had been added to the handcuffs, and she'd never rest until she learned the whole story.

And where did Parker fit?

Opening her eyes, Sage adjusted to the light streaming through a window to the left of her bed. She vaguely remembered the room from some distant corner of muted voices and incredible agony. A tray of medicine on a small table indicated this was Doc Slader's house. Ah, this was where the doc had treated Parker when Aiden's brothers broke him out of jail.

In the haze of her memories, she recalled Parker leading her down from the mountains on the back of his horse. He'd taken good care of her. She remembered the kindness in his eyes and his gentle touch. Her attention slid to the right of the bed, where Leah Timmons sat in a rocking chair with mending in her lap.

"Good afternoon." Leah tilted her head. "How are you feeling?"

How she felt was not how she needed to reply. "Better, thank you." She glanced down at her nightgown. Someone must have dressed her. She recalled wearing Parker's shirt and not knowing when that happened either. "How long have you been here?"

Leah smiled, accenting a splattering of freckles across her nose and cheeks. "I took over for Widow Bess about three hours ago."

Sage cringed. The last thing she wanted was to be bothersome. She normally shied away from other women; it always ended in disaster. "I'm sorry. How long have I been like this?"

"Better than a day."

She attempted to raise her head, but weakness overtook her. "I ... I don't remember much after getting shot. Parker and I talked some—"

Leah placed a hand on Sage's shoulder. "You just rest now. Doc Slader gave you medicine to make you sleep. He said you'd heal better that way."

Resting was for old and sick people. And she didn't own up to either one. "What about the McCaws?"

"No one's seen or heard from them. Everything around town is quiet. Oh, there is one bit of news to report." Leah stuck her needle into a sock. "A US Marshal arrived this morning. He and Parker have spent the day together."

Sage relaxed slightly. She could breathe a little easier knowing the trouble certain to come hadn't started yet. But she wanted to be with the US Marshal and Parker, not stuck in a bed under a quilt and wearing some woman's gown like a charity case. "I need to get up."

"I can get you the chamber pot."

"If only nature's call was my problem. I appreciate what you're doing, but I need to get dressed and find Parker."

Leah shook her head as though Sage had lost her mind. "Doc told me to make sure you got another dose of laudanum."

"I'm finished with that stuff. It clouds my head." When Sage saw the worried expression on Leah's face, she had to rethink her words. "Thank you for being here and nursing me, but I have things to do. I haven't forgotten what happened to Mr. Felter, your husband, and your sons."

"You sound like Parker." Leah picked up the needle and began to darn a child's sock. "I should have married him when I had the chance and not listened to Frank's smooth talk." Then she stopped, and her lips quivered. "How horrible for me to utter such a thing with Frank barely cold in his grave. He had his faults, but I loved him. Miss him terribly."

Parker had almost married Leah? A twinge of jealousy wrapped around Sage's heart, and she realized it was wrong. Yet it continued to defeat her as though a thread of hope had been snipped like a loose thread under Leah's sewing scissors.

"Parker wants us to move to his ranch, but I'm not sure what folks would say. Preacher Waller would not approve."

A lot had gone on while she'd slept. Sadness, almost grief, settled upon her, and she couldn't quite shake it off.

"Anyway, even with Parker sharing the bunkhouse with his men, it wouldn't look proper. People would talk. I think the boys and I can manage our ranch. We did all right when Frank was alive, and he wasn't home much. Parker took up the slack when John couldn't manage all of the work, and there's no reason why he wouldn't continue."

"I'm sure you'll make the right decision." Leah embodied all those things that Sage was not—a real lady and a mother.

Leah swiped at a tear. "I suppose. It's so hard to believe Frank's gone. I … I'm sorry for saying what I did about him earlier. He had his fine ways. Could always make me laugh and see the bright side of things. Even when he'd been drinking and Parker had to bring him home, he'd say something witty, and I'd forget about being angry. I keep thinking this is a nightmare and I'm going to wake up and he'll be right there beside me." She shook her head.

"Mercy, I'm talking too much. I should be thanking you for rescuing my sons and letting you rest. Forgive me for carrying on."

Maybe Leah needed to say what was on her heart and mind. Sometimes talking to a stranger was easier than talking to a friend. "I'd much rather listen to you than think about what happened in the mountains."

Leah's cheeks reddened. "I . . . I was only remembering Parker having a talk with Frank about being responsible. It seemed to help because he came home every night after that sober. He helped John and the boys with chores and brought out his fiddle. Then he got shot."

"Your husband must have been convinced that his place was with his family."

Leah pulled her needle in and out of the sock. "Parker has a way of making people feel like they can do more, be more than what they are. I suppose he learned that from all those books he reads."

What kind of books?

"He wanted to go to a fancy university and be a lawyer, but he came out here with us instead." Leah continued to darn the socks and chatter. "Now he's talking about politics." She lifted her gaze. "He'll be good."

Sage had heard enough about Parker and Leah to get herself out of bed and get on with life. She swung her leg over and nearly fell on her face. The pain in her side brought back the nightmare in the mountains, and she was weak. It took all of her might to breathe.

Leah rushed to stop her. "Please." She held onto Sage's shoulders. "You don't need to tear that wound open. None of us could bear it if something happened to you after saving my boys. Please, stay in bed."

"All right." For now anyway. "Did Doc say how long it would take?"

Leah moistened her lips.

"How long?"

Leah gently urged Sage back onto the bed and tucked her legs beneath a thin coverlet. She had a soft touch that must have come from mothering. "Four weeks if you mind him."

"What am I supposed to do for four weeks?" Sage recalled the endless hours and days it took when she'd been shot before.

"I'll visit you, and so will Widow Bess. Tomorrow's Sunday, and I'm sure Preacher Waller will want folks to pray for you."

She shouldn't have tried to get up just yet, but how would she ever lie around for four weeks? Emotions and duty had gotten tangled in her heart. She sensed the misery moving through her body at the same speed as the pain. "I can't ask you to stay here with me. I'm feeling pretty good. Really I am. I've paid for a room at the hotel. Do you know the whereabouts of my clothes?"

"Widow Bess picked them up to wash them, but I don't know where they are now." Leah proceeded to pull the coverlet up around Sage's chin. "I want you to stay here. I want to be able to sit with you in the daytime and for us to be friends."

Sage hadn't ever had a woman friend, and she wasn't sure she needed one now. Remembrances of growing up and the taunts about her Indian heritage rolled across her mind. "Leah, I appreciate what you're saying and what you've already done, but once the McCaws are arrested, I'll be gone."

"But we could write."

She sounded sincere. No wonder Parker cared for this sweet lady. If the McCaws weren't stopped, they could kill every man, woman, and child in Rocky Falls and not care a whit. Leah and her family included. "Has Parker rounded up a posse to go after the McCaws?"

"I really don't know." Leah walked to the window and stared outside. "I want them stopped. I'd blow a hole through each one of those killers and not blink an eye." She whirled around to face Sage. "Can't believe I actually said that. But I mean every word."

Sage managed a smile. "Maybe we could be bounty hunters together."

"Maybe so," Leah whispered.

"Where are your children?"

"Evan's tending to them at the parsonage. John is sleeping at the jail. He and Preacher Waller don't see eye-to-eye." Leah lifted her chin as if to say more, and Sage remembered the bits and pieces of conversation when Parker brought her into town. "Anyway, that's where we're staying until all of this is over." Leah paused as though her mind had drifted to more pleasant things than raising five children by herself. "John's my little Parker. I don't worry about a thing when he's with his brothers. My prayer is he has his father's way to make folks laugh and Parker's way of being responsible."

Sage felt the twinge of jealousy swirl through her again, and she despised herself for the sensation. "I don't think you'll have a worry with Parker looking after you."

"Oh, but he needs a wife. Don't you think? Especially if he goes on to Denver or Washington to represent us."

Of course Parker needed a wife, and it wouldn't be a woman wearing a man's clothes and doing a man's job. Or an Indian.

TWENTY-FIVE

Parker hated the hours away from Sage, but he had business to tend to with US Marshal Wirt Zimmerman. There'd been too many killings of late, and if Parker was going to have peace in Rocky Falls, the McCaws had to be caught and tried for two counts of murder. The man before him wanted to escort the outlaws to Denver where they'd be charged with even more crimes.

However, Wirt was too cocky for Parker's liking, questioning him as though Parker didn't know how to do his job. If Boulder's county sheriff didn't have his hands full, Parker would have asked him for help. In addition, he wished he hadn't told Wirt some of the details surrounding the mystery of what the gang wanted from him and Sage.

"Deputize some of the men here, and let's go after that bunch," Wirt said, straddling a chair opposite Parker's desk at the jail.

"None of them want the job." Parker swallowed his pride with the understanding that Wirt wanted the gang brought in too. "The last deputy was murdered, and no man wants to take his place."

Wirt frowned. "Don't they care about their town? Are they going to stand by and do nothing while more crimes are committed?"

"Of course they want the gang stopped. But they care more about their wives and children. We're not talking about some two-bit thieves. We're talking about a gang who's ridden together since the war. If the McCaws ride in here and start shooting up the place, then the town's men will grab their rifles. But not until then."

"That doesn't mean the McCaws can't be stopped."

Parker had begun to think the man had left his logic in Denver. "I agree, but we need trained men, not ranchers and storekeeps. A couple of the men here might go if you had professionals riding with them."

"And I believe a US Marshal and the town's marshal are enough trained professionals for any posse."

Parker wasn't in any mood to argue. After all, he and Sage had trekked out after the McCaws and barely escaped with their lives. While Leah sat with Sage, Parker put up with a US Marshal who didn't understand how an outlaw gang could break into a jail, free a prisoner, and nab two boys under the nose of the local marshal. The surly side of Parker was starting to creep in.

"Where's Sage Morrow?" Wirt said. "I want to meet her and hear her side of what happened."

"She's at the doc's. One of the McCaws shot her when she rescued my nephews." When Doc had told him that Sage might not make it, the news had scared the sin right out of him—so to speak. Odd how a woman could get to a man that quickly.

"How bad?"

"She nearly died. The bullet went straight through her side, and infection set in."

Wirt cringed. "Can she talk?"

All lawmen had to do what they could to find criminals, but Wirt could have been more considerate of Sage's condition. "Not unless she's wakened this afternoon."

"Let's head over there and see." Wirt nodded and grinned. "Heard a lot about that Indian woman. Anxious to talk to her. Is she as pretty as they say?"

Who's "they"? "I think she's comely. But there's a lot more to Sage than a pretty face. She's got a lot of guts."

"And I'd like to find out more about her. Stories say she's half woman, half witch. Heard a hawk rides with her."

Parker forced down the fury rising in him. Sage didn't need the likes of Wirt Zimmerman questioning her. She could take care of herself and put the nosey US Marshal in his place, but not while she struggled to heal. "I'll check on Sage. If she's awake, I'll ask her when you could come by."

Wirt eyed Parker. "I haven't time for special permission. Stay here if you like, but I'm going to check on the Morrow woman. I need to think through the best way to go after that gang."

Parker stood from his chair and opened the door. He needed to work with this man to bring about an end to the killings, but he wasn't the easiest fellow to like. At this moment, he'd rather send Wirt back to where he came from and figure out how to bring in the McCaws with Sage.

As much as Sage enjoyed Leah's company, the constant talk about Parker and how Leah had always relied on his help and how much he meant to her and how she loved Frank and how she once loved Parker was giving Sage a headache.

"Then there was the time that Parker took me on a picnic, and Frank found out. Just when I opened the basket of food, Frank—"

A knock at the door interrupted any more talk. Leah stood and opened the door. She was a tiny little thing with a face like a child's doll. Parker would be foolish not to want her in his life ... as badly as the thought hurt Sage. "We were just talking about you," Leah said.

At the sound of Parker's voice, Sage's heart swelled like a rock sending ripples across water. She had to fight this. What if he could read her eyes—or her heart? He stepped into the room, hat in hand, looking far too good for a man who couldn't ever belong to her. A taller man strode in behind him, but she only had eyes for one.

"Glad to see you're awake." Parker picked up a chair and set it beside her bed. "Your color's improved from ashen to white."

"I'm glad you think I've improved." She captured his gaze. How could she be disagreeable to the man who'd saved her life? "Thanks for taking care of me."

"You'd have done the same for me. John and Davis are mighty grateful. You did a brave thing."

She'd never known how to handle compliments—made her feel uncomfortable. "I'd like to get out of this bed and to the hotel. I've work to do."

He pressed his lips together and shook his head. "Doc says you'll be staying put for a few weeks. You nearly died when that bullet hole got infected."

"A few weeks?" She wanted her words to sound strong, but instead they squeaked out like a frightened kitten's meow. Then a spark of hope ignited. "Leah said four weeks. Has the doc changed his mind?"

Parker rubbed the back of his neck. "He did say four. The best thing you can do is rest so you can heal faster. Aiden is quiet right now, which gives us time to talk through what we can do next." Parker spoke softly to her like he did when they were in the mountains. But instead of comforting, his words irritated her.

"I tried to explain that she needed rest," Leah said. "But she's stubborn."

"My guess is her stubbornness is what kept her alive," Parker said. "But life's too short to take chances with it."

The longer he talked, the more Sage realized her heart would certainly show if she didn't turn away from him. "I'll talk to the doc myself. I heal fast. I understand Widow Bess has my clothes, and I'd like to have them returned."

"And I locked up your rifle and Colts. I have an idea to discuss with you later on."

"The last I heard, taking a bounty hunter's guns means a man is looking for a fight. And I thought you were trying to make friends for the upcoming election."

"Some things are more important than winning an election." The gentleness of his words confused her, especially when she shouldn't read any more into them than a town's marshal concerned for an injured woman. Although he had talked about the two of them getting to know each other better. "I expect to have my guns back in this room before dark." The pain she'd battled for the last hour grew steadily worse.

Parker gave her a slight smile. "Feisty as ever."

The other man in the room cleared his throat. Parker motioned to him. "Sage, I'd like for you to meet US Marshal Wirt Zimmerman."

She closed her eyes, torture sinking its teeth into every part of her. "I'm sorry you've come all this way to pick up Aiden McCaw." Fire hurled through her side. She clenched her fists in an effort to fight the accompanying dizziness threatening to pull her inward.

The man removed his hat. "We'll get him and his murdering brothers caught again."

Through the haze of rising agony, she studied his face, so different from Parker's — pale gray eyes and smooth skin. Some would call him handsome, but to her he seemed a bit of a dandy. "I have a vendetta against one of them."

"Why's that? You know which one shot you?"

Which time? "I didn't see who pulled the trigger." He'd killed Charles and Timothy, but that was none of Wirt's concern. "And my reasons are personal."

He peered at her as though she had two heads. "I'm looking forward to talking to you about Aiden and what he has against you and Marshal Timmons."

She and Parker both wished they had the answers to that question. "This town's seen enough trouble from that gang."

Wirt nodded. "None of it would have happened if Aiden hadn't broken out of jail."

Anger grabbed hold of her, and she couldn't let it slide. "If my memory serves me correctly, Aiden's brothers broke him out in the dead of night." She wasn't about to let her weakness stand in the way of truth. "Not much anyone can do when you're outnumbered."

Wirt chuckled. "Now that I'm here, the odds are a little better. You rest up, ma'am, and I'll check on you tomorrow."

"Looks to me like she needs to rest for a few days before you question her again." Parker stood, and the room grew eerily quiet. Sounds of the boys playing outside met her ears. Parker was challenging the US Marshal. But why? Sage fought the urge to look at Parker, to see if any animosity had passed between the two men.

Wirt opened his mouth. She could tell he had more to ask. "I'll still stop by tomorrow and see if you feel like talking about what happened in the mountains."

"Parker knows as much as I do. Even more, since I was shot."

"But I'd like to hear it from you."

The firmness of his words alerted her, as though she and Parker had been judged as incompetent. "Why?"

"It's my job to bring in outlaws and find out what they've been up to."

Sage chose not to say a word until she felt better and could size up US Marshal Wirt Zimmerman with a clear head. In the meantime, she'd guard her tongue. Or at least try.

"I'll bring supper in a few hours," Parker said. "Widow Bess asked me to stop by and pick up a couple of bowls of stew and cornbread."

"Don't forget my guns and my clothes." The pain in her side had grown worse.

"I'll see what I can do," Parker said. "Are you planning to get out of bed and go after the McCaws?"

She tossed him a glare, and he laughed.

"Are you staying here again tonight?" Leah said. "'Cause if you have things to do, I don't mind."

Surely Parker hasn't been staying here at night? He had a ranch in addition to his duties for the town of Rocky Falls.

"I'll be back. I feel better knowing she's sleeping sound."

Sage's breath caught in her chest. "You've been keeping vigil?"

"Didn't see a need for Doc to stay up all night. Someone might need him. And Mrs. Slader has her hands full with those boys."

"That doesn't make sense when you have a town to protect."

Leah wrapped her arm around Parker's waist. "Because that's what Parker does. He takes care of folks when they need help."

Twenty-Six

Parker set the bowls of stew and plate of cornbread on the table beside Sage's bed. He detected something wrong, and he wondered if her wound had grown worse. The lamp was lit and cast a soft glow on her face. How could one so strong still look so vulnerable? Mrs. Slader had helped him prop her up against the pillows so she could eat supper.

"Are you feeling all right?"

"I believe I'm on the mend."

"You seem bothered by something." Then he knew exactly what was wrong. "Wirt Zimmerman must have gotten under your skin like he got under mine."

A faint smile lifted the corners of her mouth. "I've dealt with worse characters."

"He thinks he's pretty special."

"Parker, you should be ashamed of yourself."

"For speaking the truth?"

She turned her head, but he saw the smile. "He must be good at what he does. We just have to figure out what that is."

It felt good to talk to her this way, as though serious matters weren't a part of their lives. "Can you eat a little? Bess's stew is always good."

She met his gaze, warm and tender. Ah, he'd love to get to know the many sides of Sage Morrow. When this was over, he would court her proper. "I'll try a little."

"Do you want me to feed you?"

Her gaze shadowed. "My arms are just fine, Mr. Timmons."

"Yes, ma'am." He laughed.

While he finished his meal, he took note of how much stew Sage had been able to eat. She'd lost quite of bit of weight, and she needed to build her strength. When he saw she'd finished, he took the bowl. He had a little time before returning the items to Bess.

"What were you like as a little girl?"

She closed her eyes and leaned back against the pillow. "Papa called me his wild child."

"What did you do?"

"I already told you about my pets, and there were lots of them." The lines that deepened around her eyes when she was in pain were gone. "I wanted them with me all the time. Mama and Papa didn't share in my interests."

"Did you skip school?"

Her eyes flashed open. "Who told you?"

"Hawk."

"I'll need to have a word with him." She paused. "I have good parents. Mama put up with cruel gossip, but more so from the men than the women. Seemed like the women were ready to be friends, then their husbands stopped it. That carried over to the other children. She worked very hard to fit into a white man's world. She still does.

"Charles and his family were different. He and I spent hours fishing and playing together."

Sage had lost a friend and a husband when Charles died. The thought of him being an outlaw must be harder on her than Parker thought. "Any brothers or sisters?"

"Just me."

"Thank you for telling me about the wild child," he said. "Wish I could stay and talk longer, but I've got to go."

"I'm hoping to move to the hotel."

"Who would take care of you?"

"I'll be fine. For now, I need to let my body heal naturally."

Parker took a deep breath to ask the question he'd been thinking about for the past few hours. "Would you feel more comfortable at my ranch?"

Surprise etched her features. "I don't think so."

"I could make sure one of my hands was close by. I'd be there in the evenings and early morning. You'd have peace and quiet, and my foreman's a fair cook."

"Parker, you don't need a guest with the McCaws out there. What if they found out where I was staying and killed your hands?"

He realized his desire to have her close by had taken priority over good sense. "You're right." He stood and gathered up the bowls, spoons, and cornbread tray. "Get a good night's sleep."

"I will. Next time it's your turn."

He tossed her a confused look. "My turn?"

"Yes, to tell me about your boyhood."

And he would. This was a beginning. He could be her friend just like Charles, but with a different ending.

The moment Parker left, Mrs. Slader entered the room to help her with personal needs. Sage was still weak, and it aggravated her to be so dependent when she wanted to take care of herself and her responsibilities.

She allowed herself the luxury of remembering the time spent with Parker this evening. More than she should in light of Leah's confession this afternoon. Leah needed a good man to help her with the ranch and her children. But that didn't stop the lilt of Sage's heart when she was with Parker. In a way she wondered if she was betraying Charles.

She wondered about too many things regarding Charles.

TWENTY-SEVEN

Parker had more work to do than a farmer had weeds, and at the top of his list were the McCaws and how to pacify the obnoxious Wirt Zimmerman. Though the lawman never came out and accused Parker of shirking in his capacity as a marshal, he made it abundantly clear that he didn't understand how Sage and Parker couldn't figure out their connection to the gang.

"You sleep on what Aiden wants from you and the Morrow woman," Wirt said. "Then meet me for breakfast at the hotel tomorrow morning around eight o'clock. We're going to bring an end to this gang and soon."

Parker gritted his teeth. The man standing before him had more in common with a rooster than a human being. "I usually attend church—"

Wirt snorted. "Not tomorrow. I need to get Aiden brought in, and your inability to figure out what they're after is in my way."

Parker's head roiled with all the things he'd like to say to the man—none of which were good. Now how godly was that? "If you think you can do a better job, then take my badge."

"I might before this is all over with."

"Look, we have to work together on this. We can bring in the McCaws like grown men who have a commitment to keeping the law, or we can climb down each other's throats every time we talk."

Wirt fastened his thumbs on his gun belt and leaned on one leg. "I have the jurisdiction here, and this matter will be handled my way."

Heat crept up Parker's neck. "I understand. But this is my town—my friend *and* my brother who were murdered, and my nephews who were nabbed to draw me and Sage into the mountains, and Sage who was shot. Rocky Falls is the home of my family and friends, who have the right to walk these streets in peace." He took a breath to keep the dynamite in his body from exploding. "I have more of a stake in this than any US Marshal with a fistful of credentials. This is my town to protect, Mr. Zimmerman, and I suggest you swallow that before we go a step further."

Wirt's red face could have lit the night. "I could report you."

Parker laughed. "That works both ways. Governor Eaton and I have been friends for years. And I'd like nothing better than to wire him for help to bring in the McCaws. But like you said, this is your jurisdiction. Senator Bowen was here about six weeks ago, and we discussed the same problem. So when you file your report about Marshal Parker Timmons of Rocky Falls, make sure they get a copy."

Wirt stiffened. "Eight o'clock in the morning. Be there. And for your information, the governor doesn't have a man to spare right now. I've already made the inquiry."

Parker wasn't one to call another man a liar, but he sure doubted the words flowing from Zimmerman's mouth. "I'll be there, not because you demand it, but because I want that gang brought to justice." Not to mention he didn't want to hear another one of Preacher Waller's hell-and-condemnation sermons, especially when it would probably be directed at him. He could swallow a bit of his own pride and start the day before sunrise with his own time with the Lord.

The following morning, Parker made sure he was at the hotel at seven-thirty and drinking Bess's coffee before Wirt made his grand entrance. He was determined to show a better attitude, and he'd drunk enough coffee and prayed enough to give it his best—through God's help. This wasn't the time to let a pompous

US Marshal get under his skin. He fretted over Sage and hoped he'd be able to spend a few hours at her bedside. That depended on Wirt's plans for them today.

"Do you need a friend?" Bess said as she refilled his cup.

Parker leaned back in his chair and smiled his thanks. "Oh, I need lots of things, but a friend sounds good."

"What's bothering you the most?"

He lifted a brow.

"Oh, one of those days." She eased her round shape into a chair opposite him.

"Bess, on top of everything that's been going on, I found out that a man by the name of Charles Morrow was part of a train robbery some years back."

"Does Sage know?"

He shook his head.

"I see. And you don't know how to tell her."

"And it won't happen today. I understand she doesn't need protecting, but the news would be hard while she's recovering."

"I understand." Bess picked up a knife and shined it on her apron. "Mr. Zimmerman reminds me of a puppy scrambling for attention."

He'd rather make friends with a wolf. "My observations aren't quite as complimentary."

"There's always a reason for folks to be pompous and arrogant. See, I said it for you."

This time he laughed. "I keep telling myself he has his job because he's good at it."

"And so are you."

"Thanks. I'm beginning to wonder with all that's happened. I really need a few good men of this town to volunteer as deputies. Doesn't help that Waller's accused me and Sage of … an improper relationship, when we're just two people who risked their lives to return two boys to their mama."

"State it like it is, Parker. I see immorality in this establishment from so-called proper men of the community. If anyone chooses to believe such nonsense, then they don't know you."

"Or Sage." He blew out an exasperated breath. "We were equals while searching the mountains for those boys. Not a man and a woman looking for time to be together." He took a gulp of coffee. "What's climbing my tree is how to rid this community of the McCaw gang."

"You'll figure out a way. I'm sure of it."

He frowned. "If things don't change soon, I may need to find another job."

"This town needs you, Parker Timmons, and they're all fools if they lose sight of it." Bess straightened and arched her back. "As soon as I serve up you and Mr. Zimmerman's breakfast, I'll be heading to the doc's to sit with Sage."

"I appreciate that. She woke up yesterday. Of course she wants out of bed. And she's full of vinegar because her guns and clothes are missing. Smart idea you had."

"We might have to tie her up, or have Doc give her enough medicine to put her to sleep. I do look forward to getting to know her a little better."

"She's a fine lady."

Bess eyed him closely.

"What's wrong?"

"Nothing. I just haven't ever heard you talk about a woman in that tone of voice."

Parker thought Bess had gone daft. His voice didn't sound any different than it did a month ago. He sucked in a breath and hoped he didn't give away what was brewing in his heart.

Bess patted his hand. "It's all right, Parker. I have no intention of telling anyone. You deserve a fine woman, and from what I've seen, Sage Morrow would do you proper."

How was he supposed to respond to such an observation? Did he claim it was nonsense or own up to it?

"If you're going to run for public office, you'll have to work on answering folks when they ask you about awkward personal matters. Instead of it showing in your face like a ripe tomato." Bess lifted her gaze to the stairway. "Here comes Mr. Zimmerman. Put on your best poker face. I'd slip you an ace if I thought it would help."

"Right now I'd settle for two of a kind."

"You've got a better hand than what you might think."

Once Wirt reached the bottom of the stair, Parker walked over and shook his hand. Bess left them to fetch coffee for the US Marshal and two heaping plates of eggs, bacon, fried potatoes, and biscuits. She always said a full belly was the best way for two men to discuss important matters.

Wirt sat and drummed his fingers on the table, then eyed Parker. "I've been thinking. We do need to get along, and I know I can be a horse's—well, you know what. We need to work together to stop this string of murders. I heard folks talking in the hotel and saloon last night. They're scared, and most of them are speculating on what might happen next."

The man did have a drop of decency in him after all. "Good. Let's get started."

For the next several minutes, while feasting on Bess's good cooking, Parker repeated much of what he'd previously said about the McCaws, emphasizing Aiden's insistence that Parker and Sage had something he wanted. "Sage and I had never met until she brought him in. For that matter, I never met her husband. From what Aiden has said, he believes we know what he wants." He hesitated. "I hope the rest of what I say won't offend Sage, but she didn't ask me to keep it confidential. Charles Morrow told her he owned a ranch up this way, but he didn't. Aiden also claimed Sage didn't know Charles's real name."

"It would be a sad thing for a woman to give up seven years of her life to find her husband's killer only to find out he was no better than a murdering outlaw."

Maybe Parker could learn to like Wirt. "I've thought the same."

"We could still bluff our way with the McCaws and act like we know what they want. Possibly use it for leverage."

"Offer a trade, huh? Might work."

Wirt pushed aside his plate. "The only things that appeal to men like him are money and power. You've already suggested it could be through political favors, but where does Sage fit in?" He held up his hand. "I know. We don't have any answers."

"Do we want to offer a meeting with a man we can't trust?" Parker toyed with the blade of his knife. "You know we'd be carving our own tombstones if we don't know what's driving him."

"You're right." Wirt grinned. "You might want to write down my admission. It may never happen again." He sobered. "We've got to go after them, and the odds aren't good."

Now Parker wanted that ace Bess offered. "When?"

Wirt picked up his coffee and downed its contents. "I asked for deputies last night after the men had a few drinks. Nothing there. They're like old men—rather complain than do anything about it. I'd like for Sage to go, but it might take weeks for her to recover. She certainly is an unusual woman, and her record of bringing in outlaws is better than most bounty hunters."

"She'd string us both up if we went without her. Besides, Aiden wants Sage and me together. If you and I go after them, they'll simply pick you off for target practice. It's going to take the three of us and a plan to outsmart them."

"What am I going to do for the next four weeks until she's able to ride?" Frustration topped Wirt's words like foam on beer.

Parker thought long and hard about suggesting Wirt take a job at the livery cleaning stalls. About time he nipped his sarcasm. Wasn't good for anything but putting distance between him and God. "We could work on convincing a few good men to ride with us. We could also study maps of the area and the best way to get to the gang. My guess is they're camped near the place where they held my nephews. At least for now. You and I both know a gang changes hideouts when they feel the law is getting close. Or you could ride to Denver and return in a few weeks. Maybe bring some help with you. In any event, the gang has someone watching the town. Nothing we do will be hidden."

"I'm not a patient man, and four weeks is a long time."

Nothing there Parker hadn't already figured out. "Depends on what you do with your time."

"Getting to know Sage Morrow has its advantages. She's a beauty."

That wasn't something Parker wanted to hear. He changed the subject. "I need to ride out and check on my ranch and Leah's. Her land is on the way to mine. Want to ride along?"

TWENTY-EIGHT

The sky was just beginning to lighten in the east when Aiden saddled his horse, listening to Quincy cough. No amount of whiskey cut it, and the thin mountain air didn't help a bit. Desperation had started to set in for all of them, but Aiden continued to push it aside. As soon as Rex returned from his trip to Rocky Falls, the brothers would push forward.

The one thing Aiden didn't want was to spend the winter in the Rockies. August would soon be upon them, and Parker had already proved that time meant little to him. But the cold would kill Quincy for sure. The idea of losing another brother nagged at Aiden like an old bullet wound. Just a little longer. All the McCaws needed to do was keep an eye on Parker and Sage until they made their move to leave town. Then he could take care of Quincy.

All good plans took time, and he'd spent hours laboring over the best way to draw Parker and Sage together. Money talked when it came to getting a job done, and he knew how to lace a man's or a woman's pockets. Nabbing those boys would have worked if ... A string of curses singed his mind. He hated being outsmarted, and those two would pay with more than just money.

This morning they had a little work cut out for them. "It's gonna take some time to go through both of the Timmons's ranches, but we'll start with Parker's place. If he's got something hid, it'll most likely be there," Aiden said. "Sure would be somethin' to find the money stashed at one of the ranches. Since he and Sage got together, they might have done that very thing."

"Or Parker could have the address of a bank where it's at," Mitch said.

"Let's get going." Aiden lifted the reins on his horse. "Jeb, you keep an eye out for us."

"What if we don't find what we're looking for?" Jeb said.

"That money is somewhere, and maybe we can get our hands on it. We don't stop looking until then."

"When will Rex be back?" Quincy broke into a cough and spat a mouthful of blood.

"Tomorrow. By evenin', we'll have our plans in place." What else could Aiden do? The quicker they found the money, the sooner he'd be able to get his brother to a doctor. He didn't trust the doc in Rocky Falls. And Aiden already knew it would take a fancy hospital in the city to cure his brother's cough.

"I'm tired of the waitin'." Mitch urged his horse down the ridge toward Parker's ranch. "Parker and Sage have outfoxed us for seven years. If we don't get what's due us soon, I'm going to finish what I started when we went after Charles."

Mitch and the others weren't any more frustrated than Aiden.

TWENTY-NINE

Early Sunday afternoon, Sage woke to the sound of John and Leah talking. She'd fallen asleep after the Sladers returned from church, when Bess was still sitting by her bed. Her eyes refused to open, but she could hear, and the conversation sparked her attention when she heard Preacher Waller's name.

"Wish I could write an article for the Rocky Falls News about how Preacher Waller has set himself up as God," John said.

"Merciful beans and cornbread, John." Although Leah spoke barely above a whisper, her tone indicated her displeasure. "You mustn't blaspheme."

"Mama, the truth is not blasphemy, and you know I'm right."

Leah sighed. "You're getting more like your Uncle Parker every day."

"Thanks. I miss Pa a whole lot, but I'm glad I'm like Uncle Parker."

Silence swept over the room, and Sage nearly drifted back to sleep.

"Have you talked to Mrs. Waller about the preacher's sermon?" John said.

"Of course not. I was needed here, and, besides, we'd be thrown out of the parsonage."

"Is that so bad? At least you'd be out from under Preacher Waller's thumb."

"And where would all of us go, son?"

"Back home. There's work to be done there. Lots of it. I rode out yesterday and helped Uncle Parker's men tend to the stock and mend fence. That's wrong, Mama. We should be the ones working our ranch. Besides, look what Preacher Waller said about Uncle Parker and Miss Morrow this morning. She saved our lives—Davis's and mine. How can you stay one more night under his roof?"

"You're being disrespectful to Preacher Waller and me, and I won't have it."

"Mama, I'm a man, and I'm not being disrespectful. I'm telling you the weather on any given day. And the weather at the parsonage is condemning."

Leah sniffed.

"Ah, don't cry, Mama. I'm sorry. I know all of this is hard."

"John, you're right. I need to take your brothers home. Accepting Parker's help and generosity and not saying a thing while Preacher Waller judges a godly man and a fine woman make me no better than he is. But I'm not as strong as you."

"You don't have to be." John's voice was soft and gentle, reminding Sage of Parker's tender ways. "I'm here. God's looked out for us in the past, and He will again."

"Give me a few more days to get used to the idea," Leah said.

"All right. I need to get going. I want to tidy up the jail before Uncle Parker and Mr. Zimmerman return from their ride. Tell Miss Morrow I'm hoping she feels better real soon. Her hawk is waiting on the porch for her to get on her feet again."

"I will." Leah paused and sniffed again. "Thank you for being a good son. Don't know what I'd do without you."

"I love you too, Mama. Don't worry. I'll always take care of you. I'll check on you later." The door opened and lightly closed.

So what had Preacher Waller said about Parker and her? The last thing Sage wanted was to cause strife in a family or in Parker's town. One more reason to climb out of bed and bring in the McCaws. She opened her eyes, and Leah smiled.

"How are you this fine afternoon?" Leah stood from a chair at the foot of Sage's bed and took a few steps closer.

"Feeling stronger. Doctor Slader said sleep was the best

medicine, and I'm following his advice." Sage peered into Leah's eyes and saw the cloud of sadness. "How are you and the boys?"

"John thinks we should go home." The sadness in Leah's voice said more than a widow's apprehension about the future. "I question if we're really welcome at the parsonage. It's becoming more difficult to stay there." She gathered up her knitting and sat in the rocker beside Sage. "This is not how I should honor Frank. Hiding out and expecting others to take care of us is a coward's way."

"I imagine you're cramped, and your children are used to lots of room to play." Sage hoped Leah would state what Preacher Waller had said in church earlier today. When they all returned from the service, she heard one of Doc Slader's sons ask what the preacher meant about Parker and Miss Morrow. John's comment added to her apprehension.

"I wish lack of room was all there was to it. The Wallers ... I guess, to be honest, are highly critical of others. He has his list of least favorite people, and his wife agrees with everything he says."

What had she and Parker done to upset the town's preacher? "Please tell me what Preacher Waller said about Parker and me. Leah, I can see in your eyes that his remarks were not good."

Leah paled and fidgeted with one of the knitting needles. "What makes you think something was said?"

"I heard John talking to you about it." Sage wished she felt well enough to sit up in bed without the aid of someone to help her. But the pain still reduced her to a puddle of nothing. She'd be up and moving about if it hadn't been for that infection. "I want to hear it from you."

"I'm not sure I can tell you."

"Leah, please."

"All right." Leah swallowed hard. "Preacher Waller announced to the congregation about you and Parker spending those nights in the mountains. And he had plenty to say about you wearing Parker's shirt."

Anger threatened to ooze through Sage's skin. "What about the fact Parker saved my life—and your sons'?"

Leah stood and paced the small room. "I'm ashamed to admit I didn't stand up for either of you. I cower under Preacher Waller like a whipped puppy." She stared out the window. "I owe you and Parker my life. Instead, my silence reinforces the evil accusations. It's as though Preacher Waller can't see the good in people, always looking for something that could be bad." She glanced back at Sage with tear-filled eyes. "John said his piece. Told Waller and the whole congregation the truth about how you got shot while rescuing him and Davis. But Preacher Waller twisted his words into something ugly, as though John were a boy—if you understand what I'm saying."

"I do, and I appreciate what John tried to do." Sage's temper rose. "Leah, you've sat with me faithfully, both you and Miss Bess. You've taken time from your children to tend to me." She moistened her lips. "Doesn't the preacher know where you spend those hours?"

"Yes," she said quietly.

From the tone of Leah's voice, Sage gathered the preacher had given his opinion about how she filled her hours. "My job is tracking down wanted men so folks can live without fear. You don't owe me anything."

"But I do. Without you, my sons would be dead. Besides, Parker rests easier when he knows I'm here with you."

So Leah was doing this for him? A twinge of hurt flew through her veins. She must push aside her tender feelings for him.

"Another blessing is I've found a friend. I wish I could be as brave as you are. I want to speak up to the Wallers, but I'm fearful. Afraid they'd make us leave." Leah took a few steps toward the bed. "It's like when Frank continued to drink. I could voice my anger and fears to Parker, but I couldn't bring myself to confront my husband. I was afraid, and I had no reason to be. Parker took care of it all . . ." Her voice trailed off. "I'm so very weak. To make matters worse, Parker can't bail me out of this and speak to Preacher Waller."

"Why?"

"Preacher Waller doesn't think he's fit to be the town's marshal."

And you said nothing?

Tears rolled down Leah's cheeks. "What will Parker say when he finds out I didn't defend you or him? And my children heard it all. How can I care for my brother-in-law and the woman who saved my children and watch the town treat them so shamefully? I should have the strength to try instead of being a mouse. Please forgive me."

"I understand the tragic circumstances. Soon things will be better, and you can begin to put all of this behind you." Sage wanted to spit out a mouthful of accusatory words, but what good would that do? She'd be gone soon, though Parker deserved better treatment.

"Poor Parker. I must beg his forgiveness too. Such a dear, dear man."

Sage's heart plummeted, and in her own depths of hurt she vowed Parker would never learn of her feelings. Leah did love him, and she needed him more than Sage did.

THIRTY

Parker and Zimmerman rode the thickly wooded perimeter of Frank and Leah's ranch. The land lay sprawled out over a rich valley of green, perfect for grazing cattle and horses, although many blue spruce, pine, and fir trees still needed to be thinned. The St. Vrain River flowed through this ranch and on to Parker's, making it a choice area for any rancher. The view of the mountains never ceased to steal Parker's breath.

Parker and Frank had cleared much of the land when they first arrived in the area, but over the years, Frank had ceased to keep the ranch in good condition or keep track of his cattle and horses. The livestock strayed to where they could find tender shoots of grass, making their home wherever they roamed. Rounding up calves at branding time was nearly impossible, but Frank merely raised a ruckus about someone stealing his cattle. John did his best with the aid of his younger brothers, and that was why Parker helped. He had known that someday the ranch would go to the young man who had worked the hardest at keeping it running.

"Good-looking piece of property," Wirt said, breaking the silence of their saddles creaking in rhythm to the horses' gait. He turned to look behind him. "It has the makings of a prime ranch."

"My brother's oldest son, John, has managed it for the past four years. The boy looks at work like a challenge, a reason to get out of bed before daylight. Fortunately for Leah, John has a good mind for business and loves the land." Parker wasn't ready to tell Wirt about his fears that Frank may have been involved with the McCaws.

"He isn't the first kid forced into the role of a man. Looks like he comes from sturdy stock."

"I believe you're right. My father lived and breathed the work of his hands." Parker shifted in the saddle to ease the lingering pain in his ribs.

Wirt chuckled. "Hard to believe we're starting to agree on a few things."

"I'm sure there are subjects we'll differ on." *Like Sage.*

"Any more ideas about how you and Charles Morrow are a burr under Aiden's saddle?"

The question was eating up his waking and few sleeping hours. "I'm thinking I might have arrested him for something, which makes sense if Aiden believes the man revealed information to me."

"At least it's something to go on. Did Sage describe Morrow to you?"

Just hearing him speak her name ruffled his feathers. "Brown hair. Green eyes. Average build. Nothing more."

"No help there. Do you have a record of every man you've ever arrested?"

Parker lifted a brow. "I have a file of those who've committed murder or stolen horses and cattle during the past eight years while I've been in office. I looked at that list of names and crimes last night, but nothing shook my memory. On Friday I sent a telegram to Denver with Charles Morrow's description. I'll let you know when I hear back."

"Don't miss much, do you?"

Parker bit back a laugh at the brief hint of admiration. "Try not to."

"I heard you're running for office in the next election."

Word spread fast. But Parker imagined Wirt had been asking

questions. "Those are the plans if the folks around these parts will have me."

"How does a rancher like you get interested in politics?"

Parker gazed up at a red-tailed hawk and grinned. He knew it wasn't Hawk. The bird wouldn't leave Sage as long as she remained in bed. "Don't you think I'm smart enough?"

"Not at all. Just curious."

For a few more minutes, Parker let Wirt think he was aggravated before offering an explanation. "After seeing what the war did to Virginia, I thought long and hard about being a lawyer. Didn't have any money, but lack of funds never stopped me from finding a way to do things. But Frank wanted to homestead here in Colorado and asked me to go with him. So I tagged along. Since then I've read books on law, policy making, our Constitution, and kept up with what's going on in our country and state."

"You're a strange man. Most folks care only about what affects them where they live."

"I'd like to think I was different."

"Oh, you are." Wirt chuckled.

Parker chose not to question what he meant. They'd reached the little road leading down to Leah's cabin, and Parker swung his horse south to follow it. The first hint of trouble was when he spotted the cabin door wide open. Only two possibilities sprang to mind, and neither John nor his horse was in sight, leaving only one. Parker dismounted and drew his gun.

"Wirt, steal around to the back of the cabin. I'll go in first."

Wirt nodded and quickly made his way around the small building.

Parker listened for signs of activity inside. "John, you in there?" Only silence greeted his ears. He climbed the steps and pushed the door to the wall. Chairs were turned over, and Leah's dry goods had been poured on the floor. A bear might have pushed its way inside, but an animal would have eaten the spilled food and the honey working its way through the flour. And an animal didn't wear boots or break Leah's favorite dishes with the red rosebuds. A different set of boot prints had scattered a small stack of wood.

He took long strides to Frank and Leah's bedroom. Clothes and quilts lay in a heap, and the trunk Parker had helped carry into the cabin years ago sat open—empty. With gun in hand and his finger resting near the trigger, Parker mounted the steps leading to the loft where the boys slept. Everything lay in shambles.

"Wirt, no one's here."

He heard the man's boots pound across the wooden floor. Wirt swore. "Somebody was looking for something."

Parker knew who'd destroyed Leah's and the boys' few belongings. But this ranch would have been the second stop on their search. His ranch hands wouldn't have been ready for a shoot-out. "If the McCaws have been here, they've already been to my place. Let's go."

A short while later, Parker and Wirt pulled their heaving horses to a halt in front of Parker's cabin. The front door was closed. The men dismounted and again Parker pulled his gun.

"Duncan, are you here?"

No answer, but that wasn't surprising. Fences needed mending. And yet he feared what he might find.

"What do you think?" Wirt said. "Like before?"

Parker nodded and waited until Wirt worked his way behind the cabin. He strode up his front steps and opened the door. His gaze swept around the room. The same disarray met him. Except a man lay on his back beside the fireplace. Blood poured from his chest and trailed across the floor.

"Duncan." Parker whispered and stared at the vacant eyes. Regret, fury, and grief swirled like an angry funnel cloud. Murderous animals.

A shadow blocked the light in the doorway. "A friend?"

"More like a brother."

Evening shadows traversed the sky as Sage watched Hawk through the window of her bedroom. The bird surveyed the area around him, then cast his sights through the window at her. Tall Elk told her five years ago that Hawk would be her protector, and the bird had lived up to his destiny. He watched, guarded.

Odd that she hadn't seen Parker today. Usually he brought supper from the hotel, which helped Mrs. Slader. Her nine boys ate everything but the table and chairs. Although Sage shouldn't look forward to his visits, she longed to see his face, hear his voice and the sound of his laughter. The deep voice of Doctor Slader seized her attention. He spoke the name of "Parker." She held her breath and waited until the light rap sounded on her door.

"Come in." Anticipation warmed her.

Parker stepped inside, hat in hand, his face a mask of stone.

"What's wrong?" She caught his gaze and read the misery.

He eased down onto the chair beside her bed and picked up her hand. She didn't protest, not with the agony etched across his face. "Wirt Zimmerman and I rode out to Leah's ranch. Someone had ransacked their house, left it a mess. Figuring it was Aiden and his gang, we rode on over to my place. Found the same thing, except my foreman had been shot in the chest. Then the rain set in and washed away their tracks."

The McCaws. Sage held her breath. How many more friends would Parker lose before the gang was stopped? "I'm so sorry. What about his family?"

"All in Arkansas. He … was a good man. Like a brother to me. Wirt and I took his body to the undertaker's."

"You shouldn't have come here, not with the tragic news and your duties as marshal."

He dragged his tongue across his lower lip. "This is where I wanted to be. Needed to be."

She read so much more in his words than grief for a good friend. But it was wrong. Leah and her sons needed Parker. Sage had nothing to offer but a clouded past and a heritage that would stand in the way of his aspiring future. "I have to get out of this bed and help you stop the McCaws."

"Not tonight. Not even tomorrow or the next day. The best way you can help me is to regain your strength."

His words addressed the truth, and yet she fought the urge to argue. He hurt, and she wanted to help him work through the loss. "Tell me about your foreman."

Parker lightly squeezed her hand. "Duncan worked for me about nine years. He did whatever was needed—even cooked. He listened when I needed to talk. I listened when he needed to talk. I trusted him with everything. When work at my ranch was caught up, he rode over to help John." He paused. "Before today, I made my peace with God. Gave Him my anger and bitterness about Oden and Frank. Right now I'd like to yank it all back."

Sage understood his emotions, although she had no intention of making any peace with God. "I know you'll do what is right. You're too good of a man to allow Aiden to get the best of you."

"Do you? Because right now I'd like nothing better than to kill him and his brothers with my bare hands."

"I understand. But you won't. You'll remember what is noble and follow what the law requires."

They said nothing for a few minutes, and for the first time Sage wished she could give up the blackness of her own soul.

"I need to leave," he said. "I want to talk to Preacher Waller about Duncan. Make sure he gets a good send-off into Glory."

"I'm sure you know the right words to explain how you feel."

He smiled. "Thanks for listening. I'm glad I didn't insist on you recuperating at my ranch. Because then I'd be facing two more killings. I feel better. You always make me feel better." He paused, and something in his eyes softened. "Sage, you mean a lot to me. I—"

She pulled her hand from his grasp. "Parker, don't say anything that you'll regret later."

"Are you telling me that you have no feelings for me?"

She pressed her lips together, while an inner war raged. Lying did not become her. Neither could she encourage him on a path that would lead to his destruction. He must not have heard what Preacher Waller had said about them, and she wasn't going to discuss the matter with him now. "When this is over, you'll see that you turned to me at a time when life seemed to turn against you."

Parker stood and fingered the brim of his hat. The face once bathed in despair now held only tenderness. "No, I haven't. Wait and see. You and I will be together."

THIRTY-ONE

Aiden watched Rex guide his horse up the winding mountain trail to where they'd made camp. Good thing his brothers had seen Rex get cleaned up a few days ago, or he'd been shot by now.

Aiden cursed and turned to Mitch. "We picked Parker's and his brother's ranch clean and didn't find a thing." They'd left both places in shambles—from the cooking area to the bedrooms. No hidden doors or empty areas beneath the floor. They'd even gone through the tack and feed in the barns in an effort to find the money. Parker and another man almost rode in on what they were doing at Frank's ranch. But Jeb had done a good job in warning them.

Aiden strongly considered riding into town and blowing another hole in Sage Morrow and ridding the town of one no-account marshal.

"I see that look on your face," Mitch said. "If you want to head to Rocky Falls and kill those two and anyone else who gets in our way, I'm in."

Aiden couldn't speak for anger swelling his head. He had to calm down. Riding off without a plan could get them killed. Parker could have a dozen men waiting for them.

Then there was the money. With Parker and Sage dead, the McCaws would never see it. The past two years would be wasted. Karl's death for *nothin'*. Quincy's sufferin' for *nothin'*. Aiden didn't have a choice, and he hated giving any man, much less a woman, that much power.

"Once Rex rides in, I want to see him right away," Aiden called to Jeb.

His brother waved in response. Some days Jeb acted simple, and other days he was real smart. This wasn't one of the smart days. All he'd done was complain about everything from the rain to the lack of flour and sugar.

Aiden paced the camp for the next hour until Rex rode in. Water from the afternoon downpour dripped off his brother's hat and slicker. He did look real good—almost respectable.

"Good to see you survived proper folk. Any luck in Rocky Falls?"

Rex flashed his teeth—he was the only one of the brothers who had a decent mouthful, and he wasn't one to let the others forget. "Best news came right from the preacher."

Church folk always claimed to be doing good when they were really making life miserable for others. "Come on over here and get yourself a hot mug of coffee. What happened?"

Rex traipsed through the mud and found an empty mug by the fire. He eased down on a log beside Aiden. "I stayed at the hotel. Liked to have killed me to leave good whiskey and women alone, but I did. Bought a few provisions at the general store. Talked to folks like you said. And then I went to church on Sunday morning. Got an earful."

Aiden licked his lips and watched Rex take a big gulp of coffee. "So what did you hear that we can use?"

Rex grinned. "Looks like the preacher and Parker aren't seeing eye-to-eye on a few things. The deputy's widow and kids are staying with the preacher, except the older boy. He's sleeping at the jail with Parker. The preacher said from the pulpit that Parker was unfit to be marshal because when he and Sage rode in, she was wearin' his shirt and they spent nights together in the mountains." Rex started laughing. "Aiden, do you know how stupid that is? Sage was all shot up, and the preacher's complaining about her clothes."

Aiden had to think about this for a while. If Parker wasn't wearing a badge, then he and Sage would have more use for the money. The latest twist of events might not have played Aiden a bad hand after all. "Is the preacher askin' folks to get rid of him?"

"He said only a fool would want Parker as marshal. He asked them if God would vote for a man who spent all those nights in the mountains alone with a woman that wasn't his wife."

Great luck. Yeah, this was going to work out just fine. "So Sage is recovering?"

"I heard an old woman at the hotel say she'd been sitting with Sage at the doc's house, and I watched the marshal head there a few times. Oh, and a US Marshal is in town. A yellow-headed feller who asks a lot of questions. His name's Wirt Zimmerman."

"Never heard of him. Good job, Rex. We're that much closer to gettin' our money and making them two pay for all the trouble they've caused us. I'd hoped to find it at one of the Timmons's ranches. In fact" — Aiden slapped his knee — "I think I'll send you back there in a few days to stir up some more trouble. Don't you imagine Parker and Sage are gettin' real personal at the doc's place? Makes me wonder about a marshal who spends more time with a woman than tending to his job."

"Bet so." Rex waved at Mitch and Quincy. "I'd be glad to ride back to town. Maybe I'll be Rocky Falls' next marshal. I'll see if your money has bought any more information. I saw her working the saloon, but I stayed clear."

"I bet them other girls at the saloon know that US Marshal real well too." Aiden let his mind twist and turn with the possibilities.

"I can give the preacher plenty to talk about."

"And rile folks up about the marshal spending more time courtin' than bringing those McCaws to justice for the killings they done."

"I'll spend more time at church. They have church on Sunday morning, Sunday night, and a Wednesday night prayer meetin'.

All that God and singin' and prayin' would drive me to drink."
He laughed.

Aiden took a deep breath, and satisfaction rose from his boots
to his hat. Time to bring out the bottle of whiskey he'd been hiding from his brothers.

THIRTY-TWO

With all of Sage's grand intentions to recover faster than Doc Slader predicted, she still slept much of Tuesday and Wednesday, even when she refused the wine-tasting laudanum. In her waking moments, she wondered if her past gun wounds had slowed her healing or if she'd truly been injured that badly. Doc claimed she'd overdone it with well-meaning visitors, and she was inclined to agree. She longed to be whole again—to be outside and feel the warm July sun on her face. Eight years ago, when the McCaws had finished with her, it took weeks to recover. But now she didn't have time for such nonsense. She had business with Aiden and Mitch McCaw.

Leah came by every morning and Bess in the afternoon. Parker stole moments to see her, but she wished he wouldn't. With Duncan's funeral behind him, he appeared more determined to coax the McCaws out into the open where he could deal with them. Yet he talked logically, not with the intensity of a man half-crazed by too many senseless deaths. Every time she saw him made it more difficult to tell him good-bye and ignore the tender feelings building in her heart. As much as she wanted to forget his words of endearment, they entered her mind unbidden and spun magic that she couldn't will away.

Sage closed her eyes and allowed sleep to close her thoughts and heal her body. What knowledge did Charles carry to his death? The money the McCaws killed him for? Had they been unable to locate it and were still looking? Seven years seemed like a long time for them to carry a vendetta. It had to be a tidy sum. But then again, why hadn't they come after her when she first recovered? The questions, the endless ponderings—speculations that battled her wits while the McCaws left a trail of blood in their wake.

Tuesday afternoon, Parker detected Wirt had something worrying him. Granted, all their talking hadn't gotten them a single deputy, but that didn't mean either man had given up on forming a posse to go after Aiden and his bloodthirsty brothers. Parker and Wirt sat at the hotel dining room with a map of the area spread over the table—from Rocky Falls to Estes Park and on to where the gang had taken John and Davis.

"What's on your mind?" Parker said.

"Rumors thick as mud."

"You might as well tell me."

"Why don't you tell me why you aren't on Preacher Waller's list of upstanding citizens."

Parker nearly groaned. "What's he done now?"

"This morning I overheard a couple of women at the general store talking about church. The good preacher doesn't believe you're fit to be the town's marshal."

And Parker knew why. "Let me guess. When Sage and I rode in, she was wearing my shirt. No matter that she was near dead. Waller took offense to the shirt and the nights in the mountains alone."

"That goes along with the local talk. Next time ask Aiden to chaperone. Maybe you'll stay out of trouble. Is it just me, or is the preacher a little quick to condemn?"

"The latter. But I'm not his favorite citizen right now. Did you hear anything else? Hate to be relieved of my job before rounding up the McCaws. However, I'll bring them in with or without a badge."

"If that happens, I'm deputizing you as a US Marshal. Maybe

next Sunday you ought to slip under a window outside the church and find out what's being said about you."

"Wednesday night is prayer meeting. If I went, at least I could defend myself." Parker shrugged. "My temper and Preacher Waller's self-righteousness are a grand mix. I think God's been preparing me for politics for a long time—probably as long as I've known Waller."

"Better you than me. Two things I stay away from—church and politicians."

Parker digested Wirt's words and considered what, if anything, he should do to stop the gossip. So Waller had preached one of his fire-and-brimstone sermons on Sunday. And he urged the citizens of Rocky Falls to consider another marshal—possibly Waller himself. Wouldn't be the first time the preacher had ruined a fine person's reputation.

Faye, one of Bess's girls who worked the saloon by night and helped in the kitchen during the afternoons, refilled their coffee mugs. He smiled his thanks.

He remembered when Widow Bess owned the general store. At the time, she was inviting the local soiled doves to her home in an effort to dissuade them from their current means of earning a living. Waller took offense. Called her an unfit member of the church and told her she wasn't welcome in his congregation. Then he urged the town folk to take their business elsewhere. He even drove a wagon to the next county for supplies. Bess was forced to sell out and get a job at the hotel. At least now she was closer to the women she wanted to help. With the way they listened and believed Waller unquestioningly, a good portion of the people of Rocky Falls reminded Parker of dumb sheep.

Parker may be the next to lose his standing in the community, but he'd been preparing for that fight for a long time. He'd rather be on God's side than on the side of a preacher who had no idea what it meant to be a shepherd. Of course, he still warred against the revenge in his spirit. He thought he'd moved past it until Duncan was murdered. Now he wrestled with sheer hate for the gang and all they'd done. Every day found the matter at the forefront of his thoughts as he asked the Lord to help him make good decisions. The struggle to find a way to bring in the McCaws had started to weaken him. How much longer could he take the manure slung at him from every direction?

That's when he decided to attend Wednesday night's prayer meeting.

Parker waited until the piano music ended and Waller bowed his head to pray before he slipped into a pew at the back of the church. Some of the townsfolk had ignored his greetings this week, but it wasn't until yesterday that he discovered why. Now Parker wanted to know exactly what was being said about him. He understood the gist, but to fight this with Waller, he needed to hear the accusations for himself. Waller was a coward. He rarely confronted folks, only directed his vile tongue at them behind their backs.

If Waller weren't such a hypocrite, Parker would question whether he'd thrown in his lot with the McCaws. But the gang would never put up with him. The prayer ended—Parker had his own—and Waller faced the congregation. Fortunately for Parker, evening shadows spread over the church. Candles were lit near the front, which would help conceal him in the back.

"Evenin', folks. I pray the Lord's been talking to you this week about the sins of our town's marshal."

He's not wasting any time. I might get burned at the stake by the end of the meeting.

"For eight years, Parker Timmons has held the office of marshal in our little town, and for eight years, I've prayed for his soul. It grieves me to report that my prayers and yours have gone in vain. God revealed to me this week that Parker Timmons cannot be redeemed. It's also been revealed to me the McCaw gang's activities of late—including another murder—is God's retribution on us for not doing a thing about getting rid of Parker Timmons."

Parker had to root his boots to the wooden floor to keep from standing and demanding to be heard. What was wrong with these people to believe such lies?

"God told you all that?" Bob Culpepper boomed out his question. As far as Parker could tell, Bob was unaware of Parker's position behind him. Good to know he had a friend.

"Careful, Brother Culpepper," Waller said. "This is God's house, and He don't take kindly to others disputing His words."

"My question isn't about God, but what you claim He said about Parker Timmons. Our marshal is a God-fearin' man if I ever saw one."

"Then you should have seen the rebellion in his eyes when I asked him what went on in the mountains with Sage Morrow."

"Looks to me like the woman was more dead than alive."

"God's hand, Brother Culpepper. His judgments are right and not to be questioned."

"So you're condemning and executing him without letting the man speak for himself? Even the Pharisees required a few witnesses."

Several others in the congregation ordered Bob to keep quiet. But Waller would think twice about kicking the town's undertaker out of the church. Especially when he was a deacon and owned the parsonage.

"Let's have order in God's house." Waller raised his hands as though about to pray. "We need to vote about getting rid of Marshal Timmons so our town can once more be at peace. We don't need any more folks murdered or children snatched from their mother's arms."

Parker clenched his fists and waited for the proper time to state a few biblical truths.

"Preacher Waller?" an unfamiliar voice said.

"Yes, sir," Waller called out.

"I'm new to this town, and before I bring my wife and daughters to Rocky Falls, I want to know a God-fearin' man is keeping the law."

"I understand, sir. We all feel the same way. That's why we're taking up some of God's time to discuss what He'd have us do."

"Thank you," the stranger said. "I have my eye on a homestead southeast of here, but not one penny will be spent until I can shake hands with a respectable marshal. My wife and daughters deserve to live without the threat of murderin' outlaws. And I don't take kindly to arming them like soldiers instead of delicate women."

"Who would be our marshal if Parker Timmons were gone?" a woman said. "We don't even have a deputy."

"I've been thinking on that very thing." Waller's voice echoed just like he was ready to bring down fire from heaven. In his case, it would be fire from down below. "I filled in for Marshal Timmons when he was in the mountains. I can do so again until you folks vote in a new man."

"I've worked with lawmen in the past," the stranger said. "I know how the job's done."

"Well, that's mighty fine, sir," Waller said. "I'd like to hear about your qualifications after prayer meetin'. We do believe in electing qualified men."

Murmurs rose through the crowd. Some were for pinning a star on Waller—right beside his cross—and others were against getting rid of Parker.

"I suggest we not quarrel with our fellow Christians," Waller said. "I wanted to vote tonight and be done with this distasteful matter. But we can wait until Sunday evenin'. And let me remind you the outcome is in God's hands. Be prayed up and in your Bibles. If any of you need Scripture to read, I can help you." He cleared his throat. "It's time to hear from our Lord and what He's put on my heart. Our message tonight is from Ephesians, where Paul warns the church not to be led away by wolves. We have much to learn from this letter in light of the current tragedy in our community."

Now I'm a wolf and about to be booted out of being marshal. Parker needed a few more folks on his side fast—and a deputy. *Lord, what kind of a mess have I gotten myself into?* He stood.

"Preacher Waller and all of you fine citizens of Rocky Falls. Tonight I've heard the accusations against me and Miss Morrow. And since we're in God's house, I'd like for you to hear the truth from me."

"Would you even know it?" Waller said.

Parker smiled and ignored the burning in his stomach. "I've never lied to any of you folks, and I have no intention to start now." He made his way out of the pew and down to the front beside Preacher Waller.

"Parker Timmons, I was ready to preach."

"Good. I won't take up much of your time since we're going to talk about Paul's warning against wolves in sheep's clothing. I see neither one of us is wearing a coat, so these fine people can listen with open minds and hearts."

"I for—"

"It's true Sage Morrow and I traveled together to find John and Davis Timmons. On the Sunday the gang broke Aiden out of jail and took those boys, I asked some of you men to take that trek with me, but you refused, stating your fear of the McCaw gang. The idea of going after my nephews alone against five outlaws didn't sound like good odds, and I welcomed Miss Morrow's assistance. She nearly died from a gunshot wound when she helped those boys escape, and I believe John attempted to tell you that. So the preacher is right. Miss Morrow and I did spend some nights in the mountains alone. If any of you fine men had gone with us, then she could have worn your shirt when hers was blood soaked." Parker scanned the haze of faces. Enough said. He walked back to the pew behind Bob, snatched up his hat, and walked out the back of the church.

THIRTY-THREE

Parker has been hurt enough by this town," Leah said. "Preacher Waller has turned many of the townsfolk against him with his lies."

But aren't you living at the parsonage? Sage wanted to make a few remarks of her own, but what would being disagreeable solve? She'd already heard from Leah about Parker's speech in church.

"Why, he gives and gives, and most of the people of this town don't appreciate it. They're like vultures. Those of us who love him don't know what to do."

Sage had three things on her mind: healing from her wound, tracking down the McCaws, and distancing herself from Parker Timmons. Closing her heart to the town's marshal was the hardest, but she'd find the strength. Leah loved him, by her own admission, and she'd be a good wife, too — much better than Sage. A politician's wife needed to be a genteel lady who kept a spotless home, cooked fine meals, and didn't keep wild animals as pets.

Leah wasn't scarred with bullet holes either.

Hours later, Sage woke to Leah and Wirt Zimmerman's whispering at the foot of her bed. Wirt held a handful of blue and yellow wildflowers. Goodness, she hoped they weren't for her.

"Are you talking about me?" Sage said through half-opened eyes.

"Only that you're beautiful." Wirt stood and held out the bouquet. "Prettier than these flowers."

In an instant, Sage sized up the US Marshal. He could sweet

talk the girls at the saloon or Leah or Mrs. Slader or Miss Bess —
on the other hand, Miss Bess could probably see through his
syrupy words. Sage certainly had no use for them. If she couldn't
have Parker, then she didn't want anyone else. "Thank you. But
I'd rather you were convincing Doc to let me move into the hotel."

"Parker discussed the matter with Doc this morning," Leah
said. "And he said he'd talk about releasing you in a week's time
to my and Bess's care. I was going to tell you as soon as you woke
up."

Finally a glimpse of climbing out of the four-poster prison. "I
could move today."

"Soon, Sage." Leah walked around the bed toward her, wearing a smile that rivaled Wirt's flowers. She clasped Sage's hand.
"I know how badly you want to be well and out of here. So does
Bess. One more week is not that long, considering what you've
been through. But still you'll be confined to bed most of the
time."

Leah was right, but it didn't make the waiting easier. At least
at the hotel she could get up and use the chamber pot by herself.
"What I've been through is why I want to get back to work."

"We need you well to get the McCaws," Wirt said. "You're the
best bounty hunter I've seen in a long time. Beautiful too."

Sage had never fallen for flattery, and this man was quickly
irritating her. "What about Belle Starr or Casey O'Hare?"

"I'm sure you'd find a way to befriend them."

Sage groaned. "I feel like someone has chained me to this
bed. And where's Hawk?"

"You mean that bird observing everyone from the roof?" Wirt
stepped closer and laid the flowers on her bed. With his clean
shirt and shiny pistols, he looked more like a dandy than a US
Marshal. "I'm sure he'll take his stance on the front porch rail
soon."

As if Hawk had heard every word, he flew within sight of her
window. The red-tailed hawk was better than any medicine. He'd

been gone the last time she was awake. She'd longed to have him inside with her, but Mrs. Slader wouldn't hear of it. "You have to know him to appreciate him."

"Some folks say that about me." Wirt smiled broadly.

Most likely those comments came from women, but she wasn't in a witty mood to pose that question. The man was so full of himself that the outhouse wouldn't hold all of his boasting.

"Rumors are you have a way with birds and animals," he continued.

Some days she got tired of explaining this part of her. "I believe in taking the time to understand and communicate with them." Sage moistened her lips.

"Oh, my." He patted his heart. "I think you're talking about me."

Sage blinked and bit back the laughter threatening to fill the room.

"Does a way with animals help you track down outlaws?" Wirt's words had grown soft.

"No. That's attributed to stubborn tenacity."

He chuckled. "As soon as you're strong enough to discuss the McCaws, you, Parker, and I will talk about a plan to ride out after them. Parker said you recognized Mitch McCaw as the man who gunned down your husband."

She nodded and wondered if Parker had mentioned Charles's connection to the outlaws. "I have more than one reason to bring them in."

"Anything else you've remembered?"

"Nothing at this time. I'll let you know if something comes to me."

"Good. You look sleepy, so I'll leave you in the capable hands of Mrs. Timmons. However, spending time with a beautiful and spunky woman is my favorite pastime." He glanced back at Leah. "Both of you have my heart pounding."

Does he ever stop? "Thank you for the visit," Sage said. "And the flowers are very nice." What she really meant was he could take his charms to someone who might appreciate them. Once he left, Sage threw a curious look at Leah. The woman's face was rock-hard emotionless.

"Are you thinking what I am?" Sage bit into her lip to keep from laughing.

Leah covered her mouth, but Sage saw the mirth. "He does stretch his compliments."

"Any available ladies we can introduce him to?"

"I'm not sure I'd do that to my worst enemy. But I'll be thinking about it."

They both laughed, and it eased Sage's heart.

"How long were you blessed with his company before I woke?"

"Long enough to yawn and want to tickle your feet." Leah wiggled her shoulders and lifted her chin. "However, I was the one receiving all of his attention until you opened your eyes."

Sage did value all Leah Timmons had done for her since the shooting, and that made walking away from Parker a little easier to bear.

Parker couldn't leave Rocky Falls again and put Preacher Waller in charge, especially after what he'd learned at Wednesday night's prayer meeting. Deputizing Waller would be disastrous for all the folks he cared about, even if they wanted another marshal. Some folks were not speaking to him, and others were asking him questions about his faith.

Parker's first choice for deputy was Bob Culpepper, the undertaker and a good man who didn't mind standing up for what he believed. The irony amused Parker too. Might make the ornery folks think twice about breaking laws. Culpepper used his head before his emotions, and he was loyal to Parker, as Wednesday night proved.

"Bob, you back there?" Parker called, stepping into the undertaker's office. He disliked walking into Culpepper's back room, especially when a body was laid out for preparation for burial.

"Sure, come on back, Parker."

Culpepper must be busy. What bad timing, but he couldn't think of who'd passed away for there to be a body. Parker made his way to where the sights and sounds gave most folks nightmares. Parker didn't care for how Culpepper made his living, but he wasn't superstitious. "I need a good deputy."

The bearded man glanced up from sanding a pine box. "Preacher Waller's claims eatin' at you?"

"You might say that."

Culpepper continued sanding. "In my opinion, he's trying to shove God out of His job."

"Or be His right-hand man."

"It'll backfire on him in the worst way."

Parker didn't want to be around when that happened. He had enough of his own consequences to handle. "Let's hope he comes to his senses before then."

"I can remember when he was the town's worst troublemaker."

Parker grinned, and it felt good. "Not much has changed."

"Are you heading back into the mountains after the McCaws?"

"As soon as Sage feels like riding."

Culpepper went back to sanding. "The town's divided. Hard to tell which ones are on your side. Crows always make the loudest noise."

Parker didn't want to dwell on the fact a good many of his friends had turned against him. "I figured as much."

"Waller's pushing for the townsfolk to vote you out. He gathered a few men together at the feed store this morning and started in. Along with his usual complaints about the McCaws, he added the problem with the German and Dutch miners feuding and killing each other."

"He hadn't jumped on me about the miners. I'm sure he will."

"Give him time. He probably has a list tucked into his Bible.

The McCaws have folks afraid, and he's making it sound like getting rid of you will cause them to leave the territory."

Parker should have stayed until church was over. Then he could have squared off with some of those opposing him. Instead he walked over to the hotel and broke up a few fights in the saloon—some over women or cards and others over men who allowed the whiskey to do their talking. There Parker considered leaving the town for a deputy to manage while he looked for Aiden and his gang. In fact, last night wore him out so much that he thought of leaving town period. Let the locals handle their own problems since they had plenty to say about how he handled them. The trouble was he didn't need one good man with a gun; he needed a handful. Other than Bob Culpepper, who else could he approach? Parker had exhausted the list before Frank came on as deputy, and he sure wasn't going to hand the responsibility over to John. Maybe he should send Wirt and Sage after the McCaws and stay behind. But, no, that made even less sense.

"The preacher's saying he'd do a better job as marshal," Culpepper said.

"What're your thoughts?"

Culpepper studied him—maybe wondering what it would be like to fit Parker in a pine box. "He'd want to pass a law for the folks to be in church or get thrown in jail. I'll be your deputy, permanent-like. Been talking to the missus about it, and she finally agreed. She thinks I could be of help in getting folks to understand that keeping the law is everyone's job. Besides, the wife and I refuse to trust a man who hands out impossible rules according to his interpretation of the Bible, then judges folks who can't abide by them. I'd like to see a new preacher in town."

Culpepper had put into words what Parker had been pondering. "Thanks, Bob. I appreciate your friendship. Any idea who else we could get to help put this town back to a law-abiding place for folks to live?"

Culpepper rubbed a whiskered jaw and chuckled long and

deep. "Widow Bess would do a good job. And I understand she's a good shot, but I don't think she'd take the job as deputy. Tell you what, I'll look around."

"I hear a stranger in town has asked about my job, but he's not wearing a badge until I find out more about him."

"I don't like the looks of him. Something about him isn't right."

That confirmed Parker's opinion. "My nephew John has been begging me for the job, but it'll be a cold day in—"

"Oh, I understand. I got a sixteen-year-old who thinks he's smarter than his pa." Bob laid down the sandpaper. "Were we that ornery back then?"

Parker remembered a bunch of his own shenanigans. "I was—probably worse."

The two men shook hands. "One thing, Parker. The McCaws are digging themselves in deep. You best be careful. You out-smarted them one time. They won't let it happen again. Mark my word, they're up to no good right now, and all we can do is sit and wait."

"I'm wondering how long I can stay here before heading up after them."

Bob stretched his back. "You and the US Marshal?"

Parker nodded. "The problem is, as much as Wirt Zimmerman and I need another gun, Sage is still recovering at Doc's. It'll be a few weeks before she's able to ride."

"What about wiring for more help?"

How many times had Parker and Wirt asked for more men? "I've been told there's a shortage of US Marshals, and we're to raise our own posse."

Culpepper went back to sanding. After several seconds, he lifted his head. "I've met Wirt Zimmerman. Do you think he sees this as an opportunity to make himself look good?"

Parker didn't respond. Wirt had a strange personality. At times he was likeable, and other times he had all the answers.

A man who promised to uphold the law needed to be prepared mentally and physically. If Wirt lacked in either area, someone could get killed.

"Since you're not saying," Bob said, "then I guess you've asked yourself the same question."

"My thoughts are he didn't get to be a US Marshal unless he was quick with a gun and proved himself. He's all right, and we've learned to get along."

"As I said before, be careful. I'd hate to think the man was working for the McCaws."

Parker eyed his friend. "I agree someone is feeding the McCaws information, but it's not Wirt."

"Any idea who?"

"I have my sights on a couple of people. Bess is my ears and eyes. The saloon collects the worst of characters—men and women."

THIRTY-FOUR

Sage picked her way through a plate of savory beef stew Mrs. Slader had brought in for her and Parker. Hard to have an appetite for the food she'd smelled all afternoon when she felt like she was drowning in a river of emotions, and the source of those feelings sat within arm's reach.

She couldn't get out of bed and leave, so that meant she had to discourage Parker from returning to visit her. Right now all she could do was tread water and hope she didn't get caught up in the whirlpool of his eyes or the gentleness of his voice. She had no right longing for the company of a man who rightfully belonged to another woman.

Some evenings Wirt accompanied Parker, and the three discussed the situation with the McCaws. Mostly Wirt talked and asked questions, usually ones he'd brought up before. Parker had a tendency to protect her from his hammering, but Sage could take care of herself without the marshal playing nursemaid. On a few occasions, Wirt came by himself and showered her with lavish compliments that nearly made her gag.

Some things she learned settled like a rock in the pit of her stomach—more like a boulder. Wirt insisted upon bringing up the fact Charles had lied to her about the ranch up north, and that meant he most likely lied about other things, too. Did he think she was stupid not to realize Charles's duplicity?

"The way I look at it," Wirt said earlier today, "your husband was an outlaw too. One who double-crossed Aiden, and that got him killed. But what does he want from you and Parker?"

She refused to discuss the money Aiden claimed Charles had stolen or speculate on what Aiden wanted from her and Parker. In fact, she was tired of thinking and talking about it. The time had come for answers. The only thing that mattered to blood-thirsty men like Aiden was money and power. She had neither, and Parker not much more.

A thought sickened her. Could Parker be holding out on her? Did he know what was behind all of this? After all, she'd trusted Charles, and look what happened there.

For sure Sage had to get out of bed soon. Her temperament was causing those around her to suffer.

"You aren't eating much," Parker said, pulling her from her musings to the present. "Are you feeling poorly?"

"No. I have a lot on my mind." At least she told the truth. Conversation had been easier in the mountains. *Do it. Tell him.* She moistened her lips. "Have you put together any more of the puzzle about Aiden?"

"I've been thinking about it night and day. The fact is we don't know what we have that they want. Have you brought in any of Aiden's other brothers?"

She remembered her first glimpse of them through her binoculars. "I'd never had any dealings with them until I received the wire about Aiden being wanted for murder."

"One of the brothers, Karl, was shot and killed over seven years ago. I rode with the US Marshal who was trailing them at the time. But unless you knew Adam Moore, then we're on a dead-end trail again."

She shook her head. "I heard the name once, but I never met him. He was killed before I became a bounty hunter. Could Aiden blame you for his brother's death?"

"He knows I wasn't the one to pull the trigger. Moore did that."

"I've gone over every man I've ever brought in—the ones in prison and the ones who were hanged. I've questioned if their families and the McCaws rode together—and I've wondered if they were Indian haters. My next thought is to wire the prisons to see if any of the men I brought in have been released or escaped." She pointed to a folded piece of paper on the dresser. "There's the list."

"I'll send those telegrams in the morning."

Tell him now. "I don't think you should come by here alone anymore."

He startled. "Why?"

She forced herself to lock into his gaze. No turning back now. "Preacher Waller is trying to take your job because of me. The townsfolk you've sworn to protect believe you no longer care about their safety. Your friends and supporters have become your enemies. And your spending evenings with me is destroying your reputation."

He set his partially eaten food on the small dresser behind him. "I don't care one whit about what Waller or anyone else says."

"I do, and you should too."

"Then marry me if it means so much."

His response shook her to the core. "Have you been drinking?"

His eyes narrowed. "Sage, you know I care about you. I want you in my life permanently. I think you care about me too."

Caring was not love. Friendship sealed the rough edges of marriage. But love was the main ingredient. Parker had to be tired from all his burdens, and he simply needed a way to appease Waller and the townsfolk in order to concentrate on important matters. A marriage to him would be one of convenience. "I have no desire to marry you. All of your goals for the future would be destroyed. Please, I don't want you visiting me here alone anymore."

"Why do I think there's more to this than what you're saying? The Sage Morrow I know doesn't care about what other folks think or say. And you can deny feelings for me until the moon is snatched from the sky, but I see love in your eyes."

Love? She was utterly confused. Yet she refused to give in to his proposal. Even if he did feel love for her, she could never be what he needed in his pursuit of political office. "That's ridiculous. Once I'm on my feet, we'll bring in the McCaws. Then I'm gone. You have your town ... your political aspirations ... your God." *Leah.* Later she'd cry, when night hid her tears.

"And what will you have?" He spoke each word as though he'd punched them with his fist. "A hawk and a vendetta? That's a great life, Sage Morrow. I thought you were finished with being a bounty hunter once the McCaw gang was behind bars."

"What I do is none of your business."

"Is that the way you really want it?"

She refused to cry. "Yes. I don't want to see you unless you're with Wirt."

Parker stiffened. "You prefer his company?"

She hadn't considered the possibility of Wirt as a suitor. Neither would she. "I believe your job as marshal and your future is more important than looking after me. Besides, I *am* at a doctor's house."

He blinked and glanced down at his hands before searching her face. She expected the lines forking out from his eyes to deepen. Instead they grew softer, causing her heart to quicken. "What else is wrong?"

"Nothing. Yes, there is. I want out of this bed. Bess hasn't returned my clothes, and I want my guns where I can reach them."

Parker turned and picked up his plate and cup. From the frown on his face, she thought he was about to repeat another sheep story. A candle-like light shone in his eyes, and she regretted what could never be. "I'll have someone bring your guns to you. Your clothes are up to Bess. Doc Slader is handling your healing. But let me remind you something happened between us in the mountains. You know it, and I can't forget it."

Ignore him. Don't listen to a single word. "We were two people facing death with no one else around." She crossed her arms over her chest. "I had a husband, remember? He's dead, and I don't need another one." She forced herself to stare into his face. "I believe I can choose my own company—be it Wirt Zimmerman or anyone else."

Parker gave her a brief nod. "I'll be leaving, and I'll honor your wishes and not come back alone. Even then it'll be business only. I don't understand how what I see in your eyes is so different from what you're saying. I admit I didn't ask you to marry me the proper way. But my foolhardy attempt doesn't wipe away my intentions. I'll be praying you'll change your mind."

"It's better this way."

"Sage, when are you going to let a man love you?"

After thanking Mrs. Slader for the beef stew and cornbread, Parker bid the large family good-night. The boys were seated around a long table just like he wanted his own children seated one day. He stepped off the porch onto the dirt street with regret nipping at his heels. What had changed with Sage?

He patted his shirt pocket containing her list of those she'd helped send to prison. Tonight he'd send a wire to Governor Ben Eaton to see if the outlaws were still behind bars. A good many of them were being held at the Colorado State Penitentiary, and Ben could get the information sooner than Parker. Someday when he held office, he, too, would remember those people who had tough and thankless jobs.

Parker also wanted Wirt to take a look at Sage's list. *Wirt Zimmerman.* Parker had a hard time believing Sage preferred the US Marshal over him, but maybe she did. He shook his head. Confusion had slammed into his heart and mind, and he had no answers. Women were the most difficult creatures on the face of the earth. Besides, he had a job to do. If Sage wanted Wirt, then she could have him.

Now he was lying to himself. He'd find a way to win the woman he loved. A woman unlike any he'd ever met. A woman who stood on equal ground, who didn't need a man to take care of her. A woman who was true beauty from the depth of her eyes to the wisdom of her soul. Sage Morrow was a woman who'd walk life's journey with her man.

He rubbed the dull ache at the back of his neck. Before he could win Sage, and before he could expect her to admit her feelings, the McCaws had to be stopped. This waiting for the gang to make the next move made Parker feel like a coward. What did the gang want?

He had no answers about anything, and the troubles kept piling up.

"Hey, Parker."

Parker recognized Wirt's voice. "Evenin'."

"I expected you to be with Sage. Thought I'd join you there." He held up a map. "I've studied the area again, and I have some questions."

Right now Parker wanted to be alone, but sulking solved nothing. "As soon as I take a look at some information she gave me, you and I could go over those questions."

Wirt glanced down the street toward the Sladers' house. "Can you give me an hour? Think I'd like to talk to Sage for a while."

The idea of Sage welcoming Wirt's company but not his made Parker madder than a swarm of angry bees. "I'll be at the hotel. I asked Bess to find out all she could about the stranger in town — the one looking to take my job."

Wirt tipped his hat, and Parker noticed he wore a clean shirt. Courting clothes? "I shouldn't be too long. Then again, I lose track of time in the presence of a pretty woman."

Not if I can help it. "I ought to tell you that Sage isn't feeling very good. Might be better if you wait until tomorrow. I'm afraid we've forced her to talk too much."

"Sorry to hear she's feelin' poorly." Wirt glanced down the

street, then back to Parker. "We both need her to heal. Guess I'll pay her a visit tomorrow. Take her some flowers. She liked the last ones."

If Parker had been the unselfish type, he wouldn't have lied about Sage's condition or persuaded Wirt to put off his visit. He should feel ashamed of himself, and maybe later he would. But not now, not while he stared at the moonstruck look on Wirt's face.

THIRTY-FIVE

Good morning, Miss Sage. You have a visitor." Dr. Slader's robust voice stirred Sage from her sleep.

Sage opened her eyes to see Dr. and Mrs. Slader standing at the foot of the bed with Widow Bess. Bess held out a plate of food, and it smelled like bacon and eggs.

"We told her you needed fattening up," Mrs. Slader said, who more closely resembled a fence post than the mother of nine boys. "Our dear Sage has stolen all of our hearts." The woman walked around to the side of her bed and planted a kiss on Sage's cheek. She smelled of vanilla and motherhood. For certain, what Mrs. Slader lacked in a woman's shape, she made up for in a sweet face and a kind heart. As if the shape of a person made her more or less likeable.

"I hear you haven't been eating very well, so I brought breakfast." Bess's round cheeks dimpled in a big smile. "Leah and I changed times today so she could attend church. Hope you don't mind."

"I'm being very spoiled. And I already had a biscuit this morning."

"My point," Mrs. Slader said. "You aren't eating enough to keep a bird alive." Her eyes widened. "Hawk eats more than you do."

"He's a growing boy—like yours." Sage attempted to sit up, even though every movement still pained her.

Instantly Doc Slader was at her side. "I'll help you there, Missy." He gently lifted her while his wife propped pillows behind her back.

"I sure am looking forward to getting out of this bed." She grinned at Bess. "But I believe you still have my clothes."

Doc Slader laughed, and he and his wife excused themselves. "We'll be back after church," Doc said. "Unless Preacher Waller throws us out."

Sage's ears rang with the remark. Did the preacher and Doc Slader not get along either? Heaven forbid that the Sladers had fallen under the preacher's wrath for doctoring her.

Mrs. Slader punched him in the ribs, but he simply wrapped his arm around her waist and planted a loud kiss on her cheek. The couple left the room, closing the door behind them. Sage heard the doctor shout for the boys that it was time for church, calling each one by name—all beginning with the letter *A*.

Sage focused her attention on Bess. "I want to thank you for staying with me since I've been here. I appreciate your company— all you've done for me. You and Leah are so dear to me." And she meant every word. Leaving Rocky Falls would be difficult for many reasons.

"We'd have stayed nights, but Parker shooed us out of here."

Sage wondered when he had time to sleep. But that was over now. She wondered lots of things about Parker, but it was all useless. "Most of the times you've been here, I've been asleep. Please, sit down."

Bess held out the plate of food and tilted her head. "Only if you promise to eat."

Sage reached for the food and set it on her lap. She'd learned to eat less while on the trail. "I'll do my best."

"We want to see you well. Got lots of talking to catch up on." In the distance, church bells sounded.

"Aren't you going to services this morning?" Sage took a drink of cool buttermilk.

"God and Preacher Waller don't have the same views."

Sage's eyes widened. How many others had less-than-complimentary remarks about the town's preacher? "May I ask why?"

Bess folded her hands in her lap, then unfolded them. "Did you ever taste food without salt?"

"Plenty of times. It filled the ache in my belly, but it certainly wasn't satisfying."

"That's Preacher Waller. He doesn't know how to add love to life. Instead he spouts sin like a bubbling pot and judges everyone but himself."

"Does he have a large congregation?"

"Not as many as he could have." She shook her gray head. "He has a habit of bringing to the pulpit what other folks are doing—and oft times it's not the good things. He and I parted ways when he disapproved of me motherin' the girls at the saloon. I love those girls, and I know how they earn their livin'. But if they don't have someone like me to love on them, how are they ever going to know Jesus?"

Sage agreed. She'd been separated from God long enough to know that those who really needed Him weren't in church . . . for various reasons.

"Preacher Waller condemns what my girls do from the pulpit." Bess shook her head. "Goodness, my girls know sleeping with men for money is wrong without someone constantly reminding them. All that accomplishes is making Preacher Waller look righteous and chasin' my girls away."

"He should be glad you're befriending them."

"Not exactly." Bess paused. "He said I wasn't welcome in his church as long as I associated with saloon folks."

"His church?" Sage questioned how God put up with any of them. "I thought it was God's church." Doc Slader's last comment still needled her. "Have Doc and the preacher had words?"

"I have no idea, but I wouldn't be surprised." Bess punctuated her sentiments with a nod. "Now, let's talk about something else. You, Miss Sage, nearly died on us, and look at you now. You have color in your face again."

The simple words touched Sage. All the words and actions of these kind people would never be forgotten. "As the color of my skin resembles coffee with cream, it doesn't take much to make me look healthy. But thank you."

"We all need to be expressing our gratitude for what you've done for our community. You saved the lives of two children. Those boys are our legacy, our hope for Rocky Falls." She laughed, or, rather, giggled. "And none of us can ever remember Parker Timmons wearing such a broad grin."

Sage dared not dwell on the matter, lest her own feelings show through. "You make me sound like more than who I am. It's been a long time since I've been able to call anyone a friend."

"What about your folks?"

"They live in southern Colorado, but since my husband died, I haven't been around them much."

"We widows have much in common," Bess said reverently.

"Do you have children?"

"Three. Stillborn. They're buried in the town's cemetery next to their papa."

Sage swallowed a lump in her throat. "I had a baby boy, and he's buried next to his papa too. He would have been almost eight by now."

Bess reached out and patted her arm. "I understand better now why you had to find Leah's boys. What was his name?"

Sage would rather feel the pain of another bullet than the agony of remembering her family's deaths. Still, it might be good for her to talk about what walked with her night and day. "Timothy Charles."

"It means more when you can name them, as though God can write it in His Book of Life, just like we can write their names in the Bible."

Mama had said it was important to name Timothy, but until now Sage had not truly understood. "What are your children's names?"

"Laura Alice, Mary Katherine, and Elijah James. I can't wait to meet them again in heaven." Bess blinked backed the tears.

And so did Sage. She set the fork on the side of the plate and took Bess's hand into hers, holding it tightly while gazing into the depths of honey-brown eyes. "Thank you. Some days I want to forget about my hopes and dreams that lie buried."

"We never forget. We simply push aside the pain. All we can do is shove all that nurturin' and lovin' into someone who needs it."

"Like your girls at the saloon," Sage said.

"Like you did with John and Davis Timmons. And the hawk who's taken up residence on the roof—and Parker."

So Bess knew what Sage could not utter. And in the midst of the firm grip of Bess's hand and the compassion of kindred hearts, Sage believed the woman also understood why she and Parker could never be together.

"I hear that in a few days, the doc is releasing you to the hotel."

"The sooner the better. I am so tired of this bed and this room."

"My girls could use someone else to talk to who isn't in the same profession as theirs. Between the two of us, we might be able to convince them to leave the saloon."

"I'd be glad to talk to them." She smiled. "Not sure if being a bounty hunter is much more respectable than their current profession."

"Nonsense. I'd like for them to hear of your courage."

Sage welcomed anything to keep her mind off Parker, except more bad news about the McCaws.

Parker watched Wirt pace the floor of the jail and listened to him talk on about Sage. She was smart. She was pretty. She was everything her reputation claimed and more. One more word and Parker might lay a fist alongside his jaw. How many times had he thought the same things? Too many troubles plagued his mind and made him surly. If he weren't careful, his good judgment would suffer. Widow Bess said the girls at the saloon thought Wirt was quite a catch. Did Sage think the same?

"She's the type of woman who'd convince me to settle down," Wirt said. "Never has a woman caused me to think about a home and family before. Sage Zimmerman has a nice sound to it, don't you think?"

You are not good enough for her.

"As soon as she's strong enough, we need to head into the mountains after the McCaws," Wirt said. "They've done enough killing. How many men have indicated they'd ride with us?"

Parker's mood had soured worse than curdled milk. "I might get two."

"Two? Is this town full of women?" Wirt laughed. "If they were all like Sage, I'd say we should deputize them all."

"Never can tell. I'm not so sure Sage is up to a trip into those mountains again."

"She'd follow us if we left her."

Parker realized that part was true. "We've waited too long as it is. Who knows what Aiden will do next?"

"In a couple more days, Sage will get her strength back, and then we can get down to business."

"You mean weeks. She isn't up to traveling yet." Why did he let the man get under his skin? *Lord, I'm needing more and more help here to be godly.* "I think you and I can bring them in. I have an idea about—"

"But she's the bait. They're after her."

Parker grabbed him by the shirt. "We both are. And she's not to be dangled in front of them like a worm on a hook. First you talk about marryin' her, then you want to put her in danger. I admit she can take care of herself, but what you're suggesting is wrong."

"Ease off, Parker. I was only joking."

Right. "You heard me."

"You're a mite touchy about the woman. Maybe all that talk about you and her's true. What are you going to do when Waller convinces the folks of Rocky Falls to get themselves another marshal?"

Waller's rumors had spread through town like manure, and Parker had heard them all—and stepped in a few piles. "I don't think you need to concern yourself about me or Sage. I don't have time to explain the difference between truth and lies to every person in this town. If someone has a gripe against me, let them tell it to me face-to-face. In the meantime, I have a town to protect."

Wirt snatched his hat from the desk. "I'm going over to talk to Sage right now. See when she thinks she'll be fit to ride."

"You best be asking Doc Slader that question."

"Are you ordering me—a US Marshal?"

"Do I need to? The woman's under the care of a doctor. She nearly died in those mountains, and you want her to ride back out as bait. She can handle herself better than most men, but force it?"

Wirt plopped his hat onto his head. "You don't know what you're talking about. She'll tell me today when she's ready to ride, and I bet it will be sooner than Doc claims. Sage knows the longer she's laid up, the more the chances of the McCaws striking again."

Parker couldn't argue with what Wirt claimed, and with that knowledge, he realized most of the reason the US Marshal got under his skin was his attraction to Sage. "All right, but you take a long look at the shape she's in before you jump into wanting her to ride. In fact let's talk about it over supper tonight at the hotel. I want to check in with Bess again, see if anything new came to her ears last night."

"Sounds like a good idea. Are you going to church tonight? I hear Preacher Waller wants to take an informal vote about whether you should continue as the town's marshal."

"He might need a reminder about separating church and state. But I doubt if it will make a difference. And I intend to be there. Why don't you come along?"

Wirt eyed him curiously, then grabbed the doorknob. "I'll make my visit with Sage short and meet you back here. I'll think about joining you for church. Might be entertaining."

THIRTY-SIX

The Sunday morning hours with Bess passed much too quickly. Leah was late, but she could be busy at church or the parsonage. After all, she had five sons who needed her attention, not just one bounty hunter. Sage startled. Doctor and Mrs. Slader had nine boys. If not for the McCaws, she and Charles would have had a houseful of children. *Stupid!* Charles was an outlaw. There, she'd admitted it.

Sage would have cried with self-pity if she hadn't been afraid the Sladers might return from church and find her behaving like a ... woman. Today the large family planned to check on her, then spend the rest of the afternoon at a rancher's for dinner. One of them could walk in and find the notorious Sage Morrow in tears if she weren't careful. Instead, she allowed her mind to slip back to those last few days with Charles. Had he said something she'd ignored? *I'm a fool.* If only she could get out of the bed and ride out after the McCaws. If only—

A light knock interrupted her thoughts. It had better not be Parker, because if it was, she might ... she might ...

"Sage?"

Leah. "Yes. Come in." She needed a diversion to take her mind off herself.

Leah walked in carrying something that looked like yard goods. "Sorry I'm late. Preacher Waller was long-winded today. How are you feeling?"

"Better now. I'm glad you're here." Sage held her breath. "I'm sounding as pitiful as an old woman." She pointed to the chair where Bess had sat earlier. "Make yourself comfortable."

Leah eased down onto the chair, erect and very much like a proper lady. She smiled, an impish grin that defied propriety. "I brought something for you."

Sage's gaze slid to the bundle in Leah's lap. "What?"

"If you have to stay here a few more days, and Bess insists upon holding your clothes hostage, then you can wear these." Leah held up a blue-green dress, one that reminded her of a mountain spruce. "I know you won't try to ride after the McCaws in this."

Sage wanted to jump from the bed. "Real clothes?"

"Yes, and I'll help you into them. Everything's here. I borrowed them from Bess, and I think they came from one of the girls working there. But they look respectable and should fit."

Longing filled Sage's heart. It had been years since she'd looked like a real woman. "You have made this the best day since I arrived in Rocky Falls."

"Friends do what friends do—love each other." Tears pooled Leah's eyes. "Even if you hadn't saved my sons' lives, I would treasure our times together. After a visit with you, I feel like I could do anything."

Hidden beneath the Leah everyone saw was a real western woman, and she was stronger than she realized. "You can, Leah. Don't let anyone tell you otherwise. Believe in yourself and don't turn back. Encourage the ones you love, and they will be able to accomplish their dreams." Sage meant her sons, but Parker crept into her thoughts.

"I want to help John manage our ranch without the help of anyone. And I want to grab the bull by the horns—" Leah covered her mouth. "Mercy, I sound like a cowhand." Then she straightened. "Why not?"

The two laughed, and it felt so good. When they quieted, Sage stared up at the ceiling. Dare she ask what was going through Leah's head? "Did you see the Sladers when you came?"

"They were right behind me at church with all those boys piled into the back of their wagon. Why?"

"Do you suppose after I'm dressed that I could get permission from the doctor to sit on the front porch? I despise this bed, and I don't care how much it hurts to sit out there. I want to reach out and touch my Hawk ... Enjoy the sunshine."

"I'll ask him straightaway. If he agrees, I'm sure he and one of his strapping sons would carry you outside. Oh, Sage, it's a beautiful day. Birds are singing, and it's warm, but not too warm. Before we can think twice, fall will be here. But not today."

"Hawk probably thinks I've deserted him." She stared out her window to where her pet sat on the porch rail. "I really miss him. He has a way of peering at me that makes me feel like I'm his best friend."

Leah shuddered. "Not so sure I'd feel the same way, but I'm sure he's missing you. He's stood guard on the roof or the porch ever since Parker brought you here. Behave yourself so you can ease the poor bird's heart." She giggled, as though the two were girls ready to embark on something they weren't supposed to do.

A short while later, Sage sat on the Sladers' front porch in a rocker with a pillow under her and another supporting her back. She felt awkward wearing a dress, almost naked without britches hugging her legs. A shift and ruffled drawers beneath it reminded her of the clothes packed away in a trunk in southern Colorado. Just the feel of a woman's clothes caused her to recall her life with Charles, when she'd been a full woman—when it hadn't been necessary to track down his killers. Years had passed as though she'd been in a fog, and the job still wasn't done. Why did she torture herself with the same grueling images? Especially when it looked like Charles had been one of them.

But she now had names to go with those faces, and she knew where to find them. In bringing in the McCaws, she'd find out the truth. Sage let the creak of the rocker soothe her troubled mind and carry her back in time. Her gaze moved to the mountains. The McCaws would not escape her again. Charles may have been an outlaw, but the gang had still murdered her baby.

"You look very pretty, Sage," Leah said.

For a moment, she'd forgotten about her friend. "Thank you again for the dress and underthings. I feel like a lady."

"You *are* a lady. A beautiful woman."

"Eight years ago, maybe." Sage glanced down at the dress with the tiny bit of lace around the neckline and sleeves, and stretched out her bare toes beneath it. "But I'd rather have my own clothes."

"Whatever for?"

"Those mountains are calling to me." Sage looked from the sea of dark green trees flooding the lower slopes to where the rocky crags emerged to touch the sky.

"The McCaws," Leah whispered. "Remember they nearly killed you. And don't forget what happened to Duncan."

Hawk, poised on the porch rail, turned to look at Leah as if he understood her words.

"The reminders are why I have to be going. The McCaws will try, but I'm more determined."

Leah's face paled. "Let Parker and Mr. Zimmerman go after them."

"It's not entirely their fight." How could Sage make Leah understand? "Don't you want to see them stopped before another woman is made a widow or another child is forced to grow up without a father?"

Leah nodded. "I do, but I trust the law to bring them in." She glanced at Hawk and shivered in the summer heat. Leah was afraid of too many things. She had grand dreams, but she'd need to step from her timidity to reach them.

You can survive the tragedies of life. "Once you said you could pull the trigger."

"I could—with no regrets." Leah paused and fretted with a loose thread on her dress. "I just believe a woman has her place, and men have theirs. I don't mean to be judging you like Preacher Waller—"

"What did he say today?" Sage ceased to rock.

Leah flushed red. "Nothing worth repeating."

"I know he doesn't approve of female bounty hunters. And he doesn't approve of those who have befriended me."

Leah clasped her hands in her lap. "If I repeated gossip, then I'd be no better than the rest of those loose tongues." She sighed. "But I heard it, so it's not gossip."

"Leah, what else?"

"Preacher Waller is a strange man. He lives right by the Bible—"

"If you don't tell me what he said, I'll pester you until you do—or ask the preacher myself. I'm sure he'd tell me."

Leah stared at Sage as though the decision weighed heavily on her heart. Compassion filled her face. "He reminded folks about you and Parker spending those days and nights in the mountains. And the proof of it was your wearing his shirt. He said Parker admitted his sinful life to them during prayer meeting." Leah shook her head and stood. "I don't believe such nonsense. You were more dead than alive when Parker brought you into town. And he didn't look much better. Besides, no one else would go after my boys."

Sage studied the street leading to the church and parsonage. "The gossip is ruining Parker's reputation as a fit marshal or a man running for office. What *else* happened today?"

Leah shooed away a fly. "Tonight after church, Preacher Waller is asking for the men to vote on whether to keep Parker as the marshal or not."

Anger burned in the pit of her stomach. "I thought the whole town voted on who was supposed to be marshal. A legal election is not one in a church."

"You're right. But if he gets the church on his side, then he has the majority."

Sage understood. A legal election would be a mere formality. Waller would have his way. "So would Bob Culpepper be the new marshal since he's now the deputy?"

"I don't know. Preacher Waller's been talking to a stranger who's looking to buy land. The man says he has experience with lawmen."

All of this because Parker saved her life. The unfairness made no sense. No sense at all. No wonder Sage was finished having anything to do with God. When He had spokesmen like Waller, who needed the Devil?

"This is wrong." Sage wished she could march to the parsonage and put an end to the gossip. "Is this town full of cowards?"

Leah lifted her head. "Bob Culpepper said if Waller followed through with tonight's vote, he'd make sure the governor found out."

"And?"

"The stranger—his name is Richard Edwards—said he knew those in Denver who would back up Preacher Waller."

A nest of rattlesnakes. "This town has been in turmoil since I rode in with Aiden McCaw."

"Parker and Preacher Waller weren't getting along very well before then. You came to help, Sage. Don't you dare go blaming yourself."

"But I do."

While Leah continued to protest, Sage made a decision. She'd wasted enough time at the Sladers'. She'd give herself until early Thursday morning to heal, and then she'd ride into the mountains and rest there until her strength returned. Parker may have stolen her heart, but she'd not steal his right to be the town's marshal or discredit his ability to lead the people of Colorado.

"Don't do anything foolish," Leah said.

Sage widened her eyes. "Do you think I'm going to gun down the preacher?"

Leah covered her mouth and stifled a laugh. "I shouldn't mock the man since he's provided a place for me and the children to stay until this is over. But ... he is overbearing." She peered beyond Sage to the street. "Mr. Zimmerman is walking this way. He has an eye for you."

The last thing Sage wanted was another man looking at her in the way she wanted Parker to see her but couldn't allow. "I hadn't noticed."

"I have."

As if he knew they were talking about him, Wirt waved. He'd been to see Sage a few times and talked a good yarn. She was more interested in his abilities as a US Marshal than as a potential suitor ... But seeing them together might get Parker to pay more attention to Leah.

He carried his hat and wore a clean shirt, but no matter how nice he looked, his boasting would drive a woman insane. She'd not pretend interest in Wirt for the short while she was here. Once she left town, Parker and Leah could rekindle what they'd lost years before. And their lives could resume again.

Wirt stopped in front of the porch. "Afternoon, ladies, Hawk. Beautiful day, isn't it? But it's no match for the two pretty ladies on this porch."

Sage had no desire to talk about the weather or listen to him smooth talk her and Leah. But she must pretend interest.

"How are you feeling, Miss Sage?"

"Stronger every day. Thank you, Mr. Zimmerman. And how are you?"

"Little to complain about, but if I got started it might take me all day." He laughed—by himself. "I don't want to interrupt you and Mrs. Timmons, but is there a time I could come back today and discuss a matter with you?"

Leah clearly became flustered and stood from her rocker. "Oh my. Right now is fine. I need to stop by the jail and see Parker and John before I return to the parsonage."

Sage tossed Leah a silent plea for her to stay. Being alone with Wirt was not the bright spot of her day. "Please don't leave. We haven't finished our conversation."

"I'll check back later or tomorrow. Parker needs my answer about moving to his ranch."

Leah had mentioned on more than one occasion how easy it would be for her and the children to take him up on his offer. This would definitely force Parker and Leah together. Sage should be happy instead of feeling sorry for herself. "So you've made a decision?"

Leah looked every bit as sweet and innocent as always. "I have, and he deserves to know as soon as possible."

Then Parker could ask Leah to marry him. An event Sage would not attend. "I'm sure whatever Parker is thinking would honor God's name."

"I just left Parker at the jail," Wirt said. "I'm sure he'd welcome your company."

Leah stepped around to the other side of the porch to avoid Hawk. Once past him, she hurried down the street.

"Thanks for the clothes," Sage called after her.

Wirt lifted a boot onto the porch. She could probably see her face in it if she took the time. "Mind if I sit a spell with you?"

She started to claim she was tired, but lying wasn't her style, and she needed to hear him out. He took the empty chair and studied her, seriousness etching his expression.

"Do I have mud on my face?" Sage wanted to ask more but thought better of it. Best she kept her manners intact for the few days she had remaining in town.

He smiled broadly, revealing his milky white teeth. "No, just admiring how you look in a dress." Good teeth she liked. Flattery she detested.

"It won't last. Bess has my clothes at the hotel. And I'll soon be strong enough to walk down there and demand them." The best way to tolerate Wirt was to joke with him.

"So you're healing all right?"

"It's slow, and I'm not a good patient."

He toyed with the brim of his hat. "I'm not either. Staying in bed makes me short-tempered."

She wanted to get on the trail after the McCaws as badly as he did. This was Sunday, and she didn't want to hold Wirt or Parker back. If only her body would mend faster. But weakness plagued her morning and night. No point in being too stubborn and stupid. If they chose to leave sooner, she could catch up with them.

He took a deep breath, as though he were garnering nerve to make a speech. Her mood fell another notch while she waited for him to state what was on his mind. "Parker and I are going to head after the McCaws. I know you wanted to go, but we can't hold out much longer."

Her heart sped up a notch. "When?"

"Most likely the end of this week. We're trying to get a couple of good men to ride with us."

"And you think that will happen with Preacher Waller making his demands? I heard about the vote tonight."

Wirt hesitated. "What the good preacher is planning has nothing to do with what Parker and I must do. In any event, we need to get after the McCaws before they decide to kill someone else."

Sage agreed with the urgency, but not with her staying behind. No point in arguing. She'd work it out herself. "Next Sunday noon."

"You'll be ready to leave then?"

"Yes. If you and Parker need to head out sooner, I'll catch up."

Wirt rubbed his clean-shaven jaw. He and Parker had similar coloring, but definitely different mannerisms. "I'll talk to Parker and see what he says. Have you thought of anything else about the McCaws?"

"I've told you and Parker all I know. Being laid up has given me lots of time to think, and the only point hammering against my brain is that it looks like Charles may have ridden with outlaws."

"Parker and I have talked about your husband's — uh — possible other interests." He paused. "Would you consider having supper with me before we leave?"

Sage wanted to flat out refuse him, but she saw no need to insult him. The only man she wanted to spend any time with was Parker Timmons. Besides, she planned to ride out on Thursday before sunrise. "I don't think I'd be much company, but thank you for asking."

"Would you consider allowing me to call on you when this is over?"

"I think you and I are quite different."

"Maybe not so much."

She wanted to tell him absolutely not, and later she would.

"Parker and I have been going over the map of these parts. Could we stop by tomorrow and go over it with you?"

"I'd like that."

Wirt said his good-bye and left her rocking on the front porch. Hawk twisted his head at her.

"I know he has the potential to be less irritating. Even so, I'm not interested."

Hawk continued to stare as though sizing up the US Marshall.

"He has to be good at his job, or else he'd have been killed by now."

Then she began to think about what Preacher Waller had said about Parker. The townsfolk deserved to hear the truth. Wednesday night she planned to be at prayer meeting. She might not have shoes, but she had a dress.

THIRTY-SEVEN

I feel like a schoolboy," Wirt said. "I'm a US Marshal, not a wet-nosed kid." The two men stood near the bend in the street that led to the church, waiting for an opportunity to slip in unnoticed.

"If you don't lower your voice, then the others will hear you and Waller will know we're planning to attend," Parker said. "He'll drag you down the aisle by your ear. And be sure he'd bring up every piece of Scripture in the Bible that denounces sinners." The thought of Waller grabbing Wirt caused Parker to stifle a laugh, and for a moment he let himself enjoy the sensation. He needed something to lighten the burdens weighing on him.

"I suppose you'd get away?"

Parker pointed toward the outhouse. "My hideout."

"Very funny. I understand the importance of sitting in the back and listening to what's being said, but I feel real stupid— like I've done something wrong."

"Consider it a new chapter in the US Marshal's handbook." Parker listened to the closing verse of the hymn "Amazing Grace" and wondered if Waller had ever pondered the words he sang. "The song's about over," he whispered. "Let's go."

"Welcome to tonight's services," Preacher Waller began. "Glad to have you here. We have some things to take care of tonight before I bring you a message from God and we sing more beautiful hymns about His saving grace. Let's bow our heads and ask God's blessing on all we do this fine evening."

Parker caught a glimpse of Bob and his wife on the other side of the room. Good, he didn't want to call attention to his friend again. Parker was curious about the new man in town, Richard Edwards, who claimed to be a cattleman from near Fort Worth, Texas. Parker had wired the city to see what he could find out about the man but hadn't heard back yet.

"... and Lord, give us wisdom to know how to vote about Marshal Parker Timmons. You know the immoral life he's livin' and how that's not good for a God-fearing town. Take care of our widows and orphans and help us live accordin' to Your Word. Amen." The crowd shuffled, as though the ending of a prayer meant they could breathe. "I thought it best if we vote first and get it out of our way so we can worship."

"Excuse me, Preacher Waller," Bob Culpepper said. "Our national Constitution states there's a separation of church and state. Looks to me like we're breaking the law by voting on our marshal during church time."

"That's only if someone complains," Waller said. "We're voting because we're all here together. That's not mixing church and political business. Once the voting is done, we can approach Marshal Timmons with the truth of how this town feels about him. Shall we continue with this? I think we could handle the voting through a show of hands. Get it over with and done real fast."

"I disagree with the vote and how you are going about it," Bob said. "Why don't we contact the county sheriff over in Boulder? Let him handle the problem. Or wait until someone could come from Denver."

"We've all agreed to vote on the marshal tonight, and we have thirty-three men of voting age here. If no one else has a problem with a show of hands, we'll continue." Waller cleared his throat. "All those in favor of keeping Parker Timmons as the marshal of Rocky Falls, raise your right hand."

It took all of Parker's willpower to keep from standing. Who were his friends and who believed the lies?

"That's thirteen votes for Parker. All those in favor of allowing me to take over the duties of marshal until the town can vote on a new man, raise your right hand."

Parker's spirits dropped to his toes with a wheelbarrow full of anger burning his gut. A shuffle of folks and a hum of voices met his ears.

"That's eleven who are ready to stand up for God and get rid of the sin in our midst. If my arithmetic is correct, nine of you didn't cast your vote. The Bible says God will spit out the fence sitter."

"That passage is about those who ride the fence about making a decision to follow the Lord, not taking part in an illegal election." The sound of Bob's voice whipped around the church louder than Waller's finest sermon. "And I didn't see you vote."

"Sorry, Brother Culpepper. My vote is for replacing Marshal Timmons. That makes twelve votes for replacing him. Any more discussion?"

"There are more citizens of voting age in this town besides the thirty-three here," Bob continued. "I'll be contacting Denver about this meeting and will continue to take direction from Marshal Parker Timmons. I'm not a lawyer, but I do believe what has happened tonight is clearly illegal." A few moments later, the sound of heavy boots pounded down the aisle and out the door.

Thanks, Bob. Parker tossed a glance at Wirt. The US Marshal scowled, clearly disgusted at what they were witnessing.

"I support Marshal Timmons," Jess Lockard said. "*The Rocky Falls News* will report the happenings tonight in this week's paper."

"You said last week you believed the town could use a new marshal," Waller said.

"What I said was Rocky Falls had every right to vote for a new man in the next election. I said nothing about bootin' him out of a job. He's a good man and kept the peace until the McCaws started their killin'."

The buzz of voices reminded Parker of a swarm of angry bees.

"If any of you have questions, I'll be available after the service to talk to you." Waller's voice shouted above the others. "We need to tend to our worshipin'."

Parker had heard enough. The odds were not as much against him as he thought, and those who hadn't voted were obviously torn by the situation. No need for him to stand and confront Waller. Others had handled it nicely. Unlike the other night, he'd stay until services were over. The folks here needed to see he'd attended.

Once the service was over, Parker purposely delayed leaving. He greeted men and women, and said nothing about the vote. Those who supported him clasped his hand while others slithered away and spent their time with Preacher Waller.

"I appreciated the last song," Parker said to Waller. "One of my favorites, 'There's a Wideness in God's Mercy.'"

Waller ignored him, turning his attention to Richard Edwards. Parker watched them converse for a moment. Something about the man was oddly familiar. Unable to place the stranger, Parker headed down the road to the hotel with Wirt to make plans for leaving town at the end of the week.

"That man is a clear hypocrite," Wirt said. "Especially when he used to spend a lot of time in jail. If that's the way God changes a man, then I'll never be interested."

"Wirt, I'm a Christian, and I'm committed to my faith. Don't be judging God by those of us who have a habit of sinning."

"But you're sitting by and doing nothing while Waller turns many of these folks against you."

Parker chuckled. "Bob and Lockard took care of everything tonight. And the vote shows Waller isn't swaying folks like he thinks he is."

"Maybe," Wirt muttered. "I hope for your sake that you're right."

After a long pause, Wirt said, "Before I forget, I told Sage we'd see her tomorrow to go over the map. She'll be ready to leave next Sunday."

The protective side of Parker wanted to protest, but he understood how Sage's mind worked. If she were determined, then nothing would stop her. "I'm sure she wouldn't have agreed to leave if she wasn't feeling strong."

"I'm only repeating what she said. I'm sure she's talked to the doc about it. Why else would she agree to leave?"

Because she's stubborn and she's spent seven years of her life hating those who destroyed her family.

The two men walked into the hotel. More men were taking advantage of the saloon than were eating supper. But that was all right. Bess had been too busy to talk to Parker when he and Wirt came by for dinner, so Parker had waited all day to hear what, if anything, Bess had learned since yesterday. She waved and called out a greeting the moment he and Wirt made their way into the dining area.

"Have a seat, gentlemen." Bess pointed to a corner table far from the saloon's noise. "I'll bring you some coffee."

After she brought the men two steaming cups, Bess disappeared into the kitchen for two heaping dishes of apple pie and cream. She set the dessert in front of them and eased into a chair at their table.

"Before it gets busy again, I wanted to talk to you two. I learned a few things about that Richard Edwards. He and Waller were in here last night for supper." Bess looked around for eavesdroppers. Luckily they were in a quiet area. "He's met twice here with Preacher Waller now."

"I'm hoping a telegram confirming his claims will clear up a few things," Parker said. "But go ahead and tell us what you know."

"He claims to be from Fort Worth where he has a ranch and a wife and four daughters. Wants to live out here. Says the mountain air will help one of his daughters, who has breathing problems."

"All that sounds respectable," Wirt said. "If he's telling the truth."

"Not sure," Bess continued. "He told Preacher Waller he'd worked with lawmen in Texas and knew the ropes about being a good marshal. Preacher Waller said the town could use a new marshal with experience. Edwards thanked him and said he'd pray about it." She frowned.

"What else, Bess?" Parker said.

"Well, his words say one thing, but his actions say another. After the preacher left, Edwards watched the goings-on in the saloon. He didn't drink, but he kept watching Faye. Once when I went back to the kitchen, I peeked back in and saw him slip her some money. A short time later, he went upstairs to his room. Within a half hour, she followed. I never saw her come down until the next morning."

"So the churchgoing rancher who wants to bring his family to a quiet town has a few weaknesses." Parker stole a glance at Faye, a pretty woman who was known for charging more than the other soiled doves. Parker believed she'd do whatever necessary to make a dollar. Sad but true.

Following his glance, Bess said, "I asked Faye if she was enjoying Mr. Edwards's company, but she denied having anything to do with him."

"The preacher would be all over him if he knew." Wirt poked his fork into a juicy apple slice and popped it into his mouth.

"One more thing," Bess said. "When paying me for his room, he dropped a silver piece. He used a whole string of swear words that don't belong in a church or a hotel. His breath was strong with whiskey, too."

So Richard Edwards found it necessary to cheat on his wife, drink, and use some language unbecoming to a respectable man. It would be interesting to see the report on him from Fort Worth.

THIRTY-EIGHT

Parker spread the map of the Rocky Mountain region over the floor of Doc Slader's porch. He hadn't brought up the conversation in which Wirt and Sage had discussed her leaving with them on Sunday. No point, since Parker and Sage's last discussion had ended badly, and he'd most likely make her mad. But he hadn't given up on Sage and him; when this was over, he'd hog-tie her if that's what it took to make her listen. Love sure did crazy things to a man. He shook off his thoughts and turned his attention to what lay before him.

"It took Sage and me two days of hard riding to find John and Davis. Without her tracking experience, it could have taken a week." Parker pointed to the area where the McCaws had held his nephews. "They wanted us to find them, but we have no idea where they're camped now. My suggestion is for us to ride to Flattop Mountain. They'll be looking for us."

"It's rough terrain." Sage traced her fingers over a mountain pass. "Am I right that it's just the three of us?"

Parker nodded. "I need Bob Culpepper here to watch over things. This town should change its name to Confusion Falls. The folks are scared—thanks to the McCaws—and they're looking for someone to blame. I'm hoping when all of this is over, I'll have a chance to call a town meeting and answer their questions without Waller waving his Bible."

Wirt leaned back in the rocker beside Sage and took a deep breath as if preparing for a plunge. "Before we go, I need to tell you about my background."

Parker studied the man, who was sometimes difficult to handle with his arrogance. He glanced at Sage, her brown eyes were shadowed. Did she already know what Wirt planned to say?

"I'm a city boy. Grew up in Columbus, Ohio. The only wild country I've seen is in getting here. I'm a good shot, but I've never killed a man. I tried law school for a while, but it bored me. I wanted action. Most ... well, all of my past work has been from behind a desk. I begged to deliver the bounty money and bring in Aiden McCaw in hopes of proving my mettle and obtaining bigger assignments." His face glistened redder than a ripe tomato. "I promise to do my best, but you're not looking at a veteran US Marshal."

Parker's first reaction was to punch the man in the nose. But what good would losing his temper do? It wasn't Wirt's fault he got caught up in the middle of a mess with a town petrified of a gang of outlaws and no one willing to be part of a posse. However ... "Would have been easier if you'd told the truth right from the start."

Wirt's red face said it all. "I've been asking a lot of questions because I need to know what we're up against and how not to get any of us killed." Wirt leaned forward in the rocker. "My apologies for my ignorance and lack of humility. Pride has made me real disagreeable."

Parker wavered between frustration and pity. Looked to him like he and Sage were better off alone.

"Do you even want to ride after the McCaws?" Sage spoke softly, not a trickle of condescension tipped her words. "You don't have to. Parker and I are riding a fool's trail. We know they're waiting for us."

"I have to prove to myself that I can be of help to you or anyone else in need. I've talked to Mrs. Felter and Mrs. Timmons, and I hate the hardship they face because of the McCaws. I'll not hold you back, and I'll do my part."

Taking in a deep breath, Parker added a bit of admiration to his feelings for what Wirt was about to do. He just hoped the man's inexperience didn't get any of them killed. Taking John with them made more sense. "It takes a lot of guts to admit what you just did. And I won't refuse you. But remember this—the McCaws have murdered and stolen since the war. They don't have a shred of decency. Did you fight in the war?"

"No. My father paid for another man to take my place."

A Yankee. "I fought for the South just like the McCaw brothers. I saw war take a good man and turn him into a killer. Fear and panic caused brutality and disrespect for life. Many Confederate soldiers returned home to nothing—homes destroyed, a way of life gone forever. When a man is beaten inside and out, he turns to whatever he can to fill the need for significance and survival. He has to fill the hunger in his body and soul while wondering if he can exist with the nightmare of war stuck in his mind. It's impossible to forget. For those war-torn years, all of us who fought were a part of a huge group that was told when to eat, sleep, march, and fight. It's hard to go back to thinking for yourself after that. The McCaws never changed. They're a walking, talking, stalking, prowling, murdering gang. We are nothing to them except a way to get what they're looking for."

Wirt nodded. "I'm ready. A man has to learn sometime how to do his job."

Parker glanced into the face of the woman he loved. Doubt brimmed her eyes, but what choice did they have? "Sage?"

"Wirt, I hope your lack of experience isn't your epitaph."

Things could not get any worse.

Sage closed her eyes and drank in the warm afternoon sun. For the first time, Doc Slader had allowed her to make her way to the porch alone, and she saw the new freedom as proof that she had taken a huge leap in her recovery. She heard her name being called and opened her eyes to see Bess and two young women standing on the porch.

"Good afternoon, Miss Sage. You look real fetching sitting here," Bess said.

"Thank you." Sage forced herself to sit up straighter. She must have dozed off, for she'd grown a bit stiff. "Today the good doctor let me walk out here by myself."

Bess gestured toward the two young women. "We came to visit."

Sage realized these two must work at the saloon. However, they were dressed as conservatively as any respectable woman in Rocky Falls. Her gaze fell on Bess again, and she noticed something in the older woman's hand. *Oh my goodness, she's got a Bible. What next?*

Bess wrapped her ample arm around the brown-haired woman on her left. "This is Faye, and this is Tillie." Both women smiled, and Sage returned the greeting.

Bess pointed to the empty chairs. "I brought my friends to help you while away the afternoon. I know how boring it gets for you."

"Oh, it does. Makes me lazy."

The three women eased into the chairs. "I usually sleep during the afternoon," Faye said, but the attractive woman failed to look at Sage straight on. Sage had always believed a person who could not give eye contact had something to hide. Maybe Faye was embarrassed about the way she earned her living.

"I'm glad you're here," Sage said. A second look at Tillie filled her with compassion. The woman had the saddest gray eyes. Why had these women chosen this way of life? But then again, she'd chosen to become a bounty hunter out of desperation. Life. Circumstances. Hardship. All were potential reasons for a woman to turn her back on propriety.

"I sleep most afternoons too," said Tillie, a rather plain-looking woman. "I have a little girl at school. When she comes home, I want to spend all of my time with her until evening."

"What's her name?" Sage said.

"Caroline."

"Very pretty. I had a son once."

"He died?" Tillie's shoulders fell, as though she'd experienced more than one loss.

"Yes." This wasn't going well at all. Sage should think of something more positive to talk about. She threw a helpless look at Bess.

"You're wearing Tillie's clothes," Bess said.

Sage glanced down at the blue-green dress. "Thank you so much. I'll make sure it's washed before returning it."

"Glad to be of help." For the first time, Tillie appeared to relax. "It looks very nice on you."

The uncomfortable exchange of pleasantries caused Sage to wonder who felt the most awkward. Respectable folk frowned on all of them.

"I'd like to know who taught you how to track and survive in the wilderness," Faye said.

"An Indian by the name of Tall Elk. He's from my mother's people."

Faye glared at her as though she deemed herself a better person because of Sage's heritage.

"Why did you become a bounty hunter?"

Sage didn't want to go deep into the past, but what could she say? "It's a long story—"

"Oh, no," Bess said. "Here comes trouble."

Sage lifted her gaze to see Preacher Waller headed their way. Maybe one of his children needed Dr. Slader. She caught Bess's eye and read the same apprehension. "Afternoon, Preacher Waller," Sage said. "Dr. Slader is on a call."

"I'm not here to see the doc."

She'd seen more emotion from a rock. "Mrs. Slader is inside. Would you like for me to fetch her?"

"I'm not here to see her either." He stood at the foot of the porch, first giving Bess a look of disdain and then Faye and Tillie. Sage sensed the ire rising from her toes.

"What do you need?" Sage kept her voice even.

"Looking for Parker Timmons. Figured he was with you."

"No, sir. He and Mr. Zimmerman planned to spend the morning at Leah's ranch. Maybe they haven't returned yet. Have you tried the marshal's office?"

"He's not there. No matter. He'll learn soon enough."

"What's that?" Bess said.

Waller lifted his nose like a woman who'd smelled something offensive. "The godly citizens of this town have asked him to resign as marshal rather than force an election. The company he keeps has caused us to question his morals and his ability to protect our community."

Sage wanted to spit venom more poisonous than his, but she held her tongue—by biting down on it until she felt it was under control. "I won't speak for him, but I do know him to be a man of high regard, a man who loves God and His people. I doubt he resigns."

Waller laughed. "You would. When you see him, tell him I'll be waiting at the parsonage."

"I thought the vote was in Parker's favor." Bess words sounded more pleasant than Sage's would have been.

He turned and walked back into town.

Anger shook Sage to the core. Waller had no right to judge Parker without knowing the truth. But would Waller ever listen to anyone but his own pride? She shivered at the snake of bitterness crawling up her spine. Maybe she and the preacher weren't that different.

Thirty-Nine

"Bess, I need my clothes." Sage leaned on the registration desk at the hotel. If Bess refused, she'd have to find a way to buy new britches, a shirt, and boots before heading out in the morning.

Bess appeared to size her up, frowning and puckering her lips as though someone had given her a pickle. "Looks to me like you have clothes on. Did you walk from Doc's?"

"I did. But I don't have shoes."

Bess's face flushed. "Heaven forbid, Sage. What's got into you? And why didn't you ask for them this afternoon?"

Sage ignored the question. "I'm going to prayer meetin'."

Bess's mouth dropped open. "You must still be smartin' about this afternoon."

"Yes, ma'am. Now, do I get my clothes?"

"I suppose. Tillie's dress looks more like what you'd wear to prayer meetin', though."

"Probably so. But I need my own things."

Bess reached below the desk and pulled out her folded britches, Parker's shirt, and her socks and boots. They were clean, and her boots were repaired. Not since her mother had a woman been so kind.

"Thanks for all you've done for me," Sage said.

"My pleasure."

"Parker needs to have his shirt returned."

"He told me to keep it in case you needed it." Bess continued to stare. "I wonder if I should go to church with you."

"To protect Preacher Waller?" Sage hid a smile.

The corners of Bess's mouth lifted. "To see what you're up to. Been told he's a fair shot. Might be a real show to see him get beat."

Calling the preacher out into the street might be the easy way out, but, in the end, Parker would be the one to suffer. "This battle will be fought with the truth."

Bess's eyes widened. "Sounds like you're going to do the preaching."

God would strike her with two bolts of lightning for pretending to be friends with Him. "I'm going to speak my piece. That's all. I know Parker explained his side of what happened in the mountains, but now it's my turn."

The hotel door opened, and a slender young man stepped inside. "Miss Morrow, I have a response to the wire you asked John Timmons to send for you a few days ago." He pulled a folded piece of paper from his shirt pocket and handed it to her.

Do I really want to read this? "Thanks. How did you know I'd be here?"

The young man, not much older than John, shifted from one foot to the other. "I saw you walkin' down the street." He tipped his hat and left the hotel.

Studying the paper, Sage realized the contents would answer many of the questions piercing her heart. She opened the message. Her stomach twisted and turned.

"What's wrong?" Bess said. "You're trembling."

Sage glanced up, her throat dry. "Bad news."

"Do you want to tell me about it?"

What good did it do to hide the information? "Eight years ago, the McCaw gang held up a train outside of Denver. A man who rode with them claimed to be Charles Morrow. For sure Charles must have double-crossed them, or they wouldn't have come after him."

"I'm sorry. Parker told me he suspected the same."

Another rise of deceit and betrayal settled on her like a bad cold. First Charles and now Parker. "This is proof that Charles was an outlaw." She drew in a breath in an effort to calm herself. "However, it doesn't change the fact that the McCaws killed my baby. And they are wanted men who need to be brought in."

"Bringing them to justice won't stop the hurt."

"It's what I have to do." Sage would contemplate what she'd learned about Charles later, when no one was around to see her tears. "I'll wash this dress tonight and get it back to you." She glanced around the hotel and into the saloon already filled with drinkers, gamblers, and the girls. Faye and Tillie were busy serving drinks. Their laughter was as false as the words they said to the men. "I'd sure like to see Faye and Tillie out of the saloon."

Bess planted her hands on her hips. "It's their decision, and they can't change unless it's their idea. I have money put aside for both of them. But they will have to approach me with plans to leave town before they know of it."

Sage would have liked to talk to them more—to let them know their visit today was appreciated. "Will you tell them thanks and I wish them well?"

"Of course. And don't go washing that dress. You'll set your healin' back a week. I'll stop by and get it in the morning."

Emotion tugged at her heart. After tonight, she might never see Bess again. Being a bounty hunter meant every day could be her last day. She supposed that was true of everyone, but more so when a person earned her keep with a gun. The widow had become more than a friend, and they'd shared their inmost secrets—the agony of their hearts. "You're a special lady, Miss Bess. I won't ever forget you."

The woman's eyes pooled. "You're leaving aren't you?"

"Soon."

"Parker will be upset. He thinks highly of you."

"Leah needs him. Not me."

Bess startled. "You're wrong. So very wrong about him."

Sage adjusted the clothes in her arms. "I think I'll just slip on my boots and wear the dress to church."

"You won't reconsider?"

Sage understood Bess aimed her question at her leaving town instead of attending prayer meeting. "I've already made up my mind. I hope the girls here understand they have a gem in you." She turned and left the hotel before she gave in to all the sentiments that made her a woman.

When Sage arrived at the church, the last of the congregation was filing inside. Already weakness from the walk had latched on to her, but she must do this for Parker. Integrity walked with him, and she couldn't leave Rocky Falls without making sure the town's respect had been restored.

Preacher Waller's booming voice welcomed folks to the meeting as Sage slipped into the last pew and laid her bundle of clothes beside her. Midway on the left side sat Leah and her five boys, but they didn't see her. The church was larger than most and furnished with oak pews and a matching pulpit. Three windows on each side were open to allow a bit of fresh air. The July day had grown hot by late afternoon—much like the temperature would soon rise inside this building designated as a house of God.

Preacher Waller led them through three verses of "A Mighty Fortress Is Our God." The voices rang strong, even without a piano to accompany them.

"Tonight we have some special prayer concerns," he said. "Mrs. Felter has been put to bed. Ever since her dear husband was shot and killed by the McCaws, she's not been her normal self. Grief and the fact Aiden McCaw has not been arrested has made her ill. Yesterday, Doc Slader ordered her to bed.

"Last Sunday we voted to ask Marshal Timmons to resign in order to avoid public embarrassment. Since several of you thought he should be replaced, I asked him to step down. But he refused. The Bible speaks about the conduct of deacons and elders, but I tell you that Paul's mandates are for our elected officials too."

A man shouted a hearty "Amen."

Another claimed, "That'll preach, Brother."

As though spurred on by the affirmations, Preacher Waller stepped from behind the pulpit. "Our town deserves a man who is upright and moral, a man who loves God and His laws for man. We don't have that in Parker Timmons. We will be forced to call a special election. He's—"

Sage stood and grasped the back of the pew in front of her for physical support. "Preacher Waller, I don't believe you or these good people know the truth about what happened in the mountains. So I've come to make sure all of you fine folks have an understanding about what kept Marshal Timmons and me there."

"We don't want to hear about your unrighteous behavior." Preacher Waller shook his fist at her, but she'd faced outlaws and wild animals. He'd not deter her.

Sage fought the anger threatening to unleash in a most unholy manner. After all she was in God's house, and He honored truth, not lies. "I will continue whether you like it or not. The day I brought in Aiden McCaw for the murder of Mr. Felter, Marshal Timmons had just buried his brother, who was also murdered. That night, the McCaw gang broke Aiden out of jail and beat your marshal nearly to death. Then Marshal Timmons learned his nephews John and Davis were missing. The next morning, he rode out with me to find those boys and hopefully the McCaws. He had bandaged ribs, and his face was bruised and swollen, but he had a sworn duty to perform. Not a man among you would go with him. We found the McCaws with those boys and rescued them. In the process, I was shot. Marshal Timmons could have ridden back down the mountains with John and Davis. Instead he stayed with me because he knew I was dying. Your marshal tended to my wound and prayed over me." She paused. Not a sound came from the congregation, but Waller's face blanched.

"Yes, he prayed over me more than once. The reason it took us so long to get back was because he walked beside me to make sure I didn't fall off his horse. That's not a man who is immoral. That's a man who is dedicated to preserving the law and keeping folks safe. This town and this state need more men with integrity like Parker Timmons."

Waller raised one fist, then the other. "You have no right coming into my church and blaspheming."

"Every word I've told you is true." Sage swallowed the unfairness of his accusations. "I'm not an educated preacher like you, but I do know the Bible says the greatest commandment is love. Your marshal loves this town and the people in it. I think he's a man you'd want to keep—the kind of man you'd want your children to model their actions after."

She felt every eye on her, and suddenly her anger subsided to pity. These people were following a man who they believed spoke for God. The truth rang in their hearts, while their preacher's words echoed in their ears.

Preacher Waller stepped down from the pulpit. "Get out of my church. You have no right to be here among the righteous."

Sage glared at the man who judged a person's character by his own standards. "Is it your church or God's church? Did you write the Bible or did God give the words to ancient prophets?" Gathering up her belongings, she made her way to the door and down the wooden steps to the outside, where the air did not reek of hypocrisy.

The angry voice of Preacher Waller bellowed from the church. "Leah Timmons, if you walk out of here, you are no longer welcome in my home."

Sage refused to turn around and interfere with Leah's decision. Bess's words earlier resounded in her ears. Folks needed to decide for themselves where life would lead them.

"Leah, you heard me."

*Leah, think hard about what you're doing. You may need to
be strong sooner than you wanted.*

"Preacher Waller, I'm grateful for what you've done for me
and my sons, but I think it's time we returned to our own home."

Leah's and her sons' footsteps tapped a brisk procession behind Sage. She hadn't intended to turn friend from friend, but
only for the people of Rocky Falls to learn the truth about Parker.
Her inability to stay out of the way of a McCaw bullet had caused
the uproar, but her leaving Rocky Falls would help them all to
forget the rumors and resume the peaceful life they'd known
before the McCaws went on a murdering binge.

With a heart full of regret for Leah and her sons, Sage turned
to her friend. "Are you sure this is the road you want to take?"
With Leah's bonnet shielding her eyes, Sage couldn't see her
friend's face to detect fear for the unknown.

"I am very certain. Every day at the parsonage has been filled
with lectures and gossip and ugly accusations that are wrong. I
should have taken a stand sooner. Preacher Waller also said horrible things about Frank in front of the children."

"But it means returning to your ranch with the possibility of
the McCaws seeking revenge. Or have you decided to take Parker
up on his offer?"

"This afternoon I told Parker it was time I took care of my
own family. He has his own life without being saddled with a
widow and five boys. There's work to be done at our ranch, a
means for my family to eke out a living. You have shown me how
to be strong, and I'll forever be grateful. I've always depended on
others to help me and the children when Frank wasn't around.
No more. John has been urging me to stand tall, and he's already
told me how we can make the ranch work."

"I'm proud of you, Mama." John's words were wrapped in affection. "Preacher Waller is more interested in himself than helping the folks of Rocky Falls."

"We mustn't judge, son. But I agree."

John laughed, and he sounded like Parker. "Let's get our things from the parsonage and go home."

"Tonight?" Sage fretted that Leah's and John's eagerness ruled over common sense.

"Of course tonight," Leah said—and even added a giggle. "John, you get our wagon and horse at the livery while the rest of us fetch our belongings from the parsonage before Preacher Waller calls prayer meetin' to a close. I want to sleep in my own bed and greet the morning from my own front porch."

Sage wished they would reconsider, perhaps stay the night at the hotel. "I'd be glad to pay for a couple of rooms at the hotel. You could head home in the morning."

"Goodness, Sage. There's no reason for such luxury. The wagon ride home is about forty-five minutes. The boys and I have much to talk about, and the time will fly by."

Sage couldn't let go of her concern. "What if the McCaws are watching your ranch?"

"We can't live our lives in fear of what might happen." John's deepened voice resounded around them. Yes, he was a man.

"You're right, son," Leah said. "You and I know how to use a rifle, and one of the first things we're going to do is show the other boys how to handle one too. We're staying on the land your papa bought for us."

"I already know," Evan, the twelve-year-old said. "And so does Aaron. Mark will learn soon and then Davis."

Sage reached out to grasp Leah's hand. Parker would have a fine wife in this woman. She'd even be independent and determined.

Frustrated that Leah had made a decision without consulting him, Parker left a note on his desk for Wirt stating he was riding out to Leah's ranch to check on his family. He refused to think about anything happening to them, knowing the McCaws would use whatever means they could to pull him and Sage into the mountains. Why couldn't Leah have waited until the McCaws were brought in? Danger stalked everyone in this town, and she'd already been the outlaws' target twice.

The longer Parker rode, the more he fretted with what he might find, until he saw smoke curling from the chimney and the older boys working outside. Parker and Wirt had cleaned up the house after finding it torn apart, but not the barn. The family had plenty of work to do, more than these boys could manage. John met him by the well.

"What's going on?" Parker didn't attempt to hide his displeasure.

"We're home where we need to be." John wiped the sweat from his brow. "No more running from the McCaws and cowering under Preacher Waller."

The determination in John's words told Parker it was useless to try to talk him out of staying. "You've seen the McCaws in action."

John pointed to his rifle propped against the well. "This family is sticking together, and I dare anyone to try to stop us."

No point in arguing with an eighteen-year-old who thought he had all the answers. Besides, Parker had the same stubborn pride. "Let me talk to your mother."

Early the next morning, Parker rode out from Leah's ranch and back to town. He'd spent all of the preceding day helping John and his brothers put the barn in order, then checking on the cattle and mending a stretch of fence that the McCaws had destroyed. He'd lectured and warned and scolded, but it did no good. Leah was as obstinate as her sons. Parker grinned. It was good to see her full of gumption, and he could only pray they'd be safe.

With sunrise bringing in a new day, he needed to concentrate on how to go after the gang and how to handle Waller. His first stop would be to see if he could convince Sage to rest up another week. She probably wouldn't want to see him, but he didn't care. After yesterday, he was ready to tie her to the bed and put a lock on her room at Doc's.

Then he learned from Doc that Sage had left sometime before sunrise yesterday, and when Parker checked the livery, her pony was gone. As Parker placed one foot in front of the other on his way to the hotel to find out what Bess and Wirt knew about the situation, he hoped no one got in his way.

He flung open the door of the hotel and smelled coffee and breakfast. Both sent his stomach to complaining about lack of food, but he had business to tend to first.

"Bess," he called out. "You'd better not be hiding from me."

She walked from the kitchen with a towel in one hand and a mug of coffee in the other. "A pleasant mornin' to you, too, Parker."

He scowled, trying to find his manners. But fury had grabbed hold of him, and it would take wild horses to rein it in. "What is happening around here?" She held out the coffee to him, and he took it. He needed it.

"My guess is you found out about Sage attending prayer meetin' Wednesday night."

Bess knew it all. He could feel it in his bones. "That's just part of it."

"Perhaps Sage has left town?"

He blew out an exasperated sigh. Of course she knew Sage had left town. Women talk, and Sage considered Bess a friend. "I deserve to know what went on the other night."

"Why? Did she break the law? Did Waller file charges against her for disrupting his prayer meetin'?"

"'Cause I'm the marshal. At least I am today, and I'm not resigning."

Bess pursed her lips, then lifted her chin. "Parker Timmons, I suggest you calm down and drink your coffee before you come in here demanding things."

She was right; he was acting like a bear after a spring thaw. He took a big gulp of the hot brew, which he sputtered down the front of him, and forced a smile. "I'm sorry, Bess. Just don't like surprises, and I suppose you know Leah and the boys are back home."

"Good for her." She handed him a towel to wipe the coffee from his shirt. "That's better. Hold on to your temper, Parker Timmons, or you might find my iron skillet across your head."

Outlaws were easier to handle than a provoked woman. "Would you *please* tell me why Sage left town? She didn't say good-bye, and I'm worried about her."

"She did come by here on her way to prayer meetin' to pick up her clothes. I have no idea what went on there, except she was perturbed about Preacher Waller's condemning you for saving her life and trying to replace you as marshal."

Parker had been privy to more of what had gone on in a couple of the church services than he cared to mention. "I wish she'd have let me handle it."

"Your life is none of my business, but if you want my opinion, I'd be glad to give it."

He would have laughed if he'd not realized she was serious. "I want to hear it." He paused and thought about the evening Sage asked him not to visit her alone again. If she wanted a relation-ship with Wirt Zimmerman, then why did she confront Waller?

"Why do you look so mad?" Bess frowned.

"Because I am. Sage is the most confusing female I've ever met in my whole life."

"Listen to yourself. If you don't know what the problem is, then I'm not so sure I should tell you."

Bess was fast becoming as exasperating as Sage. "I'm calming down." He moistened his lips and took another generous gulp of coffee.

"That's better. I was told she defended you against Preacher Waller's accusations."

"I heard the same from Bob Culpepper. I'm sure Waller found plenty of Scripture to back up his claims."

"I'm sure she held her own."

Once more he affirmed the stirring in his heart about Sage. "I don't understand why she left town when the doc claimed she needed another two weeks to heal."

Bess shook her head. "She left because of the obvious."

"What obvious?"

Bess looked around as though she didn't want anyone else to hear. "Are you blind? She's in love with you. But for some reason she thinks you and Leah are supposed to be together."

"Leah?" Where had she gotten such a ridiculous idea? Parker had been overwhelmed in his life—fought in a war in which his side lost, faced down outlaws, been bitten by a snake and chased by a bear, and buried his brother—but he hadn't expected the woman he loved to leave town because she thought he should spend the rest of his life with another woman. Didn't he ask her to marry him? Didn't that stand for something? Sometimes Sage aggravated him to the point he didn't know if it was sunup or sundown.

"Say something," Bess said. "For the best marshal in the Rockies, for a man who is better than most with a pistol or a rifle, for a man who is getting mighty close to forty years old, you're downright pale with the idea of a woman loving you."

How did Bess manage to lay out his raw emotions like she could read his mind? He swallowed hard. "I don't suppose you'd understand how a man could feel like his rear had been filled with buckshot over something good." He downed his coffee in hopes he'd look more in control. "So she left town because of me?"

"Oh, I'm sure there's more to it. She might think you hung the moon, but you didn't hang the stars too. The McCaws murdered her husband, and she's dedicated a few years of her life to bringing them to justice. Then she found out something else about her deceased husband."

"As the marshal, I need to know what it is."

Bess shook her head. "Would you stop this 'I'm the marshal' talk? The only reason you want to know everything about Sage is because you're in love with her."

Bess's words clamored like a bell in his ears. If she had read the truth, who else knew his heart?

"What's got your tongue?"

Get a hold of yourself. "I still need to help bring in the McCaws."

"Yeah, ignore me. Can't tell me you don't fancy yourself married to her." Bess wagged a finger at him. "She found out about Charles being a part of the McCaw gang when they robbed a train in Denver some years back."

"And I suppose she thinks I knew about it?"

"Probably."

Parker nodded while his heart thumped against his chest. "I want to ride after her. She needs another gun to bring in those outlaws."

"She might need to hear how you feel about her."

He knew he loved her. *She* knew he loved her. What was he supposed to do, send up smoke signals? If only he didn't have so many other things to consider. "You're right, Bess. I don't want to lose her."

"Don't waste a single minute. Wirt Zimmerman is packing his things to go after her too. He's been talking mighty big about how he could settle down with a woman like Sage Morrow."

"We'll see whom she chooses." Parker handed her the empty coffee mug. He grinned. "I'm still the town's marshal and not a dandy of a US Marshal."

FORTY

Thursday morning, Sage and Hawk rode into the foothills, heading west to the mountains as sunrise graced the eastern horizon, her favorite time of the day. Pastel colors streamed across the sky, then faded into a brilliant blue. Charles used to call sunrise one of God's promises, just like a rainbow after a hard rain. The man who turned a phrase like a poet might have been an outlaw. At least the evidence stacked against him. If Charles had been part of a train robbery, he could have killed and robbed innocent folks. Yet . . .

Charles, a liar and an outlaw?

She swiped a tear and shoved the perplexing thoughts from her mind to focus on what needed to be done now: find a place to rest for a couple of days until her body regained strength. Riding west to where the small band of Ute camped had entered her mind, but she didn't want to burden Tall Elk. He cared for her, and she understood the pangs of unreturned love. Why would she want to put him through the same heartache? Better she camp alone and ponder the relationship between Charles and the McCaws than cause a good man to grieve.

Parker had said he loved her, but even if he really did, she wasn't the right woman for him. At least she was smart enough to see that.

The sun warmed her back, and she wanted to think it brought healing to her body and spirit. Hard to believe this beautiful land with the sounds of singing nature and bubbling streams and the beauty of summer growth could turn on a person with a change of weather. Like a friend who deserts you when the road gets steep and rocky. Had that been the circumstance with Charles and Aiden?

In the valley, bighorn sheep grazed on tender green shoots and drank deeply from the narrow Falls River that gushed and gurgled over smooth rocks. The animals' majestic stance and surefootedness contrasted to the type of sheep that Parker often spoke of. *Parker.* When would she be able to push him from her mind?

Purple and yellow wildflowers sprouted from obscure hideaways tucked in the rocks, defying what farmers called the nurturing of rich earth.

She remembered a satisfied life filled with contentment, when the difficult times were few and not so treacherous. People died but were not murdered. People laughed and babies were born, drowning the traces of any sorrow. Perhaps someday those moments could be recaptured in her life. She'd thought Parker might be the man to help her forget the ugliness of the past, but she'd been incredibly wrong. Finding love again only to lose to another, more-deserving woman only increased the ache in her heart.

No, she would not reach out to Tall Elk. Once she'd turned to him when Charles died, and she refused to do the same again because of Parker.

Parker and Leah deserved a good life after they had been separated as young sweethearts. Leah understood her need to be a strong woman for what lay ahead—from widowhood and comforting her growing sons who missed their papa to a future with Parker. Leah made a huge step last night in church when she stood up to Preacher Waller. Truth had a way of dividing those who attended church from those who clung to God. She'd like to find that relationship again.

By midmorning, exhaustion had depleted Sage's strength. She pushed her pony to a higher elevation where she could make camp. A rushing waterfall filled her ears, flowing around pine trees and over branches tossed across its waters. A deep sadness swept over her, much like she remembered when Charles was killed. She needed no explanation for the source, for the realization of who he had been and what he'd done hurt worse than his death. Before, he had been an honorable man who was murdered. Now he lay cold in the grave as an outlaw and a liar.

The longer she rode, the more she grieved. Yet she understood her tears and anguish were necessary. Hawk flew close by, as though he understood her shattered heart. But even with his shadow a frequent reminder of his presence as it slipped back and forth across her horse's neck, she had never felt more alone.

God, if You are really there, if You are the God I once trusted and believed, why has my life been broken? Am I being punished for something? Show me what I am supposed to learn.

When she heard nothing around her but the familiar calling of the wild, she realized one more time that God had deserted her.

Parker needed answers fast. Overnight a few things had changed, and he wasn't happy about not being consulted. Uncertainty began when Wirt announced that Sage planned to be ready Sunday noon to trek back into the mountains. The man was using her to get the McCaws, and the thought infuriated him. And Wirt's confession about his lack of experience didn't help Parker's mood.

To make matters more complicated, last night John didn't come back to the office after prayer meeting. Parker hadn't been concerned, thinking Leah might have wanted her son at the parsonage. But this morning he learned from Bob Culpepper about the ruckus during prayer meeting, and the undertaker-deputy said he'd seen Leah and her boys driving out of town just as the meeting let out.

FORTY-ONE

Aiden finished skinning the doe he'd brought down a few hours before. Already he could taste the roasted venison, but that wouldn't happen until tonight. Soon this time in the mountains would end, and the McCaw brothers would be eating and sleeping in a big fancy hotel. California sounded good. He'd never been to San Francisco, but he heard the weather was easier on a man's bones. Might even try ranching in New Mexico. Many parts were wild there, and the law would leave them alone.

Until then, he'd keep Parker and Sage on the trail after them in these mountains.

Late last spring, Quincy had the idea of paying Faye to supply them with information. Usually Quincy didn't have much to say, but he saw the warm weather would be coming to an end, and spending the winter in a frozen death trap didn't sit well with his steady cough.

A twinge of anxiety attacked Aiden, as if he had found himself about to step on a rattler without his boots. None of the McCaw brothers were getting any younger. No wives. No young'uns. Ever since the war, Aiden had looked out for his own, promising them a good life if they'd just stick together. They'd lost one brother in the war, the only one who had red hair besides Aiden. And Karl had died because of Charles Morrow and that no-account marshal. Mitch had grown harder through the years. He masked it with jokes, but Aiden had seen him blow a hole right through a man for looking at him strange. Rex was their best shot, but he'd met a girl in El Paso and wanted to get back to her. Jeb's simple mind often put him in the middle of crossfire, and Quincy had been spitting more and more blood with his coughing.

If ever Aiden had a reason to get the money due them, it was now. He hated Parker Timmons and the Indian bounty hunter worse than anything he'd come up against since the war. They'd turn over his money, and then they'd pay.

"Mitch," he called. "We're too close to Rocky Falls and need to move on."

"All right. I'm ready to end this."

"We all are. It's time to pull our ace. Sage rode across the foothills and into the mountains. My guess is she'll follow the Falls River and on across the Moraine Valley. We all know Parker will follow."

Mitch left the horses and made his way to where Aiden knelt beside the doe. "Have you heard from Rex?"

"I met him midway between here and Rocky Falls day before yesterday. We took a steeper trail so no one could follow our tracks. He's done a fine job churning trouble, and now he'll be trailing Sage."

"Is Quincy or Jeb going with me?"

"You don't need anyone. Tell our man Sage is in trouble and needs him."

FORTY-TWO

Friday, late morning, Parker checked the amount of ammunition in his saddle bags, and then added more. Nothing worse than being pinned down and out of ammo. He glanced at Wirt, who was securing his Winchester to his saddle. Earlier, he'd cleaned the rifle—twice.

"Sure you want to go?" Parker had a bad feeling about Wirt's inexperience. A real bad feeling.

"Yes. Time I did a few things besides sitting behind a desk and filing papers."

Parker nodded while queasiness pitched havoc with his stomach. He stared off down the street. The horses were saddled and supplies packed. Bob Culpepper stood on the boardwalk outside the office. The sun picked up a glint from the deputy's star above his heart.

Parker swung up onto his saddle. "Bob, I appreciate what you're doing."

"I'll do my best to keep things quiet."

"Parker!"

He turned at the frantic sound of a woman's voice. Bess hurried down the street. Ordinarily, her stout figure rushing toward him would have been comical, but the look on her face wiped any thought of humor from his mind.

"Parker, don't leave. I have to talk to you." She caught her breath, her face red.

He waited as she fanned herself. "What's wrong?"

"I think one of the girls at the saloon has been giving Aiden McCaw information."

"Who?" Parker dismounted.

"Faye." She sucked in another breath. "A few minutes ago, I overheard Tillie talking about Richard Edwards giving Faye money for information."

"Is Edwards still in town?"

"I don't think so."

Parker nodded at Bob. "Let's go see what Faye has to say. She can be your first arrest." His pulse sped to racehorse level. "With the mood I'm in, you might have to hold me back." Vivid images of Oden, Frank, Duncan, and Sage caused him to consider the consequences of responding to Faye like she was one of the McCaw gang.

"Are you all right?" Bob said.

"Yeah. I'm fine and ready to question Faye."

At the hotel, Faye hadn't climbed out of bed for the day. Bess walked up the creaky steps and pounded on the woman's door while Parker, Bob, and Wirt waited below. "I need you downstairs. Marshal Timmons wants to ask you a few questions."

Parker doubted if he'd have been as genteel.

Two more times, Bess pounded on Faye's door with no response.

"Bess, can't you open the door?" Parker's patience had worn thin. He needed to talk to Faye, and he needed to get on the trail.

Bess attempted to open the door. "It's locked, but I have a key."

Nearly ten minutes passed before Bess found the key and finally managed to open the door. "Faye, I've called out for you until I'm blue in the face." She gasped and stepped back into the hall.

"Bess, what's going on?" Parker lunged up the steps, yet he already knew what had happened.

"Blood everywhere." Bess's face paled as she stared into Parker's. "She's dead."

Richard Edwards. Parker now remembered where he'd seen the man. He was Rex McCaw.

Parker and Wirt rode on through the foothills, following Sage. She hadn't disguised her trail, as though she wanted him to ride after her. Or maybe she was offering herself as bait for the McCaws.

Parker hadn't intended for Bob's first duty as deputy to be tending to Faye's body. Her killer had slit her throat, typical for Rex McCaw—his brand on his murder victims. Faye's life had been snuffed out, and, regardless of what the woman had been or done, Parker felt a deep regret for the senseless killing. Why hadn't he noticed the resemblance between Richard Edwards and Rex McCaw? The outlaw had cleaned up and shaved, but the basic features were still there, and Parker had missed them. Overlooking the obvious frustrated him. He *should* have recognized Rex.

Faye had betrayed innocent people and caused their deaths, but she didn't deserve to die at the hands of a murderer. No one did.

"How long has Faye lived in Rocky Falls?" Wirt's voice broke through the quiet sounds of nature.

"About six months, I think. She rode in on the stage and immediately went to work at the saloon. The timing fits with what has happened. Aiden paid her for information, and she supplied it."

"What do you think she told him?"

Parker had contemplated the same thing. "She may have overheard a conversation between Bess and me or Frank. My brother spent a lot of time in the saloon. Aiden is clever." Parker paused. Faye's death had prompted him to consider a plot of seemingly impossible depth, yet Aiden had already proved himself a highly intelligent man. "If he had devised a plan to put Sage and me together, then he had someone trailing Sage and someone watching me. Faye fit the latter, and I'm sure Aiden could have kept track of Sage's travels."

"But the timing of this is crucial. How could Aiden have known when Sage was in Denver to time Oden Felter's murder and force you to contact the sheriff's office there for help? That's a far-fetched idea."

"Do you have a better one? Maybe he hoped Oden's murder would prompt her to respond. No one coerced her. I know it sounds ridiculous, but Aiden is desperate for whatever it is that Sage and I have. If it has something to do with Charles Morrow, then he's had seven years to plan. Sage believes it's the money the gang claimed Charles had. If that's the case, it must be a large sum."

"Has it occurred to you that her husband was killed about the same time their brother Karl was shot?"

Parker nodded. "Hadn't put the two deaths together. Anyway, I'd be to blame for Karl's death, not Sage. About four months later, the US Marshal who killed Karl died too. No connection to Sage."

"So if I'm hearing you correctly, you think Aiden had people watching you and Sage until the opportune time to bring both of you together—for an unknown reason."

"Purely speculation, Wirt. But that's what I'm thinking."

"Sounds like you've been drinking. No one goes to that much trouble without making it known what he wants."

Parker wished he knew more about Charles Morrow. "Ruthless men, no matter what side of the law, are ruled by money, power, or vendetta."

"Maybe you'll find out the truth."

Or maybe Parker would go to his grave with the questions still hammering in his head.

"I trust you have the map and we're on the right trail." Wirt said, as Parker led them along the foothills toward the mountains.

"You scared?" Parker had heard enough of the US Marshal

and how he knew he'd be true to his badge—and his feelings for Sage—when it came to facing the McCaws. *Bravado* best described Wirt. Parker should have left him in Rocky Falls.

"What makes you think I'm scared?"

"Oh, you haven't shut up since we hit the foothills. Good thing we weren't planning to sneak up on anyone."

"Just making small talk, Marshal." The irritation in his voice told Parker to back off. No point making an enemy when he'd need the man to cover his back.

"How long have you been a US Marshal?"

"Five years."

"I 'spect they appreciated what you learned in law school."

"It helped."

"What did you do before then?"

"School and farmed."

Hearing bad news was not one of Parker's favorite pastimes. And he'd heard so much of it lately that he craved good news. "Ever do much camping in the woods when you were a kid?"

"Are you checking my credentials?"

"Nope," Parker said. "Just making small talk."

Wirt chuckled. "Guess I had that one coming since I wasn't honest up front."

So the man had a sense of humor. "The way I look at it, if we're working together, we need to work harder at knowing each other."

Wirt nodded. "Some would say your reasoning is why we shouldn't."

If this man would only shove his pride into his back pocket. "I look at it this way. If I like you, then I'm going to do all I can to make sure you don't end up in a pine box."

"And if you don't, then I'm a dead man?"

For the pure stubbornness of it, Parker decided not to answer. They rode on about another half mile.

"How did you become a lawman?" Wirt said.

"A US Marshal was a friend of mine. I admired his guts and determination. He knew how I wanted to help the people of this state grow, so about eight years ago I decided to run for town marshal."

"What's his name?"

"Adam Moore. Got shot. Don't know how it happened. One of the finest men I ever knew."

"Friends are hard to find and even harder to replace. I never met him, but I heard enough from the other marshals to know he was respected."

Maybe Wirt wasn't so bad after all.

"I've lost two good friends who were marshals," said Wirt. "Made me stop and think about my choice to come out here, but I couldn't handle being a deputy behind a desk any longer. I wanted the opportunity to bring in a wanted man. My own reasons may have been selfish, but after talking with the family of those killed in Rocky Falls, I want to see this ended."

"You picked a bad gang."

"I realize all outlaws care only about themselves. And I never expected to meet up with Sage Morrow. Other bounty hunters keep their names quiet to protect themselves, but a woman like Sage is a different story."

Did Wirt think about her night and day?

"I bet she's at home in those mountains." Wirt pointed to a distant snowcapped peak. "They sure are pretty. But I'd rather look at them than ride over them."

"Better hope your horse is surefooted."

"I agree. Why is it when I bring up Sage, you get all riled? Are you sweet on her?"

Parker changed his mind about giving the man a chance at being a decent human being. "You haven't been shy about your feelings for her either. Besides, a grown man doesn't refer to his affections for a fine woman as 'sweet.'"

"So you are."

"I didn't say anything of the kind. Just correcting the way you talk about her."

"When this is over, we'll see whom she chooses."

Parker buried his anger, gazing off at a herd of bighorn sheep. Must have been fifty of them. Beautiful animals. "What do you think about sheep? I mean the kind some folks raise."

"Sheep? I don't know. Some folks eat them, but not me. Why?"

"I like stories about sheep that remind me of men." When Wirt didn't respond, Parker kept going. "There's a story about a shepherd going after one sheep and leaving ninety-nine behind. That's how I feel about Sage. If we weren't trailing the McCaws, even if it was the dead of winter and twenty below zero, even if it meant riding through these mountains alone and she despised me, I'd still be looking to find her."

FORTY-THREE

Sage felt refreshed after a restful night's sleep and had ridden farther into the mountains to where she had first found Aiden. She'd found yarrow to brew and had been drinking it steadily. The waterfall cascading near her flowed down into a steady stream that contained mountain trout, and she'd caught one yesterday and today. Long ago Sage realized that understanding how to survive in the mountains took away the fear of traveling over them. Tall Elk had shown her how to take the tender bark of a balsam fir, grind it fine, and mix it with fat for a filling meal. He'd also shown her how to use the inner bark of spruce and some pine trees for food. Ute children often ate the inner bark of a Trembling Aspen as a treat. Many plants, berries, and edible pods of the area would keep her alive and healthy. Tall Elk and his people — her people — had taught her wisely. But when Tall Elk wanted her to become his, to show her again the way of a man and a woman, she'd refused. He deserved a woman who loved him with all of her heart.

Why her mind whirled with memories of Tall Elk was a mystery. Or maybe the preoccupation was a way to keep the truth about Charles from breaking her completely. Her thoughts should be consumed with the McCaws and how to outsmart them. They could very well be watching her, calculating the right time to walk into her campsite. Yet she felt certain they wanted her and Parker together. It was the why. Always the why. Only Aiden McCaw knew the connection, and he hadn't offered it.

Saturday morning, gray fog blanketed the mountain peaks.

Normally she anticipated its lifting to behold a sun-kissed day. But this morning it seemed to stalk her like a veil of death—for that was where she headed. She finished a mug of tea and went back to sleep. Maybe her dreams would be better than reality.

Sage slept into the midafternoon, and when she awoke a strange eeriness enveloped her. She'd fallen asleep with her rifle in her hand, and immediately she was alerted to something. But what?

Not five feet away, Hawk perched like a regal guard keeping vigil. He turned to look at her, but nothing about him indicated trouble. She studied the thick variegated green brush and trees. A light breeze whispered through the branches and touched her face. Was a storm forming even in the midst of the brilliant sun-light brimming off the stream's whitecaps?

She shivered in the knowledge she was not alone. And the presence did not take the form of man or animal. Hawk widened his wings and lifted gracefully into the air, leaving her alone. She started to call him back but changed her mind. A mixture of fear and awe wrapped its cloak around her. The unseen enemy always had the advantage. Sage stood and waited with her finger resting on the trigger of her Winchester.

Before living with the Ute, she had no concept of or use for the mystical. She discarded their beliefs in the spirit world, leaving their superstitions behind. But this was unlike anything she'd ever experienced or heard about from her mother's people.

Could it be God had decided to answer her prayers for His presence? The thought frightened her and filled her with an awkward hope, as though she could rationalize the strangeness. The sweet aroma of pine wafted through the air, the most fragrant of all mountain scents. Swinging around to an aspen tree, she expected to see someone or something.

"God, if You are here and want my attention, I'm listening." Her own words shook her. The great Creator didn't speak to those who had abandoned Him, those who were angry at how He'd directed life.

"What have I done that You have made a mockery of my feelings for Charles?"

She remembered how God had spoken to those in the Bible, not in the fury of nature or in deafening splendor, but in the still, quiet breeze. Like now.

Heat filled her boots, as though she stood too close to a fire. But she stood on brush. The sensation slowly moved up her legs, and she didn't know what to think of it. Was this a way to die? The heat circled her thighs and hips, ever mounting. Her heart raced, and she wondered if she should step into the cold stream. The sensation rose to her waist and up to where the bullet had pierced her flesh. Sage held her breath. She steadied herself to keep from toppling over from the intensity, but the pain stopped. Gasping, she searched the skies for answers that did not come. The heat climbed higher to her heart, where the misery of bitterness and the piercing of her soul nearly consumed her. A burden lifted. Was she dreaming? For the first time in years, she felt free and whole. The heat continued, swirling around her neck and face until it spiraled to the top of her head and vanished.

She knew without hesitation that she'd been touched by God. He did love her. He had answered her prayers in a way so like God but so unlike what mere flesh expected. Few would ever believe what had happened. She wasn't so sure she believed it herself. Most folks discredited miracles, saying they only happened in the Bible. But God had not only healed her heart and softened it once again for Him, but He'd also healed her body. More important was the knowledge He had reached down to restore her to Him. The chasm of her soul had been filled.

With tears streaming down her face, she walked beyond the thicket to the edge of a rock precipice. Sage breathed in deeply and forgave Charles. The years of hate for the men who had killed him and their baby washed over her. But she must put aside the bitterness. With supernatural courage, she forgave the McCaws.

Hawk called out to her and flew to her side. "The mysteries of God." She stroked his soft plumage and laughed. "Who can explain them? I'm back, Hawk. I'm back to where I'm supposed to be." She swallowed the emotion. "I've always been under God's care. Just didn't have the sense to know it."

FORTY-FOUR

S age made better time than I expected." Parker kneeled beside a narrow path that wound up into the mountains. "Be glad it hasn't rained. Someone's following her. My guess is Rex McCaw." He'd figured the McCaws were watching Rocky Falls for signs of anyone coming or going. Made him feel like a fool. If only he and Wirt had been able to round up a posse or figure out what they wanted.

"Do you have any idea where she might be?" Wirt pulled his binoculars from his saddlebag.

"Possibly near where she found Aiden. Let's see where this trail leads us." He watched Wirt study the mountains. "See anything?"

"Nothing. What are you thinking?"

"She needs time to heal, so she's probably hiding out a few days until she's feeling better. Remember she said Sunday noon."

"You think we'll find her today?"

"She'll most likely find us." Parker glanced in all directions, looking for signs of Hawk and taking a panoramic view of the valley floor, the trail behind them, and where she'd ridden into the mountains. He'd spent enough time with Sage to understand she was a woman of her word. Yet in the back of his mind lingered the nagging thought about the McCaws getting to her first, and her injuries slowing her response time. That kept him focused and pushing ahead. He continuously reminded himself she had learned survival skills from the Ute, and determination rode with her as faithfully as Hawk.

"Only thing I see are a few deer on the other side of the valley." Wirt handed Parker the binoculars. "When does winter hit the lower elevation?"

"Around September."

"Not long off. Are the McCaws from these parts?"

Parker appreciated Wirt's line of thought. Getting to know the enemy gave a man the edge. "Mississippi is where they're originally from. They went through the war together and lost a brother, but they never went home. Rumors are they were part of Quantrill's Raiders. That's where they learned how to raid. About nine years ago, they rode through this area, killing and stealing. Then they moved into Texas for a while, always avoiding the law. This area seems to suit them best. Hard for me to figure out since this is where their brother was killed."

"How many brothers?"

"Five of them are still alive. Karl was the one shot a few years back. Aiden, Mitch, Quincy, Rex, and Jeb."

Wirt whistled. "I'd like better odds."

"I'm sure the folks they killed felt the same way." They led their horses around a rocky incline.

"Whenever you're trying to stop outlaws who'd rather see you dead, it's bad."

Parker noted Sage's pony's tracks stopped abruptly at a fork. He bent to study the sparse brush choking its way up from the rocky path. She'd purposely covered her tracks to keep the Mc-Caws or even Parker from following her. "I've lost the trail."

"She didn't disappear."

"Stay here while I scout around." Parker searched around them, looking for the obvious path that a woman who nursed a bullet wound would take. But she wouldn't take the easier path. Not Sage Morrow. He left his horse and hiked several feet over the roughest terrain until he found the faint imprint of a boot on the opposite side of a fallen fir. A short while later, he led Wirt on her trail again.

The horses splashed across a narrow stream, the whitecaps lifting and falling as though in a hurry to get somewhere. At times his life had seemed that way until Sage rode into town. He smiled in remembering how she claimed not to like lawmen and politicians. He was mad enough that day to forget she was a woman. His heart had taken a big dive since then, and, like a fish flopping around on dry land, he didn't know how to act. He wanted to find her now—not to convince her to marry him or make sure she was healing proper but to gaze into her eyes and see what her lips could not say.

"You're a praying man," Wirt said, not as a question, but as a statement.

"I am." He stopped to listen to the grating call of a raven to make sure it was a bird and not a man. He gripped his rifle. The bird flew from the branches of an aspen and eased his mind. Its blue-black feathers reminded him of Sage's hair.

"Do you pray before you shoot a man?"

Parker hadn't thought about what he did in those terms. "I pray for lawbreakers to be stopped, and for God to use me in whatever way He sees fit. If I enjoyed killing a man, then I'd be no better than a murderer."

They rode toward a clearing but hid themselves in the outer trees. When the forest grew thick, they dismounted and walked their horses. Just when Parker was certain he'd lost her trail, he'd see a break of twigs or trodden brush.

"Why did you ask about my faith?" Parker said.

"Curious. That's all. My folks never understood why I became a US Marshal. In fact, they told me not to come around."

"Why?"

"They're Quakers."

A Quaker was the last thing Parker ever thought Wirt might be. "What changed your mind about peace-loving folks?"

"Oh, it's a long story. Sometimes I think my folks found me on their back porch." His nervous laugh told Parker the man had a few doubts about the choices he'd made. "I never had an argument about how Quakers view violence and life in general. But I wanted to make a difference in the West, make it safe."

"Have you tried talking to your folks about how you feel?"

Wirt didn't answer right away, as though he had to pick and choose his words. "There's more to it. I was supposed to marry a Quaker girl who didn't see things like I did. Left her at the altar, so to speak. Chose law school over her. Didn't handle it proper."

Parker thought back over the messes he'd made in his life. More than one regret had left its mark. "In my opinion, the best way to get rid of guilt and bad feelings is to face them head-on."

"Have you ever done it?"

How many nights had he lain awake, thinking about the times he'd flown at Frank about his lazy ways? He never had a chance to make it right with his brother before he was killed. "Not as often as I should have."

"I still think about her now and then."

Was Wirt pursuing Sage out of real affection or rebellion against his parents' way of life? "What about Sage?"

"She's special. I won't deny that. Life sure can be complicated."

Parker reined in his horse and held up his hand to silence Wirt. To the left of them, Sage stood on a high boulder. She waved and motioned them on. Her black hair flowed down her back, and he could envision her earth-colored eyes and sweet smile. Parker glanced up at the sky and laughed: high noon.

Sage had thought long and hard about what to say to Parker about mending her relationship with God. In the end, she decided the best way to show her change of heart would be for him to see it. She still loved him, and she still believed he and Leah should recapture what they once had. But when she said her final good-bye, he would know she had turned her life over to God. Right now the serious matter before all of them was capturing the McCaws before anyone else was killed.

The questions about Charles remained unanswered, and she knew her own temperament well enough to know she'd not rest until the past made sense. No matter how difficult it was to face.

"Hawk, we have company." Sage lifted her gaze to a slender-branched birch tree. Of course, he'd seen Parker and Wirt coming long before she did. She shook her head and inwardly laughed. Two men and one woman alone in the mountains. Preacher Waller would have much to talk about in the coming weeks. She hoped they all lived to hear it.

By the time Parker and Wirt climbed the narrow path to her camp, she had coffee brewing and a rabbit roasting over a fire.

"You're in time for dinner," she said.

Parker dismounted. He looked pleased to see her, or maybe what she saw was wishful thinking on her part. "We followed our noses and our grumbling stomachs. You gave me a tough trail."

"Good. I had things to do before today." She tossed Wirt a smile. "I told you Sunday noon."

He returned the gesture. "You look real healthy for a woman who took a bullet."

"Might say I'm a miracle."

Parker tied his horse to a sapling. "The mountains have a way of curing whatever ails you."

In more ways than she cared to divulge. "Any trouble getting here?"

Parker shook his head. "Had a feeling we were being watched. Wirt here kept looking over his shoulder."

"Just covering our rear."

"Any problems in Rocky Falls?" She thought about Preacher Waller and his influence on the small town.

"Another death," Parker said.

Her gaze flew to his. "Who?"

"Faye, one of the girls at the saloon. Bess overheard a conversation about giving her money, but before we had time to question her, she'd been killed."

"Edwards was working for the McCaws?"

"I think he's Rex McCaw. My guess is Faye's the one who supplied Aiden with information."

An image of the attractive woman rose in Sage's mind. "I met her. She came with Bess to visit me earlier this week. I'm sorry to hear what happened."

"So am I." Parker walked her way. The thought of stepping into his arms nudged at her, but she locked it deep in her heart. Instead, she turned her attention to the rabbit, crackling and spitting over the fire. "If you have mugs, the coffee is ready." She gave in to the pounding in her chest and stole a glance at Parker. He stared back, and for a brief moment she allowed the joy of love to fill her. With a catch in her throat, she turned away before he could read the truth. Parker and Wirt retrieved their mugs from their saddlebags.

"How are you feeling?" Parker said.

"Better than I have for a long time." That part was true. She reached for her knife balancing on a rock by the fire and cut off a chunk of meat to give him. "It's a little hot." She did the same for Wirt and then herself.

"Did you leave Bob Culpepper in charge, or did other men step forward to help?"

He bit into the rabbit. "Only Bob. The ones who wanted to ride with us or be deputized weren't old enough."

"Like John?"

"Exactly. I'm not yanking our future to fill saddle space."

She studied him. His words and his heart would be a part of her forever.

Parker grinned. "Bob said he'd take over as marshal if I got killed."

Wirt laughed. "He said he'd catch 'em, hang 'em, and bury 'em. He'd be Rocky Falls' one-man show. Maybe those who can't obey the law will think twice about an undertaker wearing a badge and carrying a rifle." Wirt took a bite of the rabbit. "This tastes mighty fine, Sage."

"Thanks." She started to comment about his mama raising him with good manners, but chose not to. This wasn't a time for small talk. Instead, it was a time for figuring out how to stay alive and bring in the McCaws. "What else is going on?"

"Found out about the telegram you received from Denver," Parker said.

The one naming Charles in a train robbery. "Did you know about his involvement? Looks like Charles lived two lives."

"I'm real sorry."

She could tell he meant every word. "It definitely helps us unravel the connection between him and the McCaws. All we have to figure out is what links all of us together, and what they want from you and me."

Wirt studied her, making her feel more than a little uneasy. He needed to look at her like ... like she was a man. "Are you sure you're all right?"

Parker choked on something.

"I'm fine," she said. "The McCaws and I have a history, and I intend to be part of stopping their future. They've roamed this country for too long, frightening people with their murdering and thieving ways."

"We need a plan," Wirt said.

"That's why we're here." Parker tossed a piece of rabbit Hawk's way. "They have greed on their side. We have our wits."

"I've been thinking about where I first found Aiden," Sage said.

"My thoughts are kin to yours," Parker said. "My guess is they're not far from there."

"We need to clear this campsite, or they'll be on us by sundown. I built the fire to alert them. Possibly throw them off."

"Let's clear the ground and pile some stones around it before we leave." Parker pulled out his knife and cut another piece of rabbit. "I'm not hightailing it back down the mountain this time without the McCaws."

Hawk lifted his wings and soared into the air. The bird called out, possibly alerting her to danger. "Sunday dinner just got cut short." She stood and watched the direction in which Hawk flew. The beginning of the end.

FORTY-FIVE

Aiden intended to stay hidden from Timmons and Sage until Mitch returned. Then everything would fall into place. He'd learned the man riding with the pair was US Marshal Wirt Zimmerman. No threat there. Aiden had learned his lesson from the last time Parker rode with a US Marshal. Karl was buried in these mountains as a reminder.

Parker and Sage obviously thought the McCaws could be brought in. Were they fools? Charles was dead. Sage nearly killed. Parker beat unconscious. What a joke when the law had been trying to catch them for over fifteen years. The folks of Rocky Falls would know what happened to anyone who double-crossed the McCaws when they found three bodies dumped outside of town.

Quincy had a bad night, coughing up blood and breathing hard. This morning he couldn't hold his mug of coffee for the shaking. Scared Aiden a bit, but he'd not let on. "Cain't you stop that hackin'?"

Quincy continued to fill the air with a raspy, breathless sound. Aiden sucked in his own breath, wishing it to end. Soon they'd get Quincy to the finest doctor in Denver. He'd be fixed up in no time at all.

Jeb made his way to Aiden's side and sat down beside him. "You think Quincy's gonna die?" he whispered.

Aiden fought the urge to knock him flat. "That's a stupid thing to ask." He cursed. "Don't let me hear it again."

"I heard Quincy say it. Yes, I did," Jeb said. "He said he'd probably die before we got our hands on the money. What about the rest of the money from the other jobs? I wanna know. Tell me, Aiden, where's the rest of it?"

Aiden grabbed him by the shirt. Jeb didn't need to know the money was gone. "It's hid in a good spot. Plenty of it. But we need this to set us square from Karl's dyin'. Understand?" He released Jeb and sent him flying backward over a fallen log.

"I don't want another brother coming up dead," Jeb said.

Aiden refused to think about any of them dying. He reached over and offered Jeb a hand up. "He won't die from his cough. I'll get him to a doctor soon." He tossed a look at Quincy bent over with a hoarse sound that seemed to come from his toes. "How about a little whiskey to cut it?"

Quincy nodded, but he still couldn't speak for his gasps of air.

Aiden headed for his saddlebag and the whiskey. He was ready for this all to end.

Forty-Six

Parker made sure all three of them took turns keeping a careful vigil on the rocky path that led to their new campsite. Allowing no surprises from the McCaws bettered the chance that the three would stay alive. Their plan was simple: wait until nightfall, overpower the guards, grab their weapons, and hobble the gang's horses. But things were never as easy as they sounded, especially when desperate outlaws were willing to take a gamble. For that matter, though, Parker believed he and Sage were just as desperate to bring the gang to justice.

"My turn to keep an eye on the trail," Wirt said with one hand wrapped around his rifle barrel. "Who knows? There may be one less McCaw after my watch."

"Make sure it's not one less US Marshal," Sage said as Wirt headed to the top of the hill that overlooked a deep gulley and a narrow trail leading up to them.

"I'd have it coming for trying to bring in outlaws with no experience."

"No man wanting to uphold the law has a bullet coming to him," Parker said.

Wirt swung back around, his face pale and his features drawn. "I wanted to do this myself—be the brave US Marshal. I looked forward to handing over the bounty money to Sage and escorting Aiden's rear to Denver." His gaze lifted to the higher elevations, then settled on them again. "When this is over, I'll find some way to make it up to you."

Parker nodded in the heavy silence and read fear and regret

in Wirt's face. What was he not saying? Or had reality settled on the man? Wirt headed to his post with slumped shoulders. They all had their demons who poked fun at their semblance of courage and called them cowards. Parker hoped they all lived to talk about the tense hours leading up to capturing the McCaws.

Parker leaned back against a rock as tall and wide as a man and studied Sage across from him. With her hat pulled down over her eyes to shield them from the sun, he couldn't read her well. He caught her attention where she sat cross-legged on the ground. "You scared me when I found out you were gone. I mean, I know you can take care of yourself, but—"

"Oh, Parker, I bet you were madder than a wet hen."

He grinned. "I was that too."

She stretched her legs and scuffed her heel into the dirt. "This part of my life will soon be finished. Not sure what I'll do then." She sighed. "I've done this for enough years. It's time I put roots down again." She tossed him a smile. "Wear dresses more often than britches."

Did that mean there was hope for the two of them? "What about family?"

"My folks still live in southern Colorado. I need to apologize to my father for the way I acted when he voiced his misgivings about Charles. Then I need to figure out what I want to do with my ranch." She picked up a rock and bounced it in her hand, as though nervous. "Living where Charles and I began has too many memories."

"You could settle down in Rocky Falls." He chuckled. "I could deputize you, and together we'd keep the no-accounts out of town."

She didn't respond. At least she hadn't turned down the idea. With his heart hammering like a hummingbird's wings, he dared to venture a little closer to this woman who had come to mean so much to him in so short a time. He sat beside her on the hard ground.

"I never heard the name Sage before. Most beautiful name I could ever imagine."

Sage's gaze snapped to him, wide-eyed. Almost fearful.

"What did I say?"

She blinked and glanced away. "Parker Timmons, too many times I wonder about you."

"In a good way?"

"You frighten me."

How could he frighten her? He was a man in love with a beautiful, courageous woman. He willed his skittish nerves to calm a bit. He stared at her, but her gaze flitted everywhere but at him. "Tell me how your mama and papa came up with your pretty name."

A smile crept over her full lips. "Papa wanted his daughter to seek out truth and wisdom above all other things."

"I see that in you."

"You're kind." She toyed with the rock in her hand. "I continue to tell you more than I should—about my life."

"I want you to trust me. And I apologize for not telling you about Charles being involved in a train robbery. We've been through a lot in such a short time. Makes people ... a man and a woman close." If he could take her into his arms, he would.

She slowly turned to face him, and her eyes were moist. Could it be he'd chiseled a hole in the wall of her heart? "Parker, Leah and those boys need you."

"My invitation to Leah was to give her and her boys a safe place to live. Nothing else. I fretted about her not being strong enough to be a mama and a papa to those boys." He still could not read her emotions and so ventured on. "I'd rather have a family of my own, eight children with black hair and brown eyes the color of rich earth. I'd like them all to be girls who were independent and determined to reach out and take a fistful of life."

Sage paled. Had he gone too far? "I think ... I think a few boys would be nice."

His throat went dry. "Then we need to figure out how to get out of these mountains in one piece."

"Are you sure about this?" Her lips quivered.

"I love you, Sage, and I want us to spend the rest of our lives together."

"What about your dreams of being a politician? What would your friends and opponents feel about a half-Ute woman as your wife?"

"That she loves and supports her husband. And if he doesn't do a good job, she has a hawk that will put him in his place."

She trembled. "I'm so unsure."

"Do you love me?"

She stared at the dirt and then upward at the cloudless sky.

Before Parker could form his next words, Wirt signaled for them. Parker and Sage hurried to his post.

"Two men have found the other camp." Wirt handed Parker the binoculars. "One of them is a man I've never seen, but the second man wanted your job as marshal."

Parker grabbed the binoculars and studied both of the Mc-Caws. "That's Quincy, and the other one must be Rex, all cleaned up, which is why we didn't recognize him in town. He must have gotten a good laugh at us." He handed the binoculars to Sage. "Let's see if we threw them off our trail."

"Can't believe we're this close," she said.

"Wish we were a little closer," Wirt said. "I'd like to pick them off."

"No, Wirt," she said. "Leah and Mrs. Felter could split the reward money and take care of their children. I want the whole gang to face trial and let justice prevail."

Wirt threw her a curious look of admiration and awe. Parker assumed he was wondering how he could win her for his own. Except it wouldn't happen now.

"I'll honor your wishes, Miss Sage, unless a McCaw has a rifle pointed at one of us." Wirt stared back at the area where they'd originally met up with Sage.

"It may be quicker than you think." Sage handed Wirt his binoculars. "They're looking hard for our trail. I'm going to saddle up and be ready to ride out after them. Lead them in a circle."

"I agree," Parker said. "Wirt, you keep watch, and we'll get your horse. Tonight we'll have them trussed up like pigs."

"And it'll finally be over," she said and tossed a smile at Parker.

Parker shoved his emotions into his pocket while they readied the horses. For now, bringing in those killers took precedence over any affairs of the heart or what the gang had done to Oden, Frank, and Charles.

"Parker, we all have a job to do, and we have to work together." Sage's voice lifted barely above a whisper. "This has nothing to do with hatred or revenge but a chance to bring in a gang of killers. Both of us might lose our heads with this, but we can't. You've lost a brother and friends. I've lost a husband and a child. What we feel is what others experience when selfishness and greed destroy a loved one. I'm praying for the three of us to have wisdom."

Her words, the sound of her voice, the calmness clear in her eyes puzzled him. "Things have changed with you," he said.

"Yes. I let God bring me back to Him." She swung up onto her saddle. "Once you asked me why I wouldn't let a man love me. I left that Sage behind. I do love you, and—"

"They're riding off," Wirt called.

The words he longed to hear would have to wait. "Later we'll talk," Parker said. "Later we'll plan our future."

Sage allowed Parker to lead the way after the McCaws. He knew this part of the Rockies better than she, and she trusted him more than she'd done in the past. Odd, the confidence came easily, one of the benefits of faith. Wirt rode behind her. The only sound from any of them came from the creak of their saddles and their horses clomping over the terrain. Neither a bird nor an unseen creature in the woods uttered a cry while Hawk flew in and out of her vision.

They climbed the lower elevation of a taller peak and then steadily higher, holding back from the two McCaws but always keeping them within sight of the binoculars. She watched Parker continue ahead until she memorized the ripples of his back beneath his shirt and the way he carried himself in the saddle. Once she'd done that with Charles. She hoped it wasn't a bad omen.

Why had Charles married her when he'd led another life? For the past few days, she'd given a lot of thought to the idea that maybe he had intended to leave the outlaw life behind and live respectably. His mother claimed she never knew where he traveled other than to his ranch farther north in Colorado.

Another matter needling her was that after his murder, neither the local law nor the state would go after his killers. Did they know about Charles's dealings and didn't want to tell her or any of the family? Maybe they thought she'd survived enough tragedy without learning the truth about her deceased husband.

Parker held up his hand, and she and Wirt stopped. Sage glanced ahead to a roaring waterfall rushing over slippery rocks, then crashing straight down into a green swirling pool. Her gaze flew back to the middle of the stream where two black bears splashed and fished. Two cubs wrestled on the bank close to where the three rode. One of the cubs cried out, sounding very much like a human baby. Perhaps the other cub had gotten too playful and bitten, but one of the two adult bears—obviously the mother—whipped her attention to the three riders. Fury rode on her haunches as she splashed her way toward them.

Wirt's horse screamed. Sage held on to her pony while glancing back to check on Wirt. He held on to his panicking horse, but the mama bear seemed to have targeted him. The horse bucked, sending Wirt flying into the bear's path. Sage whirled around and placed her pony between him and the advancing bear, who looked to be around three hundred pounds. She clicked her teeth, and blew out her fear and anger. None of Sage's instinctive ways with animals could stop a bear who sensed her baby had been hurt.

"Grab your horse," she said.

Wirt scrambled to his feet and grabbed his horse's bridle and then the reins. Sage held her breath, praying for time as she yanked out her rifle. Her pony had pranced back and left a clear path for the bear to get to Wirt. Teeth bared, the she-bear moaned and swatted.

Sage lifted her rifle and aimed. She hated firing the shot and allowing the McCaws to know where they were. Pulling the trigger, she sent a bullet flying into the bear's neck. Another shot sounded after hers. Parker had fired too, but a quick glimpse showed he had problems with the second bear. Wirt snatched his rifle from his saddle and fired into the bear that was still moving toward Parker. The bear ceased to move. Only the cubs survived.

The quiet that followed gave all three of them time to catch their breath and survey the landscape. Sage found Hawk nearby—agitated with the turmoil.

"We've got to get out of here," Parker said. "Before all of the McCaws have us trapped."

Sage nodded, wondering about the cubs, who sniffed at the female. Maybe they were old enough to find food. She hoped so. The part of her that cared for animals wanted them to survive ... just not at the expense of Parker's and Wirt's lives.

Wirt struggled to calm his mare, but she remained skittish, not allowing him to lift his foot into the stirrup.

Sage dismounted. "Take my pony."

"I don't need a woman to handle my horse." He jerked on the mare's bridle in an effort to gain control. The mare snorted and pranced, her eyes wild and full of terror.

"I can calm her," Sage said. "Let me try so we can get out of here."

"Put aside your pride and let her do what she does best."

Parker's voice echoed around them. "If the McCaws had any doubt as to where we are, they don't now."

Wirt stepped out of Sage's way and slapped the reins into her hand. "See what you can do."

Keeping her gaze soft and unfocused, she stood in front of the fallen bear and gave the horse a loose rein as far back as possible. Sage wished they were in a closed area so she could release the horse. "Step back. She needs as much space as possible to calm down. Does she have a name?"

"No," Wirt spoke softly. He finally understood.

Sage used her body language and voice to invite the horse to approach, keeping her own posture nonthreatening. "The bear's dead," she whispered repeatedly. "It won't hurt you." As the horse calmed, Sage inched closer. "Look to the side of you. See the grass? Take a nibble."

Slowly the mare ceased to tremble and began to look around her. Even as she approached, Sage kept her position between the horse and the bear. Soon she rubbed the mare's withers and gently examined her for any injuries. She straightened and patted the horse's neck, then placed her cheek next to the mare's nose and slowly exhaled. "See how calm you are? It's all over. I'm going to lead you around the dead bears, but you're going to be all right. No need to jump. No need to panic."

Sage wished she could feel as confident about the time ticking away, knowing that each moment brought the McCaws closer to them.

FORTY-SEVEN

Twice Parker lost the two McCaw brothers' trail, and twice Sage helped him find it again. They worked well together. Hopefully that was a sign for the future.

Parker focused on every twig that snapped and bird that flew from the treetops. A crack of thunder added to his growing list of concerns. The question piercing his every thought was did the two McCaw brothers know they were being followed? Dangerous odds as far as Parker was concerned. Too dangerous for his liking. Uneasiness swept over him like a chill before a fever. This could backfire, but he refused to give in to any of it. Up ahead was a rough trail that the three of them could take and not only cut off the two brothers but also be able to see if they were riding into a trap.

He glanced back at Sage. She appeared as engrossed in the surroundings as he was. The long glove on her left hand was empty, and Parker looked at the sky over their heads. He'd begun to think of Hawk as a fourth gun. Something about the bird gave him a bit of reassurance. Right now Hawk had disappeared.

Rifle fire broke through the afternoon's stillness. A second and third shot cracked to their right.

"Drop those rifles," Aiden called from somewhere above them. There was no sign of the gang. Only Aiden's demands. "I won't ask ya a second time."

"How do we know there's more than one of you?" Parker focused above and around them. Nothing.

"Do you want to find out for sure?" That voice wasn't Aiden's, and he remembered it from the night the others broke the outlaw out of jail.

Parker slowly lifted his weapon from across his saddle and dropped it to the ground. He heard the thud of Sage's and Wirt's rifles hitting the rocky trail.

"And those pistols. Slow and easy."

Again Parker and the two behind him obliged. Three men rode into their path. One of them was Aiden. Another man stood atop a boulder to their right. The fifth was missing. "I don't see Mitch."

Aiden laughed. "He's waiting for Sage with a little surprise."

Parker refused to acknowledge Aiden's remark. Instead, he studied the man before him, looking for a vulnerable point.

"What kind of a surprise?" Sage's voice rang with control. "I forgot my party dress."

"Before the night's over, pretty lady, the McCaws will have their own party with you."

The vile thought sent a ripple of fury coupled with fear up Parker's throat, but he shoved it back down. This wasn't over yet, and they weren't that much outnumbered.

"I'd rather take you on knife-to-knife," she said. "But you know I'd slice you to pieces."

Any other time, Parker would have cheered on her spunk. He hadn't heard her forceful tone of voice before or the shrewdness in her twist of words. Right now he had to figure out how to keep them alive.

"Where's that hawk?" called the man on the boulder.

"He's above your head, waiting for the right time to attack." Sage tossed him a look harder than the stone he was kneeling on.

The man tensed and glanced all around him. Parker recognized him from past dealings as Jeb, the one who'd received a head injury in the war, which had left him a bit simple. Yet he'd still retained his deadly aim.

"She's lying to you." Aiden turned in the saddle and studied the trees and sky. "Any of you see that bird, kill it. I've heard what it can do." He rode toward Wirt. "Got me a US Marshal too. They ain't worth ..." He swore.

Wirt said nothing. A wise choice. Parker knew how the Mc-Caws felt about the man's chosen profession.

"Let's get 'em back to camp," Aiden called. "I've waited a long time for this special reunion."

Sage had a mouthful of questions to spit at Aiden, but as she started to pose the first one, caution curbed her tongue. The first person Aiden would kill was Wirt, and she refused to have the man's blood on her conscience because of her sassy mouth. Whatever the McCaws wanted from her and Parker was about to unfold—and not only that but also the mystery about Charles. She'd learn the truth before dying. Somehow it didn't make taking another McCaw bullet any easier.

She rode behind Parker just as she'd done all afternoon, still viewing his shoulders ... but no longer dreaming about a life with him. Thunder rumbled closer than before, but Parker didn't budge. Some dangers were worse than nature's fury. She studied the position of each McCaw from the corners of her eyes, silently measuring each man's strengths and weaknesses.

She thought about the two men with her, and a renewal of determination rose inside her. She wasn't ready to see either man's blood spilled out for the sake of the McCaws' greed. There was a way out of this—but how? She desperately wanted Parker and Wirt to live. Leah and her sons didn't need to lose another family member so soon. And somewhere Wirt had those who cared for him too.

Lord, I ventured down this path not caring about what happened to me. But these two men have full lives ahead of them. I beg You to spare them.

Odd how prayer had come back to her as easily as breathing. She'd left God; He hadn't left her.

FORTY-EIGHT

I t's time to tell us where your husband hid our money," Aiden
said for the second time. He circled a blazing fire at their
campsite. "Or maybe the question is, where have you and Parker
stashed it?"

Sage saw the outlaw's patience had worn thin. "Charles never
talked to me about any money."

Aiden stomped to where she, Parker, and Wirt sat on the hard
ground with their hands tied behind them. He bent to her level,
his nose next to hers, his breath reeking like his filthy body. "Let's
start all over. First of all, let's call your man by his right name.
The one he didn't use when he double-crossed us and killed our
brother."

She had no inkling of what Aiden was talking about or demanding. Neither could she conjure up something to momen-
tarily pacify him. "His name was Charles Morrow. We grew up
together in the same part of southern Colorado. I knew his parents. What more can I tell you?" *Stall him.*

"He went by two names, and you aren't makin' me happy
by playin' stupid. Call him Charles Morrow if you want to, but
he was a no-good US Marshal by the name of Adam Moore—a
black-haired devil who led us into a trap."

Sage's mouth went dry. She couldn't utter a word. Of all the
suspicions that had hammered against her heart and mind about
Charles, his being a US Marshal was not one of them. Adam
Moore—the US Marshal who had died mysteriously ... the man
who died about the same time as Charles? Could the two men

have been one and the same? But it didn't matter. "Charles did not have black hair." She hoped her words sounded stronger than she felt.

"Adam Moore?" Parker's voice hung in midair.

"That's right, Parker. You can stop playin' stupid too. I done figured you out a long time ago."

Sage swung her attention toward Parker. She shook, not from fear, but from the unknown. "Tell me what's going on."

Parker's stoic face stared into the leaping flames. He turned to Aiden and then back to her. "Adam and I were friends. Good friends. He was a US Marshal who worked these parts and broke up a train robbery near Denver. Later he was killed, but I never learned how. Why didn't I put it all together? Adam penetrated the McCaw gang. Rode with them." He swallowed hard. "Told me once his hair wasn't really black, that he used bootblack to dye it. He wanted to hide his identity from the McCaws."

"But that doesn't mean he was Charles." Had she resorted to sounding like a frightened woman?

Aiden laughed. "We followed him from the train job in Denver after Karl was killed. Saw how he spent time with Parker and learned he was a US Marshal. No point being ignorant. The railroad company said the money wasn't returned. Adam, Charles, whatever his name took the money for himself." He spit liquid tobacco on Parker's boot. "Two years ago when I learned she hadn't died, I figured out you and Sage had the money."

"We've waited long enough for what belongs to us." Quincy started to cough, then doubled over.

A man who fought to breathe was one less man to fight.

"He didn't steal it," Parker said low. "He returned it to the Colorado Central Railroad. You got wrong information on that one."

Rex tossed another log on the fire. "Remember the day you stood in the sheriff's office in Denver?"

Sage remembered well. She'd been studying the wanted posters.

"Remember the man who nudged you and said it would take a good bounty hunter to bring in Aiden McCaw?" Rex laughed. "I knew you'd bite on it like an animal biting down on bait in a trap. Worked too."

So the bounty hunter had become the hunted. All of it had led her and Parker into a trap. She desperately wanted to believe Charles had been a US Marshal and not an outlaw. It must be true, for the truth spoke around her. Now she understood why he had been gone for days and weeks with only a vague accounting of where he'd been. He'd kept the truth from her and his family and friends to protect them. She swallowed the tears of thankfulness and regret. Charles had changed his name for the federal marshals and used his real name with the outlaws. In his boots, she would have reversed it, but there would never be any explanation for his thinking. He'd taken that to his grave.

Aiden grabbed Parker by the throat. "Filthy liar. You and Sage have been plannin' this for seven years. You thought I'd forget, didn't you? Took me a while to realize she hadn't died but become a bounty hunter. I hate waitin', so I suggest you remember where the money is before I start in cuttin' and shootin'."

"There's nothing more to tell," Parker said. "Leave her out of this. She didn't even know he was a US Marshal. Adam never told me he was married."

"We'll see."

"Aiden," Jeb called. "Mitch's ridin' in."

"Is he alone?"

"Nope."

Aiden laughed and turned to Sage. "You'll talk now. I guarantee it."

Her heart had not ceased its incessant pounding. She watched the man who had killed Charles and their baby ride into view. *Dark curly hair and hollow, wide-set eyes. Mitch McCaw ... the* mere sight of him sickened her. The time she'd spent with God praying about forgiveness had cleansed her conscience, but the bitterness rose again. The McCaws had to be stopped and brought to justice. But it was looking more and more like the McCaws would ride free again. Pulling at the ropes binding her wrists, she tore her gaze from Mitch and looked at a second man riding an Indian pony behind him. His hands were tied behind him, and the brown-rumped animal looked familiar ... Sage's heart plummeted. The man was Tall Elk.

FORTY-NINE

Sage searched Tall Elk's face for a sign of emotion, but he revealed nothing. The man had taught her how to survive the tragedies that came with living. He'd been hard at times, and he'd been patient in his teachings, asking for nothing in return. Even when he shared his heart, he'd not condemned her for refusing his love. She loved Tall Elk for his sacrifice, but she'd never dreamed his cost would be his own life. Struggling with the ropes binding her hands, she longed for McCaw blood. Bitterness rose like a poison. Where was God now? Where?

Mitch pulled him from the spotted pony and shoved him toward the fire where Sage, Parker, and Wirt sat with their hands tied behind them.

"Take a place beside Sage," Mitch said. "Since you're so willin' to come to her aid."

Tall Elk spit in his face. Mitch responded with a rifle barrel across his neck and shoulder, knocking him at Sage's feet.

She gasped. "He isn't a part of this. Let him go." Her plea brought a round of laughter from the McCaws.

Tall Elk rolled over and caught her attention. His eyes spoke what his lips could not. He did not blame her in this. For an instant, she saw the caring and the compassion from days gone by.

Mitch kicked Tall Elk to a position beside Sage. "Now, we're ready to find out where our money is."

Tall Elk stared into the fire. "Think like one of us," he said in Ute.

Sage realized Tall Elk sensed her emotions powering over a

sound mind. She swallowed and tried to be strong. Sage recalled what Parker had told her about a US Marshal infiltrating a gang. If a marshal was caught with the outlaws, he'd be pulled out. But if he were killed or discovered by one of the outlaws, there was nothing anyone could do. He worked alone. His choice. *Charles's choice.* He'd been killed while working in disguise ... a hero, not an outlaw. A man of integrity who sought to make this country a better place to live. Now she understood why the local sheriff and the governor refused to help. No doubt they'd been told to leave the situation alone.

The memories of what happened the day she and Charles were shot repeated ... Charles's words to get her rifle. To use it. He knew the men were there to kill him, yet he didn't say a word. What could she have done if she'd understood the circumstances?

The four of them sat bound beside the fire. Words she'd never be able to speak to Parker and Tall Elk and even Wirt would follow all of them to their graves.

"Since no one knows the whereabouts of our money, you're all useless." Aiden raised his gun. "I'll begin with the Injun."

"No!" Sage's voice echoed around them. She'd tell them whatever they wanted to know—make something up—but not this.

"Where's the money? And don't give me the story about Charles returning it to the railroad."

"It's deposited in a bank in Denver."

"She's lying," Mitch said. "We checked every bank in Denver, and none had an account with her name on it. Or Charles or Adam Moore or Parker Timmons." He walked over to where she was tied and bent to her level. He grabbed her chin and squeezed. "So you either tell us or we're going to cut up your Injun friend before blowing a hole right through his head. Then we move on to the good marshals here. You know how we McCaws feel about the law. You will be the most fun of all." He tossed a sneer Parker's way. "Your brother was just a warning of what was to come. Fool man stumbled into our camp and tried to arrest us."

Frank had been innocent too. He had left a fine legacy for Leah and their sons. *Think, Sage.* How could she stall for time and tell them something believable? She did have a little money in a bank in Durango, but not the amount they were looking for.

"I'm waiting," Aiden said. "Or this Injun here will find out what a little fire and a knife can do."

Horror swelled like a snake poised to strike. Her heart cried out for Tall Elk's deliverance. "Charles never talked to me about any money. As far as I know, he never had any."

"Kill 'em all and be done with it," Rex said. "I'm tired of chasing fool's gold." He lifted his rifle and aimed straight at Tall Elk. "I'll make a respectable marshal for Rocky Falls. Got the preacher on my side."

"We already have a marshal," a man's voice boomed.

Sage startled. Whose voice split the night air?

"Come on out and show your face," Aiden said, looking around him.

"Believe me. We have two for each one of you. Isn't that right, fellas?" Several men responded from different directions. "Put down those rifles before one of you pays, and I'll start with the devil who claimed he was fit to be our marshal."

Where had she heard that man's voice?

Rex raised his rifle, and a bullet ripped into his right shoulder. He grabbed his bleeding flesh and dropped his weapon. Curses fell like the rain threatening to release on them.

"Aiden, you're left-handed, so I know how to get to you. I'm counting to three. One. Two."

Aiden's rifle fell against a rock, along with his brothers' rifles. Sage watched Bob Culpepper step out from the brush, followed by Doctor Slader and John Timmons. John reached her first and cut the ropes binding her wrists. With one hand on his rifle, he freed Tall Elk while the other two men untied Parker and Wirt. The men of Rocky Falls had remembered their dedication to Parker Timmons.

Preacher Waller slipped from behind a boulder. "Marshal, what do you want me to do with these outlaws?"

That was his voice she'd first heard?

Parker laughed and stood. "I never thought I'd be glad to see you."

"Me either," Wirt said. "I figured you'd be preaching my funeral."

"Guess I had that comin'. My old days of bluffing and using a gun came in handy. The Lord had some use for those days after all. You and I have some talking to do later on. But what do you want us deputies to do with the McCaws?"

John laughed. "Looks like I got deputized after all."

Still grinning, Parker caught Sage's eye. "Take them in alive so we can collect the reward money. I believe the town has a few widows and orphans who could use some help."

"I was looking forward to building them pine boxes," Bob said, yanking Rex's gun from his belt. "Had the boards all sanded nice and smooth."

"And I was ready to dig their graves." John spoke firm, confident.

"Yeah, and I was lookin' forward to giving them a good send-off before the hanging," Waller said.

Sage stood and took in a deep breath. What had happened to the preacher who had successfully turned the town of Rocky Falls against Parker? Then again . . . God had singled her out. She turned to Tall Elk who gave her a brief nod.

An arm clamped against her throat, and a knife's blade pressed against her flesh. "Now it's my turn," Aiden said. "Y'all drop your guns, or I'm going to slit her throat."

And he would. She was sure of it.

In the firelight, the townsmen's faces turned solemn, and they silently complied. Sage stole a glance at Parker. They'd lost their chance at whatever happiness they could have found together because Aiden would not let her live. He had too many years of hate blackening his soul.

"Just let her go," Parker said. "Ride out of here while you can."

Aiden chuckled like a devil, the deadly evil that marked him. "She's going with us to ensure you boys don't follow. We'll drop her along the way." He threw a quick glance at his brothers. "Get your rifles and then to the horses."

"We're not fools." Parker's voice steadied. "Get to your horses and leave her here. We'll give you a good head start."

"Maybe you'd like to watch?" Aiden took a step back toward the horses, dragging Sage with him. She felt the knife scrape across her flesh.

She knew he'd kill her in front of them. That was Aiden's way. The truth swept over her; Unlike she expected, she was ready to die. She'd made her peace with God, and the eternal weighed more than the present.

"Take me instead of her," Parker said.

"How noble." Again Aiden's satanic laugh filled her ears. "It's not going to happen your way. I have plans."

"A posse of US Marshals is right behind us," Waller said, his voice shaky and lacking the intensity she'd heard earlier or what she'd just heard from Parker.

"Right." Rex covered the distance between himself and Waller. "You're nothing but a sniveling coward, trying to run your town with a Bible. Now you think you can scare a McCaw." His clenched fist smacked against Waller's jaw. "Shut up, preacher man. No one here is listenin' to you."

John took a step forward, but Rex's rifle aimed in his direction and stopped him.

Aiden continued to pull Sage toward the horses. A gut feeling told her the McCaws would attempt to shoot all of them before the townsmen retrieved their own weapons. Seconds passed, and she heard the horses snorting behind her. "You think you can outsmart me?" he said. "The wolves will be lappin' up your blood within the hour." The knife pressed against her throat, the blade digging deeper into her skin.

A flap of wings and Aiden's screams pierced her ears. He dropped the knife, and she struggled loose while Hawk buried his talons and beak into Aiden's neck and shoulders. The outlaw's hat flew through the air, and Hawk continued his attack on the man's head and face amidst the outlaw's screams.

Sage fell to the ground and grabbed Aiden's rifle. Mitch raised his gun and fired, and she fired a moment after him, sending a bullet into his leg. In the midst of the confusion, Parker and the townsmen took control. She whirled around. Aiden lay with his head and face a bloody mass, and Hawk lay on the ground still, his leg bleeding from Mitch's bullet.

A gasp flew to her lips, and she kneeled beside her companion. "Oh, Hawk, don't die on me too."

Arms encircled her shoulders, and Parker whispered her name. She peered up into his face and didn't try to blink back the stinging tears. "I've got to help him."

Parker eased down beside her. "He is still breathing, and he's strong. Will he let you tend to him?"

"I believe so." She reached out to soothe the bird. "Easy, Hawk. Let me look at your leg."

Sage swallowed, hoping to gain control of her feelings. Even if the bird hadn't been hurt and frightened enough to fight back, the number of humans around him would have made him aggressive. Tall Elk bent to her other side. "The hawk is strong, and he has a will to live."

"Can I help?" Sage recognized Doc Slader's deep voice. "I brought some things with me in case someone needed doctoring."

Sage nodded. "I'll keep talking to him. It looks really bad."

"So did you a few weeks ago, and you healed just fine." He patted her shoulder and disappeared, no doubt to get his medical bag.

"Parker, what about Aiden. Is he alive?"

A moment of silence slipped by. She didn't want to look at the outlaw. He embodied all that was evil. "He's gone," Parker said. "Hawk took care of him. The bird did what the rest of us could not."

She remembered the small bird that Tall Elk had brought to her—the bird she'd trained and poured out her devotion on. "I don't want him to pay with his life."

"Doc will do his best."

She turned to Tall Elk. "And you're all right?"

He nodded, and even in the darkness, she felt his love. His bronzed body, skilled hands, and endless wisdom represented a part of her she treasured. In many ways they were alike and inseparable. Tall Elk lifted his gaze to Parker. "Take care of Sage. She is a fine woman." The broken English, the language she'd taught him, reminded her of the time spent with the Ute.

"I will. I promise to always take good care of her."

"Good." Tall Elk stood, and his gaze bored into hers. "If you ever need me," he said in Ute, "you know where to find me."

Sage bit into her lower lip and lifted her chin. He needed to see her strong, not weak and imprisoned by emotions that left her speechless. "May the Great Creator of the earth ride with you."

Tall Elk turned and disappeared. A rush of memories continued to sweep over her. All good ones. All ones she'd one day share with her own children.

A man cleared his throat, and she caught sight of Preacher Waller. "I'll do some praying for the bird," Waller said. "God may not have been listening to me in the past, but I think He will now. I owe a whole lot of people an apology, and you two are at the top of the list."

"Accepted," Parker said. "What happened to change your heart?"

Sage kept her eyes focused on Hawk, and her ears trained on Waller's words.

"I overheard my youngest daughter playing. She was pretending to be me, and her perception wasn't anything about God. In her story about David and Goliath, I was Goliath. In that moment, God grabbed me by the shirt collar and let me know how far I'd slid away from Him. How I'd tried to be a god. How I thought I had all of the answers. The more I reflected on my daughter's play, the more I realized how much I'd disappointed Him." He snorted. "When I think back about how I was the worst character in town before God cleaned me up ... and how I became such a hypocrite ... Well, if my life hadn't belonged to God, I'd have pulled the trigger on myself. But I'm a changed man, and I hope you and the rest of this town will give me an opportunity to prove it."

"Sure we can," Parker said. "You saved three lives tonight. And I'm grateful to be in one piece."

"And I owe you thanks for taking in my family when Pa was killed," John said.

"Thanks. I'm a preacher—maybe a poor one, but the last thing I want is your job."

Parker lifted his arm from Sage's shoulder and reached up to shake his hand. "We'll get along fine. Thanks for bringing this posse."

"Bob liked the idea, and it didn't take long for these fine men to grab their rifles."

"I'm grateful for all of you," Wirt said, his gun fixed on the remaining McCaws. "I wasn't ready to meet my maker. Maybe I ought to find out how to do that right."

Preacher Waller chuckled and shook Wirt's hand.

Doctor Slader bent to the ground with his bag. He dragged his tongue over his lower lip. "If you'll watch your hawk's beak and talons, I'll bandage him up."

"Sure." Sage stroked Hawk's feathers. "The bullet cut a hunk of his flesh, but it's not lodged in his leg."

"Like someone else I know." Doc forced a nervous laugh as he worked. Within fifteen minutes, Sage cradled Hawk in her lap.

The townsmen had the McCaw gang tied and ready to take back to town and Aiden's body thrown over his horse.

"Go on ahead," Parker said to Bob and the preacher. "I want to make sure Sage and Hawk have a little more time to rest before heading back."

"I'll keep my eye on the marshall's office," John said. The boy had become a man.

"Take as long as you need," Waller said and tipped his hat.

Yeah, the man had changed, and she hoped it lasted. She watched the posse disappear into the night with the understanding the men would spend at least one night in the mountains. How strange, but the thunder had ceased its roar and had taken the threat of rain with it.

Sage glanced down at Hawk. He breathed heavily but not worse than before. "I'm going to spend the rest of my life taking care of you. That's the least I can do for you for saving my life."

Parker wrapped his arm around her waist. "I'd like to do the same for you."

Sage's stomach did a little flip. Parker's promise to Tall Elk repeated in her mind, along with what they'd talked about earlier today. "I don't want to be a bounty hunter any longer." Her words were more of a whisper than a declaration.

"So you'd trade the life of a bounty hunter to be Mrs. Parker Timmons?"

Her mouth had turned dry; the idea of a new life both excited and frightened her. "Not sure how I'd manage in political and social gatherings."

"You'll do just fine. And you can have all the pet wolves, wildcats, and hawks that you want." He lifted her chin and placed a light kiss on her lips. "I love you. There could never be anyone for me but you. I don't know where God is leading me or us, but I can't take another step without you in my life. Will you ease this heart of mine and marry me, Sage Morrow?"

No doubts plagued her mind. All she could see was a future with a man she loved. She shivered. "I think I've loved you from the moment I saw you walking down the street of Rocky Falls. Yes, I'll marry you and help you be the best marshal or politician Colorado has ever known."

FIFTY

DENVER, COLORADO
SUMMER, 1892

S enator, a messenger has arrived, stating you are needed at home immediately."

Parker glanced up from the legal documents awaiting his signature to the anxious aide before him. He focused on the clock on the fireplace mantel: 2:00. The baby must be coming. "Would you kindly get my carriage ready?"

"I've already tended to it, Senator."

Parker stood, a grin spreading across his face. He remembered Sage handing him his morning coffee and making her announcement. "Expect a messenger at two this afternoon. Your daughter will be here before supper."

"Are you sending Hawk?"

"Not this time. I'll be more proper since I know we're having a girl."

He kissed her soundly, wrapping his arm around her swollen waist. "And after three sons, you're sure this one is a girl?"

"Without a doubt. So make sure you're here on time. Your daughter will be very demanding."

"I will, Mrs. Timmons." He kissed her again, taking the time to enjoy her soft lips. "Will Melanie Elizabeth have a way with animals, like her mama?"

"She just might. The boys have already started a menagerie, and she may need to stand on her own against them."

"I suspect she will learn fast and have her papa in the palm of her hand just like her mama does." He toyed with a pearl on her necklace. "We've come a long way together, Sage. Have I ever thanked you for marrying me?"

Sage smiled. "Many times. But you can again."

"You are my joy. I will spend every day of the rest of my life thanking God for bringing you to me. Nothing I am today or ever will be is possible without you beside me."

"We have hope, my love. Hope and dreams from a God who is faithful. What more could we ever want?"

He kissed her lightly, remembering how he'd fallen in love in the Rocky Mountains with a woman called Sage.

Special thanks to:

Louise Gouge; Mona Hodgson; Barbara Oden;
the Colorado Historical Society;
and Dean, who always edits me with flair.